C29 0000 0916 037

D1346051

The Summer Birdcage

L. C. TYLER

The Summer Birdcage

CONSTABLE

CONSTABLE

First published in Great Britain in 2022 by Constable

A CIP catalogue record for this book
is available from the British Library.

ISBN: 978-1-47213-508-7

Typeset in Adobe Caslon Pro by SX Composing DTP, Rayleigh, Essex
Printed and bound in Great Britain by Clays Ltd, Elcograf S.p.A.

Papers used by Constable are from well-managed forests
and other responsible sources.

Constable
An imprint of
Little, Brown Book Group
Carmelite House
50 Victoria Embankment
London EC4Y 0DZ

An Hachette UK Company
www.hachette.co.uk

www.littlebrown.co.uk

With much gratitude to Krystyna, who amongst other things shares and has encouraged my interest in Nonsuch Palace

'Tis just like a summer bird-cage in a garden: the birds that are without despair to get in, and the birds that are within despair and are in a consumption for fear they shall never get out.'

John Webster, *The White Devil*

Cast in Approximate Order of Appearance

Mistress Kitty Burgess – who would consider being mentioned first as no less than her right, a young actress who does not think it necessary to learn lines, an interesting approach in no way endorsed by . . .

Thomas Betterton – actor and manager of the Duke's Company, which is currently performing *The Summer Birdcage*, a comedy written by . . .

Aminta, Lady Grey – one of the nation's leading playwrights, whose most fortunate husband is . . .

John Grey – that is to say myself, the author of this strange and scarcely believable tale, a lawyer and magistrate, but no great frequenter of theatres, deeming modern plays (with the exception of my wife's) to be bawdy, conceited and inconsequential, unlike . . .

Mister Samuel Pepys – a lover of comedies and young actresses indiscriminately, Clerk of the Acts to the Navy Board and the loyal servant of . . .

James, Duke of York – Lord High Admiral etc. etc. and currently heir to the throne, but this last only until the King produces legitimate children to add to his many illegitimate ones by various mothers, an awkward position for the Duke to be in, though he does of course wish our reigning monarch a long and prosperous life, as does . . .

Henry Bennet, Lord Arlington – the King's most obsequious and obliging servant, owner of a nose patch, Secretary of State for the Southern Department and spymaster, who has known for some time that he could not do his job efficiently without the assistance of . . .

Mister Joseph Williamson – one of the rare honest men (possibly the only honest man) at the court of the aforesaid . . .

King Charles II, the man who rules our happy, contented nation and is himself ruled very effectively by his various mistresses, notably . . .

Barbara, formerly Lady Castlemaine – now raised to being Duchess of Cleveland and proprietor of her own royal palace, which clearly gives her precedence over lesser mistresses such as . . .

Mistress Nell Gwynne – who is neither duchess nor countess nor ever shall be, but who knows how to keep the King amused, as once (many years ago) did . . .

Eleanor, Lady Byron – who shared the King's long exile during the 1650s, and gave him her unwavering support and half her bed, just as . . .

Edward Hyde, Earl of Clarendon – in a very different capacity, served His Majesty faithfully throughout their forced sojourn in Paris, Bruges and Brussels (and as Lord Chancellor after his return), and was eventually rewarded with dismissal from office and banishment for giving the King too much sound, cautious advice, whereas . . .

Anthony Ashley Cooper, Lord Ashley – was variously a royalist and a parliamentarian during the late wars, whichever seemed the more prudent, and is now the King's Chancellor of the Exchequer and also, for reasons that remain obscure, the protector of . . .

Mistress Elizabeth Needham – a young lady who has lived much of her life in France under the care and tutelage of . . .

Lady Mary Tredway – steely-eyed Abbess of the English convent in Paris and of . . .

Father Christopher – an English chaplain who is very happy not to have to live in England, unlike . . .

The Reverend Reginald Norris – Aminta's cousin, the contented vicar of a most pleasant parish in Hampshire and (more reluctantly) guardian of . . .

Mistress Kitty Burgess – of whom you have already heard and who, as we speak, is just coming off stage after the opening performance of *The Summer Birdcage*, a play with which you will also become quite familiar very soon. More familiar, perhaps, than Kitty is herself.

Prologue

Summer 1670

The Queen removed her crown and placed it on the small table in front of her. It had, she reflected, seen better days. Its outline, once symmetrical, was now wayward and haphazard. Several of the smaller jewels were missing. Previous queens – the idle little sluts – had not taken care of it as they should. Titania, it is true, had prudently removed it before her reconciliation with Oberon, but only yesterday Lady Macbeth had thrown it across the stage in a piece of wholly unscripted business that had caused Betterton to take her to one side after the performance and threaten to deduct the cost of repairs from her wages.

They did these things better in Drury Lane, at the King's Company, but the players there were a conceited bunch of jumped-up nobodies, as she had discovered to her cost. She wasn't sorry she'd decided to move to the Duke's Company, even if some of her new colleagues were already showing only too familiar signs of jealousy. The Queen wasn't the main part in *The Summer Birdcage*, of course, but she knew the stage had belonged to her, and only her, every minute she was on it. And, though she was still sworn to secrecy, there were even greater things to come. It was true that it had not been made entirely clear to her what this promised role would be, but she had been informed, in the most flattering terms, that she was perfect for it. She had been left in no doubt that it would surpass anything she had done before. Perhaps anything anyone had ever done before. It would be, theatrically speaking, her apotheosis.

'I wouldn't be too downhearted, Kitty,' said a voice behind her.

'I beg your pardon?' said the Queen, turning to the older woman.

Her fellow actress smiled sympathetically. 'Your performance tonight. You shouldn't be too despondent about it. It happens to everyone at some time.'

'What does?' the Queen demanded. Meg might have more lines to say than she did, but Meg's role was merely that of a countess.

'Forgetting your words,' said Meg, not unkindly. 'All of us do it occasionally, Kitty. And we had a cruel audience in tonight. A thoroughly nasty crowd – especially the idiots in that so-called Wits' Row. I mean young Herbert and Sackville and their rake-hell friends at the front of the pit. Wits? Pig ignorant, I'd have called them. And rotten drunk. Still, they should have known better than to call you those horrid things.'

The Queen shook her head. 'I didn't notice them,' she said. 'When I'm playing a part, I lose myself completely in the role. I am transported to another, higher realm.'

'Well, that's very nice for you, I'm sure,' said Meg. 'Though, if you'll take my advice, Kitty, you'll try to learn your lines properly for the second performance tomorrow evening. It's not a big part, after all. Lady Grey will be in the audience. She got you your job here – when you had to leave the King's Company under circumstances we don't need to go into now. We mustn't let her down, must we? Not her ladyship. She thinks you have a great deal of promise, if you would just work at it. Like everyone else has to.'

'Some of us,' said the Queen, 'have natural talent. Lady Grey told me. That's why she wanted me in her new play.'

'Yes,' said Meg, 'but I'm sure she also said that you still have a lot to learn, because she's nobody's fool, and frankly you have. You're very young, Kitty. I wish I was your age again, I do, truly. But it's simply a kindness to you, I promise, when I say that you have to try a lot harder than you did tonight if you want to make the stage your career. At the very least, my girl, by the opening night you should have known your words. And I don't mean just some of them.'

'If I forget a few lines, I can always make up new ones,' said the Queen. 'It's easy enough.'

'Is it? Well, I wouldn't try it tomorrow, not with Lady Grey in the audience. Writers tend to think what they've written is perfect and don't like people making changes. Unless you really want to annoy her, don't mess around with her script.'

The Queen smiled inwardly. She rather thought she'd improved on Lady Grey's text. Playwriting was clearly much easier than acting. Anyway, her days of learning lines for minor parts were already over.

'*The Summer Birdcage* – I think it's the best thing Lady Grey has written,' Meg continued, happily unable to read other people's minds. 'There's nobody in London to touch her now, not for comedy. And you do have a gift for comedy yourself,

Kitty. We could have a long run in this, with regular money coming in for the whole cast. Just so long as one of us doesn't spoil it for everyone else, if you'll understand my meaning.'

'I like Lady Grey,' said the Queen, idly twisting a lock of golden hair. 'She's not stuck up, like some people, even if she is gentry.'

'She used to be a viscountess,' said Meg. 'Before she married Sir John and just became the wife of a knight instead. Still, proper gentry, as you say, with a fine house in Clavershall West.'

'Where's that?'

'In Essex somewhere, I think.'

'I met Sir John once,' said the Queen. 'Bit dry. Bit of a puritan, I'd have said. I don't think he enjoyed the play very much. Why has he got that scar on his face?'

'Sir John's a lawyer and a justice of the peace. But they say he used to be a spy in his younger days. He worked for Lord Arlington.'

'Doing what exactly?'

'Best not to ask, eh? I'll leave you to learn your lines, then. Especially the ones you didn't know tonight.'

'There's no need. I may as well tell you now that I won't be here tomorrow.'

'Not here? Tomorrow's performance isn't going to be a rehearsal, Kitty. It's not just Lady Grey coming to see how we're getting on – there will also be several hundred other people. People who pay our wages. Betterton took you on only because Lady Grey asked him to. He'd heard rumours from the King's Company – you know exactly which ones I mean – and he wasn't keen to have you. Lady Grey got you a second chance, because Betterton respects her judgement. But he'll sack you there and then if you don't show up tomorrow.'

'I've had a better offer.'

'Who from? There's only us and the King's Company in London. And I can tell you, they won't take you back.'

'From a very important gentleman.'

'Oh no, Kitty . . . Look, we all get offers like that from the men who come to watch the plays. And a few actresses do very well by becoming some duke's or earl's mistress. For a short time anyway. But you're just an understudy for his wife, with no prospect of ever playing the main part yourself. It's not a proper career. Why should a man who has learned how to be unfaithful to his wife suddenly decide to be faithful to his whore? You could make a decent living on the stage – a respectable one, almost. Send your admirer a message saying that you've got some lines to learn and he should look for somebody else to make his wife jealous. Preferably somebody from the King's Company.'

'You think I'm going to be his mistress? That's not what he wants me to do.'

'Listen to me, Kitty. Listen very carefully: *he won't marry you.* Do you think the King will ever marry Nell Gwynne? Of course not. This fine gentleman, whoever he is, he'll just use you. You're young. You don't know about men, or not as much as I do. You can't trust anything they say, even when they're sober. At least wait and talk to Lady Grey – she'll give you good advice.'

'If I told you who he was, you'd see you were wrong.'

'No, I wouldn't. I'd just know who you were sleeping with. Oh God . . . it's not the King, is it? Please tell me it's not the King. He's got more mistresses than he knows what to do with already.'

The Queen smiled enigmatically, as befitted her new station in life. 'He's coming at nine o'clock. In his coach. With six horses.'

'The number of horses,' said Meg, 'is completely beside the point.'

'I need to get this greasepaint off my face and change out of these robes,' said the Queen. 'Can you fetch me my blue silk gown from over there?'

'No,' said Meg. 'I can't.'

Kitty laughed the small tinkling laugh that made half the company want to strangle her. 'I won't need fake ermine and coloured glass jewels after this evening. And I won't need any of you. I shall have whole armies of servants. In livery, with yards and yards of gold lace. Now, if you'll kindly stand to one side, Countess, I'll fetch the gown myself. For one last time.'

'So, did you talk to Kitty?' asked Thomas Betterton.

'Yes,' said Meg. 'I did.'

'And do I have to fire her, or has she promised to learn her lines? Because it's one or the other, Meg. I'm not having a second evening like this one, with her spouting the first bit of nonsense that comes into her head and the rest of the cast waiting, open-mouthed, for a cue that never comes.'

'She says she's done with learning lines.'

'What?'

'She's found a new situation that likes her better, or so she claims.'

'She's going to be the mistress of some City vintner or a Welsh baronet?'

'Whatever it is, it comes with six horses.'

'I hope she's got a big shovel, then. Kitty's finished here, Meg. She'll never get another part from me. You can tell Charlotte she's playing the Queen from now on.'

'Charlotte won't be as good. Nothing like. I'll speak to Kitty again, if she hasn't already left. Maybe I can talk her round, eh?'

'Don't you dare. With the King – I mean the real King – coming here tomorrow, I'll sleep easier tonight knowing I have a cast who won't let me down.'

'Lady Grey will be here too. She'll want to know why we've sacked her. Kitty's almost kin to her ladyship.'

'I'll explain to Lady Grey. I'll tell her we did our best for Kitty, but I couldn't risk keeping her. My Lady will understand that we can't let her latest play get a bad reputation before it's even properly launched on the town. It's a cracking little piece, *The Summer Birdcage*. All very cynical and perfect for a London audience that likes to think of itself as jaded and world-weary. And some of the dialogue is as close to obscenity as I could risk. With the right cast we could have a long run with it. But I spoke to Killigrew at the King's Company this morning, and he warned me Kitty was trouble. I shouldn't have let Lady Grey persuade me otherwise. Kitty Burgess only ever had two boats and now she's burned both of them. It's a thousand pities, but there it is.'

'I'll tell Charlotte to learn the part, then. It won't take her long. She's a good girl. Charlotte doesn't have Kitty's presence, but she's reliable.'

'Kitty's was only a small part, when all's said and done,' said Betterton, with a sigh. 'A bit like the one I'm playing next week – in that revival of *Henry V* we're doing.'

'Which part is that? The French King? The Dauphin?'

'Chorus. I come on in the Prologue in Act One, and sort of explain what's what – for anyone coming to the play who doesn't know who the various characters are.'

'A prologue? That's always useful, if a bit dull.'

'True,' said Betterton. 'But at least, once the Prologue's out of the way, you can then get on with the actual story.'

'I do hope Kitty isn't going to do anything really stupid,' said Meg.

'I suppose that's what we're all about to find out, isn't it?' said Betterton.

Chapter One

In which there is a change of cast

From this box, high up in the theatre, I have a fine view of the stage and the audience, both lit by the flicking light of I know not how many dozen good wax candles. Outside, the sun shines, but here a new and better day has been made to dawn for our benefit, a day that will end not when God ordains, but when it pleases London. The stage is still empty, though a painted canvas indicates that the first scene will take place in a garden – as I know well, having read my wife's script several times and even dared to suggest one or two very minor changes. Music is playing, but the voices of hundreds of theatregoers below, all trying to talk louder than each other, make it difficult for me to make out what the music is – a country dance, I think. 'Cuckolds All in a Row'.

Aminta enters the box with a furious frown on her face.

'You will never guess what that silly girl Kitty has done!'

Since the play is about to start, it seems best to simply

admit that I won't. I have only met Kitty once, and do not share Aminta's high opinion of her. 'Tell me,' I say.

'Yesterday, she informed Betterton that she was quitting the stage for ever. After all I've done to get her a job here, she having already annoyed and insulted everyone at the King's Company!'

'You have been very good to Kitty,' I say. 'But you shouldn't blame yourself for putting her forward. You were, after all, under an obligation to your cousin, Reginald.'

'I would not put somebody into one of my plays, John, just because their guardian happened to be distantly related to me. I have more respect for the theatre generally and my own work in particular. I'd seen her act under Killigrew's direction and, frankly, she was slapdash and under-rehearsed. But she showed promise – real promise. When she could be bothered, in fact, she was magnificent. If she played a countess, for a few moments you believed she was actually a descendant of Charlemagne. If she played a country wench, you'd have trusted her to milk one of your cows. If she played a witch, you kept your head down in the front row of the pit, just in case she put the evil eye on you. I knew Killigrew wouldn't be able to manage her, but I really thought Betterton could make the lazy little madam work. Instead, he's allowed her to be carried off to be somebody's mistress. I've told Betterton I'm furious with him.'

'And are you?'

'A bit. But unless you make yourself absolutely clear with men they can often miss the point. When a woman is angry, the man's first response is always to assume it's something unimportant that she'll get over quickly if he politely ignores it. He now knows that's not going to happen. I've told him, he has to find her and get her back. I hold him responsible.'

'Since he is neither parent nor guardian,' I say, 'Betterton has no legal duty of care towards her.'

'That's what Betterton thought until five minutes ago.'

'Ah,' I say succinctly. *The Summer Birdcage* is about to begin. King Charles and his entourage are here and have taken their places, very visibly and very audibly, in the royal box. Two characters, who must have been waiting in the wings with some trepidation, have now appeared on the stage – an old king and his new young wife, Queen Belinda. But it soon becomes clear that the story really concerns Prince Bellair and his intended bride Emilia. Queen Belinda is already trapped in the golden birdcage of the play's title. Emilia, at first attracted by the glitter of the court, is now having second thoughts about marrying the heir to the throne, seeing the Queen's predicament. Snarkly, the Prince's friend, confidently advises him on the best way to Emilia's heart, though he is having no success himself with Emilia's friend, Livia, and is also unadvisedly flirting with Emilia's maid, who tells her mistress everything. The audience suspects Snarkly's advice may not be the best. Aminta has of course arranged things so that all will be resolved in the concluding act, and everyone will marry somebody appropriate to their station in life, because that is what her customers are paying to see. But she will make some of the characters sweat a little first. It will be good for them. The King, the Queen, Snarkly, Bellair . . . they will all emerge better people. Perhaps that is the real point of the story. Perhaps it is the real point of most stories.

'I thought the part of the Queen was played competently,' I say, when the painted, counterfeit king and the other players have made their final bows and the audience has begun to depart, in the wake of the real king, his courtiers and a representative selection of his mistresses.

'But with no spirit,' says Aminta. 'How could Betterton lose Kitty Burgess before I'd even seen her in the part? And His Majesty was also clearly displeased at the change in the cast. He had come to see Kitty. I would have expected more of the manager of the best theatrical company in London.'

'What haven't I done, my Lady?' asks Betterton cheerfully as he sweeps into our box. He is still wearing his costume as the Count, Emilia's father. It is a fine robe of scarlet plush with a large fur collar, but he will need more than that to protect him from the cold wind that is about to blow. He's clearly forgotten he's in trouble and Aminta is about to remind him.

'You didn't follow Kitty as she left the theatre,' says Aminta, counting his faults off on her fingers. 'You didn't stop her boarding the coach that had been sent for her. You didn't follow the coach to see where it went.'

'All very true, though her departure was observed nonetheless. I've just spoken to Neville – the idiot footman in your play. He happened to be outside the theatre, on the other side of the lane that runs along the back. He saw a large black coach draw up, with six black horses. They were driven by a coachman dressed in a black cloak. Very satanic, according to Neville.'

'Very theatrical anyway,' says Aminta.

'Neville felt obliged to conceal himself in a doorway, just in case things were as bad as they looked at face value. He observed Kitty emerge, also wrapped in a black cloak, but with a fine blue silk dress in evidence beneath it. She approached the carriage and conversed briefly with somebody inside. Then she took a step back and raised an arm as if to fend off a blow. A hoarse cry escaped her lips. She appeared about to swoon.'

'Really?' says Aminta. 'She actually did all of that?'

'Neville has always had strong opinions about how scenes like this should be played. Some of that concern may have unfortunately crept into his narrative.'

'I'm glad we cast him merely as a footman,' says Aminta.

'Indeed. But, to return to Neville's account, Kitty was apparently drawn against her will into the coach, as if by some supernatural force. The door closed behind her. There was a thunderous crack of the whip, and the coach sped off with the horses tossing their heads.'

'The lane is quite narrow. Speed would have been inadvisable.'

'Neville gave me no reason to believe that either party was acting prudently.'

'And Neville followed, of course?'

'He said that, by the time he reached the end of the lane, there was no sign of the coach.'

'So, he didn't follow at all, then. Oh well – maybe I wouldn't have followed a black coach that could suck you in off the street and carry you away to everlasting hell fire.'

'Neville has always struck me as a cautious man, and slightly awkward in his actions. I have never risked casting him in a part that required him to use a sword on stage.'

'How unpopular had Kitty managed to make herself since she joined your company?'

'To be fair to her, she achieved a lot in a very short time. From the first day, she made it clear that she considered herself very much above the rest of us. She would arrive late for rehearsals, which meant that we all left late as well – that endeared her to nobody. And she refused to learn her lines. In private, we all had to admit she was quite good, but that just made the other actresses worry that she would soon be taking the best parts. The cast do of course wish her well and some hope that she has not actually been abducted by the Devil.'

'They were right to fear her,' says Aminta. 'I've seen her at the King's Company. She could play young girls, old women, maid servants, duchesses, fairy attendants, witches. She had a way of transforming herself that went beyond applying a layer of paint to her face.'

'That is very true,' says Betterton. 'You'd see her in one part and simply not recognise her in another. I swear that I could scarcely tell you what her real face looked like, and as for her voice ... It was as if I had half-a-dozen actresses at my disposal, though I had the chance to cast her only in a handful of plays before we began rehearsals for yours.'

'Do you think whoever carried her off had seen her perform here?'

'That is usually the only way an actress would come to the attention of the owner of a coach and six. So, yes, here or at the King's Company. One or the other.'

'Nobody had noticed her with an admirer?'

'Here? She either did not give them cause to hope or was very discreet. I can't say what she did at the other place in Drury Lane. Killigrew's own morals are not the best and that can rub off on people.'

'The King seemed very disappointed not to see her,' says Aminta thoughtfully. 'In spite of the fact that it was not a large part.'

'I never saw her encourage him in any way.'

'The King requires no encouragement. Quite the reverse. Genuine reluctance and modesty merely spur him on. Of course, simulated reluctance and modesty work equally well. So does no reluctance and no modesty. He's an easy man to please.'

'I am sure that she could simulate anything,' says Betterton. 'But you have a longer acquaintance with her than I do, my Lady.'

'Not really. Apart from the distant family connection and having seen her on stage at the King's Company, I hardly know her at all. When she was starting to make life difficult for herself in the King's Company, my cousin wrote to me asking if I could find her a position elsewhere. Don't look at me like that, Mister Betterton. I still don't think I did you a disservice in recommending Kitty to you. If we can find her, I'd suggest you take her back – after I've given her a little firm advice.'

Betterton looks very doubtful indeed. 'I would, as ever, bow to your judgement in these matters, my Lady, but I have no idea how I'd even begin to locate her.'

'We'll leave that to my husband,' says Aminta. 'He used to be a spy, you know. Hence the rather dashing scar on his face.'

'Arlington never asked me to track down missing actresses,' I say.

'Your luck's changed, then,' says Aminta.

Chapter Two

In which I meet an old friend

Our own coach – midnight blue, rather than black, and with newly upholstered seats of shiny yellow leather – makes its way slowly through London's crowded streets and lanes. The iron-shod wheels scrape and spark on the cobbles, the leather strapwork squeals and occasionally our coachman cracks his whip to impress stray dogs and small children. Another long summer day is coming to its end. Shops are closing. The dust of the city is finally settling down. Our theatre audience has already dispersed to their homes and to taverns and to whore houses of the better sort. Some have headed to St James's Park, where, under the cover of the fast approaching night, all manner of things may be done beneath the friendly stars that cannot be done in the more judgemental light of day.

'We could have walked more quickly,' I say.

'I agree that, as an obscure country magistrate, you might have walked, but as the husband of London's fourth or fifth best-known playwright you have a duty to ride in a genteel manner. Anyway, we are not paying our coachman and postillion to sit around in the stables all day.'

'Everything in London travels so slowly that I think Mister Neville could have followed the black coach very easily,' I say. 'Had he chosen to do so.'

'Fear slows a man even more than gout,' says Aminta. 'But hopefully the trail has not yet gone cold. I have every confidence, my dear husband, that you will find her.'

'We don't know yet that she needs to be found. Or wants to be. She may turn up at the theatre tomorrow as if nothing had happened. Or she may have actually been adopted by a rich and amiable protector, who will indulge her fantasies of grand living. There is little in Neville's account of her abduction that I would credit if I were hearing the case as a magistrate.'

'The one part of Neville's story I do believe is that, at the very last minute, Kitty doubted whether what she was doing was advisable. Our little bird paused before she hopped into the cage. Then an invisible thread pulled the door shut behind her and now she must go where her cage goes. Though I hold Betterton responsible for her loss, I hold myself responsible too. My cousin is after all a clergyman, who probably considers he brought Kitty up in a respectable manner. I promised him I would find her a place that suited her – not that I would lead her into gilded captivity.'

'And it is therefore, in some way, my responsibility to put things right?'

'Both morally and legally.'

'Legally?'

'Since you are a lawyer, you will know that, as a married woman, I can scarcely be said to have any legal existence at all. My goods and chattels are your goods and chattels.

My debts are your debts. My missing actresses are your missing actresses. But I shall assist you as far as a legally non-existent person can.'

'Thank you,' I say. 'And where do you propose that we start?'

'Back at the Duke's Company, I think. Tomorrow morning, before rehearsals if possible, we'll talk to Mister Neville and see what a little editing will do to the currently overblown piece of storytelling in front of us.'

Theatres always seem grubby places when they are empty, redolent of orange peel, yesterday's candles and sweat. Some curtains have been drawn back, however, to let in light and windows have been opened to let in different smells – mainly woodsmoke, combined with the distant and complex aroma of the Thames. The addition of daylight too is a mixed blessing: it reveals that the green cloth of the padded benches is stained and torn and that the scenery has been painted with only the most cursory nod towards Truth and Beauty. There is an untidy heap of props on the stage, to be sorted, repaired and placed in the correct locations for tonight's performance.

'I've already told Mister Betterton,' says Neville grumpily. 'She's gone with Satan or Lord Rochester. That's all there is to it.'

'You say she went reluctantly?' says Aminta.

'I am certain of it. I saw her face very clearly. It was the face of one who realises that she has been much less clever than she thought.'

'But could she not have run back into the theatre if she was really scared – if she suddenly discovered that her hoped-for protector actually was one of the two gentlemen you mentioned?'

'The Devil will find you, however far you run,' says Neville. 'If you but let him into your heart, you will carry him with you wherever you go.'

I think Mister Neville might have a career as a jobbing preacher if he ever decides to quit the stage. His latest aphorism does not, however, take us very far forward.

'On second thoughts,' says Aminta, 'since time is short, let's ignore the possibility that it's Satan, and just talk about people who actually own a black coach and six.'

'If that is your wish, my Lady,' says Neville stiffly. He is a bull-like man, heavy and largely unyielding to argument. He resents having been taken away from whatever he was doing. He has yet to smile in our presence, let alone laugh. Looking at him, it is difficult to see what drew him to acting. There must be few dramatic roles for which he is suited. An old and disgruntled family retainer perhaps, or a cuckolded husband from the very depths of the country. Somebody who has amassed much resentment over the years but who has few words to articulate it. Somebody who is suspicious of anything on his plate that isn't quite clearly cabbage.

'You didn't see the man's face at all?' I ask.

'Just his arm. Fine, red velvet, it was, with a yard of linen sleeves billowing out and a lace cuff halfway down his fingertips. A gentleman's hand without doubt.'

That's probably true. Farm labourers don't usually travel around in a coach and six, any more than Satan does.

'Was there a coat of arms on the door?' I ask.

'Yes.'

'Whose?' asks Aminta.

'I'm an actor, my Lady, not a herald.'

'Not the King's arms?' asks Aminta.

'I know the King's one, obviously. It's a bit like the Duke of York's and we have that above the stage. It had animals on it, though. I can tell you that much.'

'Lions?' I ask.

'No.'

'Leopards?'

'No.'

'Eagles?'

'No.'

'Unicorns? Bears? Boars? Stags? Dragons? Griffins? Hounds? Elephants? Martlets? Camelopards? Cockatrices?'

'Maybe camelopards. What do they look like exactly?'

'Long legs and necks. Thin, pointed faces.'

'I'm not sure they had necks at all.'

Rather like Neville himself, then. He rubs his bristly chin. I'd wait to see if further inspiration strikes him, but that may not happen this week.

'Well, if you do remember what they were, please let me know,' I say.

'I'll do that,' he says, though it seems unlikely that his recollection will become sharper with time. Then he adds: 'Not that I want her back here, of course. Not that any of us want her back here. She can stay with the Devil in hell if that makes her happy.'

I nod noncommittally. If Kitty's in hell, she's probably not happy – it's more likely she wishes she were back here, learning her lines.

'You didn't like her, then?' I say.

'In all the time she was here, I don't think she said a single civil word to me. Not one. You'd have thought I was her servant off stage as well as on. And no part was ever good enough for her. Never the right length or with sufficiently witty lines.'

'Which roles did she play?' asks Aminta, who clearly thinks she gave the Queen, and indeed her idiot footman, one or two good bits of dialogue.

'She was Mistress Lucy – Sir Frederick's wench – in *Love in a Tub*,' says Neville. 'Not a bad little part, but she wanted to play Graciana. And she was a fairy or sprite or something in *Midsummer Night's Dream*. She wanted to be Hermia in that and have a few of Helena's best lines added to her own. She has a nice voice, I'll grant you. She can sing a bit when it's required. And she can turn her hand to any part. But she's lazy. And she's putting on weight. That's not good. You can pad an actress out for a part, if needed, but you can't shrink her back down. Or not overnight.'

'She never spoke to anyone of leaving?' asks Aminta.

'Only to Meg. And she wouldn't tell Meg any more than you know already.'

'And there were men in the audience who took an interest in her?'

'Why shouldn't they? It's normal. It's why most of them come here. But there was a rowdy lot of young bucks in the pit that evening – they shouted all sorts of things at her. Nasty things. Things a girl of her age shouldn't have understood. But I couldn't tell you who they were, except that brute Philip Herbert. And Mister Pepys was there. He wanted to see Kitty afterwards but she said no. Well, she knew what he was after and wasn't planning to oblige him. Sought her out two or three times after a performance, Pepys has. He's got a coach, but it's yellow unfortunately. Do you know where to find him?'

'Oh yes,' I say. 'I know where to find Mister Pepys.'

*

Aminta has declined the dubious pleasure of accompanying me to the Navy Office. Pepys welcomes me warmly because, though it irks him that I have a knighthood and he doesn't, he still sees me as an ally in Lord Arlington's camp, and one who may be of some use to him in future. He is dressed in his summer costume of a long black bombazine coat and waistcoat, both closely fitting and almost reaching his knees; black breeches, white stockings and black shoes with gleaming silver buckles complete the outfit. Or almost. The ensemble is brightened this year by a new fashion: a broad, fringed sash in scarlet and gold, which crosses the coat diagonally and from which hangs a very neat sword. He is massaging his little finger, where he might be wearing a signet ring, but isn't. Perhaps it became too tight. Pepys is looking plumper and more prosperous than when I last saw him a few months ago.

'Ah, Sir John!' he says, as I am ushered into his office by one of his growing army of minions. 'We see you and your good lady far too little in London. You are here for your wife's play, of course?'

'That and other things,' I say, 'but mainly that.'

'I hope you went to the second performance and not the first?'

'Yes,' I say.

'I was at the first,' he says, shaking his head sadly. 'That pert little miss, Kitty Burgess, almost marred the whole thing with her foolishness – speaking lines she had made up on the night rather than those your wife had written for her. A pretty enough girl, of course – quite charming off stage but very careless on it. I heard Betterton replaced Kitty with another actress on the second night? That was very wise of him, especially with the King present. George Etherege's *She Would if She Could* was a fine play but it failed entirely due to the poor way in which it was acted. I should have been very sorry if the same fate had befallen *The Summer Birdcage.*'

'Indeed,' I say, knowing how many months of hard toil, brief moments of brilliant invention and long and debilitating periods of self-doubt have gone into it.

'Well, I hope Kitty will learn from it. I would not wish to see her vanish from the stage either. She has a fine figure, even if she has grown a little plump of late, and a very good leg to play breeches parts. And she has much talent, of course.'

'She has vanished from it already,' I say. 'Gone into a coach and six the evening before last, and not seen since. She had implied that some admirer was coming to take her away, and she was taken.'

'Then her conduct much surprises me,' says Pepys with a primness to which he is in no way entitled. 'She made some claim to maidenly modesty. To me at least. I had not expected her to be seduced away so easily. But enough of her. To what do I owe the pleasure of your visit today, Sir John?'

'To the very lady we have been talking about, I'm afraid. Kitty Burgess is the ward of a kinsman of my wife's – a clergyman in Hampshire, with whom she has lived for some years, since the death of her parents. Aminta recommended Kitty to Betterton, when she fell out with Killigrew at the King's Company. Her departure from the Duke's Company was unexpected and a witness suggests that she may not have gone willingly – or at least that she had second thoughts at the last. Aminta is understandably concerned and wishes to find out what has happened to her protégée.'

'She knew Kitty well, then?'

'Far from it. I don't think she'd met Kitty before she came to London a year or so ago, and even after that Aminta really only saw her on stage. But my wife feels a moral responsibility for what has happened.'

Pepys frowns. 'Responsible? I cannot see why she should feel that. Not in any way at all. Kitty would appear to have acted very foolishly – indeed, immodestly – but if the clergyman who has been so long her guardian could not instil Christian virtue into her, then it is unreasonable to expect your wife to do so in a twelvemonth.'

'I nevertheless wondered if you might have heard anything about where she had gone.'

'Me, sir? Why should I know that?' He rubs his finger again. I think I can still see a dent where the ring once was.

'You know both the court and the theatre as well as any man in London,' I say. 'And you yourself said she was charming off stage, so you must have spoken to her.'

'Ha! Yes, of course. We talked of this and that. When we chanced to meet. Which I suppose we did occasionally. But it does not mean she confided anything of relevance. Indeed, now I take time to think about it properly, I doubt I have spoken properly to Kitty more than once or twice.' He smiles and spreads his hands before him, showing that he is concealing no actresses from me.

I wonder whether to inform Pepys that, though he may claim to have spoken to Kitty only once or twice, I have Neville's assurance it was two or three times. No, on balance, I don't think it's worth it.

'You haven't heard that any nobleman has recently taken a new mistress – I mean an actress?' I say. 'She implied she might have had such an offer from a duke or somebody of similar standing.'

'Ha!' he says again, to impress upon me how much at ease he is. 'Ha! Like you, Sir John, I avoid vulgar gossip as much as possible. I am not in a position to hear rumours of every nobleman's latest paramour – not even every duke's.'

'What about the King? You would at least know if His Majesty had another companion.'

'Sometimes I know before the King does,' he says with a smile. 'The King's ministers vie with each other to supply the royal larder with fair, fresh meat from the country. We hear of those who are being put forward as prospective candidates by my Lord Buckingham or Arlington or Ashley.'

'The King was said to be disappointed that Kitty was not on stage last night.'

'I do not doubt he was. But the King would scarcely need to snatch an actress off the street in the way you describe. Why would he employ a press gang when there is no lack of willing volunteers – ladies of rank and good breeding – to serve His Majesty? Nor can I think why anyone else would abduct an actress in that way. Heiresses, it is true, have been seized and forced to marry some rake against their will – Lord Rochester did exactly that. But nobody seeks to win a mistress in that fashion. And I can assure you that Killigrew wouldn't have tried to kidnap her on behalf of the King's Company. They thought themselves well rid of her, sir!'

'True,' I say.

'I think, Sir John, that you and Lady Grey have done your best for the girl. She was only a distant cousin of your wife's?'

'Not even that,' I say. 'It is only Kitty's guardian, Reginald Norris, who is related to Aminta by blood and even then not closely.'

'In that case, I would not waste your time further. Whether she entered the coach willingly or not, no lady who makes an assignation of that sort can claim she acted prudently or with due modesty. Whatever happens to her is her fault and her fault alone. Anyway, I'm sure Betterton can replace her quite easily. The part of the Queen is not a big one, when all's said and done. Like our own dear Queen in Whitehall, your wife's fictional version languishes somewhat in the shadows. The others can carry the play very well without Mistress Kitty Burgess.'

'You think so? That's reassuring. I shall let Aminta know,' I say.

Pepys nods. He is pleased he has solved my problem for me. He rubs his little finger again and makes a very good attempt at a smile.

'Does Pepys ever think of anything except his own narrow interests?' asks Aminta.

'I believe that he may have also considered your narrow interests,' I say, 'and indeed Betterton's. It is merely Kitty's that we can be certain he has ignored.'

'How well acquainted was he with Kitty?'

'I think he avoided answering that question as much as he could. But he undoubtedly knew her. His indignant remark about her claiming to be virtuous suggests that any proposals he may have made were rejected – on the grounds of decency or practicality. That blow to his self-esteem, in itself, explains his indifference to her fate.'

'Do you think Pepys told you less than he might?'

'Pepys, like Lord Arlington, always tells me less than he might as a matter of principle. And he would have told me nothing that was to his discredit, which may mean he left out a great deal. But I think he probably knows no better than I do where Kitty has gone.'

'It's as well, then, that my own investigations were more successful,' says Aminta. 'After you left to visit your good friend, Samuel, I decided to call in on Killigrew at the King's Company.'

'It was very early to call on any drinking companion of the King's,' I say.

'I think his head was not as clear as either of us might have wished. But my mentioning Kitty's name sobered him up immediately. It really is far worse than we believed. He sacked Kitty for her own good. She'd upset everyone in the company, except possibly Killigrew himself, who is not easily offended, drunk or sober. She had ideas of her own importance that could be accounted for neither by her parentage nor by the effort she put into her performances. He said that feelings were running so high against her that he needed to get her out for her own safety.'

'But nobody there would have decided to abduct her?'

'Killigrew thought Kitty's former colleagues took a more charitable view of her conduct now she was disrupting things in the Duke's Company rather than their own. Anyway, actors can't afford a carriage and six. But the interesting thing was this: Killigrew told me that the reason nobody would have seriously considered murdering Kitty, however much she deserved it, was that it was widely believed she had the King's protection. His Majesty apparently wished to make Kitty his mistress, or had done so already. Killigrew thought it could be true and Killigrew has better information on that count than anyone I know, being in receipt of all court gossip both factual and libellous. He said the King undoubtedly visited the theatre more often on nights when Kitty was performing than nights when she was not. And His Majesty openly praised

Kitty's acting in front of Nell Gwynne, which was a brave thing to do.'

'It is believable that the King may have been enamoured of Kitty, and that may have gone some way to turning her head. But I agree with Pepys that it is inconceivable that he would abduct Kitty. He prefers lower hanging fruit, and best of all he appreciates it if one of his friends should act as his fruit picker.'

'So do you think somebody abducted Kitty on his behalf?' says Aminta. 'I can believe that his drinking companions may have decided to steal her as a favour to the King or simply as a joke to while away an hour or two on a long summer evening.'

'Betterton and Neville both said there was a disorderly crowd of young rakes in the pit – Herbert and Sackville and their companions.'

'It wasn't Rochester anyway – or not in person. Killigrew was drinking with him when it happened. It is unfortunate that Neville was unable to identify the coat of arms, other than to rule out camelopards. That would have helped us a great deal.'

'While not denying you have discovered more from Killigrew than I did from Pepys,' I say, 'I'm not sure we are much closer to knowing where Kitty was taken, whether she went willingly and whether she is now safe or in the greatest danger.'

'Have you considered speaking to your former employer?'

I sigh. 'I suppose I could if I have to.'

'Her abduction seems, in my view, both calculated and underhand,' says Aminta. 'And it may well have been done to ingratiate somebody with the King.'

'I agree,' I say. 'There is therefore a very good chance that Lord Arlington knows all about it.'

Chapter Three

In which I read a letter

Henry Bennet, Baron Arlington, Secretary of State for the Southern Department, is in conference with his assistant, Mister Joseph Williamson, but I am nevertheless admitted to his office, with only a modest delay. I am in favour, even if I'm not sure why.

Arlington, seated at his desk, observes me over the black patch that he wears on his nose. He must have almost forgotten at which battle he received the wound that apparently still necessitates the thin strip of plaster, but it would now seem odd – almost improper – seeing him with a completely naked nose. Underneath his flowing black wig, his real hair may be a little greyer than it was when we last met, and his face may be a little more lined. But the expression of friendly contempt is completely unaltered. Williamson, standing before his master, towers over him, but he hunches himself up slightly so as not to appear impolitely tall. He gives me a quick nod and a longer smile. I'm pleased I can talk to them both. Arlington has the power to order almost anything, including a covert death or two if that would oblige me. Williamson has the efficiency to ensure that Arlington's orders are carried out. And Williamson is, up to a very carefully calculated point, on my side. At least he was when I last spoke to him.

'My clerk said that you wanted to talk to me about an abducted actress,' says Arlington. 'I would urge you to be brief, Sir John. The French Ambassador, who has been waiting impatiently to see us for over an hour, may feel that the treaty he wishes to discuss is of considerably greater weight than a missing player.'

Williamson smiles sympathetically. We both know that Arlington at present favours an alliance with the Dutch. Or the Spanish. Or the Swedes. Or the Polish-Lithuanian Commonwealth. The King conversely seems committed to an alliance with France, though appearances can be deceptive. And anyway, even if it has to be the French, there's no reason for Arlington to make it too easy for anyone. There are many good reasons for keeping a French Ambassador pacing up and down for a little longer, speculating on why Arlington won't talk to him.

'The lady concerned is Kitty Burgess,' I say. 'She's an actress with the Duke's Company. She has a small part in my wife's latest play. Kitty informed the management that she had a better offer from elsewhere – a promise from some powerful individual. Somebody came to collect her that evening in a coach and six. At the last minute, Kitty seems to have doubted the wisdom of getting into the coach, but was taken nonetheless. She hasn't been heard of since.'

'And why should any of us be concerned?' asks Arlington.

'The King may possibly have been interested in her. He may have been thinking of making her his mistress. Or somebody may've been thinking of it on his behalf.'

The mention of the King's name means that I now have Arlington's full attention. If Kitty was the protégée of one of his rivals, then that is of interest to him. If she has been kidnapped by one of his other rivals then that is also of note. On the outcome of such peripheral acts may rest the future of some greater or lesser courtier, which in turn might increase or diminish Arlington's own influence to an extent that would be almost measurable by those who measure such things. He puts his head on one side, thoughtfully.

'You clearly don't know whose coach it was, Sir John, or you would have told us,' says Williamson.

'No,' I say, 'I don't. An actor named Mister Neville saw Kitty depart though she may not have noticed him, concealed as he was in a doorway. The coach bore a coat of arms, but unfortunately Neville knows nothing of the art and science of heraldry.'

'A much neglected field of study,' says Williamson. 'Every child should be taught it together with their alphabet, the rule of three and elementary cryptology. I am still not sure how you think we can help you, Sir John.'

'Nor am I,' says Arlington.

'If the King did have plans for her,' I say, 'then you may hear rumours of those plans at court. He might, for example, have recently purchased a house at a suitable distance from the palace. Or Lady Castlemaine may be visibly vexed at the prospect of yet another rival. Or Lord Rochester may have penned a particularly obscene poem on the subject. Or, my Lord, one of your agents may have heard a rumour. Or your wife may have mentioned it in passing over dinner. Any or all of those.'

Arlington shakes his head. Nothing like that has happened to the best of his knowledge.

'If we hear anything relevant, then we shall certainly let you know,' says Williamson. 'You can trust me on that, Sir John.' His easy manner and the last remaining hint of a northern accent are reassuring, even though I know he works for Arlington and would not have survived a month in his service if he is as open and honest as he seems.

'Thank you,' I say. 'Then I won't take up any more of your time, gentlemen. I'm sure that the French Ambassador must be ready by now to agree to whatever you were about to propose.'

Williamson looks sideways at Arlington, who nods almost imperceptibly.

'There is just one other thing, Sir John,' says Williamson with a friendly smile that puts me instantly on my guard.

'Yes?' I say.

'Since you are here anyway,' he says.

'So I am,' I say.

'The Earl of Clarendon,' he says.

'The former Lord Chancellor,' I say.

'As you know, he has been exiled by the King and currently lives, somewhat reluctantly, in France.'

'He left the country a couple of years ago,' I say, 'after he was deprived of his post. Our defeats in the Dutch war had made him unpopular with the people, he had annoyed the House of Commons through some technical violations of habeas corpus and, most importantly, he bored the King to death. Nobody wanted him around any more. He was forced by the King to surrender his seal of office and then he had to flee London, lest the mob tear him limb from limb.'

Williamson nods. 'Precisely. But the French King sees his presence there as an unwelcome hindrance to the alliance he has long desired with England. He has therefore ordered the Earl to leave France several times, but Clarendon has nowhere else much to go. So he remains in Montpellier to the satisfaction of nobody. King Louis is willing to turn a blind eye to that as long as Clarendon doesn't try to visit Paris.'

'The Earl is well?' I enquire.

'That is not a question that any loyal subject of His Majesty could possibly answer,' says Williamson, 'since it is treason to correspond with him. Even his own children are forbidden to write, which I fear he resents deeply.'

'I apologise for asking,' I say. 'I did not mean to suggest you were in any way disloyal.'

'Of course, we have agents in France,' says Williamson, 'simply in order to reassure ourselves as to the Earl's happiness, safety and wellbeing. And to monitor any visitors that he has. We also, purely as a matter of courtesy, intercept and read his post. His son, Lord Cornbury, occasionally forgets that he may not write to his father. We do not prevent him doing so.'

'It would be cruel to cut off all contact with his children,' I say.

'Prevention would also stop us knowing what Lord Clarendon was thinking,' says Williamson. 'Cornbury's letters are full of helpful information in that way. Lord Clarendon's replies are more circumspect, of course. But then he was one of the King's ministers for very many years. We provided him with much useful intelligence. He knows how we got it.'

'I suppose he does.'

'One way and another, it has been brought to our notice that the former Lord Chancellor was, somewhat improperly, in Paris a couple of months ago and is back there again now. On his first visit, he wrote a rather interesting letter, which came to our attention in the usual way. It was mainly about his health and was written in plain English and good quality black ink. He used a code and lemon juice, however, for the postscript. Almost invisible until heated. Almost.'

'Lemon juice! He must think we are half asleep,' says Arlington. 'He must also think we have no idea where he sent it from. King Louis would take a dim view of Clarendon's unauthorised presence in the capital, if we were to tell the French Ambassador of it, as we really should.'

'Then something very important must have happened that justifies the risk of a double journey to Paris,' I say.

'We thought that too. But we still don't know what. It occurred to us, when our clerk told us you were in the waiting room, that you might be able to assist us,' says Williamson. 'So, we decided we would share what we know with you.' He passes me a sheet of paper. 'This is the hidden postscript decoded.'

I skim it quickly, then read it out loud. 'As we feared, the convent records show clearly that the Byron girl died there in 1658. We shall need to decide how best to conceal this. I have spoken again to the Abbess and to Father Christopher, who will testify in an acceptable way, as will I. Everything is in place. You now only have to proceed with things in London. I shall see to the rest.' I pause for a moment. 'I don't understand,' I say. 'I assume the convent is in Paris? But who is the Byron girl?'

'We pondered on that for some time. Back in the 1650s, Eleanor, Lady Byron, was a mistress of the King's, when he was in Paris. She died in 1663, not 1658 – and in England, not Paris. That is a matter of public record. And even when she was the King's mistress, she wasn't exactly a young girl – twenty-four or twenty-five, I think. So we don't think the letter refers to her. She was not without significance, of course. The

King promised her, and very occasionally paid, a staggeringly generous pension for services rendered while he was in exile. But there have been many mistresses since then. More than most of us can count.'

'But the Byron *girl* . . . Could Lady Byron have had a daughter?' I ask. 'A daughter of the King's? Is that its meaning? And she died in 1658 in Paris, before the King was restored?'

'That was our thought too,' says Arlington. 'But we have made some careful enquiries – even, obliquely, to the King himself. Nobody admits to the knowledge of a child – male or female. Clarendon, who was with the King at the time, might know better – possibly even better than the King. That may be why he has left the relative safety of Montpellier and risked his liberty, or even his life, in travelling to Paris – in order, apparently, to conceal her death. That's not the only mystery, though. There's also the question of Father Christopher and what he might testify to.'

'Who is he?'

'The English chaplain in Paris,' says Arlington.

I shake my head. 'It is an interesting problem, to be sure. But I cannot see how I can help.'

'We wondered,' says Williamson, 'whether you and Lady Grey would care to visit Paris. We do of course know where Clarendon is lodging, even if the King of France does not. I think your wife knew his lordship quite well in happier times?'

'Reasonably well,' I say.

'Excellent. So, you and she could go to Paris – with some plausible story that we would provide as to how you had obtained his address – and call on him without arousing his suspicion in any way. He'd trust you – or, more to the point, he'd trust your wife. You could find out who or what the

Byron girl was and what he would have used her for, had she still been alive. And why her death now needs to be covered up. With luck he might give you letters to bring back to his friends in England. Letters you could pass to us. He lacks truly reliable messengers, as is apparent from the ease with which we obtained the document you have just read.'

'I'm sorry,' I say. 'But my wife needs to remain in London for the next week at least. And I doubt she would be happy to leave England while Kitty is still missing.'

'You yourself knew Clarendon during his first exile – I mean during the days of Oliver's tyrannical rule.'

'I met him once or twice,' I say cautiously. 'In Brussels.'

'Remind me,' says Arlington, 'what were you doing in Brussels?'

'I was spying,' I say. 'You know that perfectly well.'

'For anyone in particular?'

'Cromwell,' I say. 'The head of the lawful government of this country at the time. You are also aware that I have shown my loyalty to His Majesty many times over since then.'

'I would have thought you would have welcomed a further opportunity to demonstrate your gratitude for the King's failure to punish you for working against him in the days of the Republic.'

'If the scar on my cheek, earned in the King's service, isn't a visible enough sign of my loyalty, then a pleasant trip to Paris probably wouldn't help me.'

Arlington's hand instinctively reaches for the patch on his nose. Williamson laughs. 'Well said, Sir John. And you are not the only person in London to have once served the Republic. But what if the safety of the country depended on it? How say you then? Could you refuse us?'

'I would advise you to find somebody younger and more desirous of adventure.'

'Well, at least think about it,' says Williamson.

'Of course,' I say, though we all know that my thinking about it won't help them very much. Then I add: 'So, to whom was this possibly treasonous message sent? Who in London is plotting against the King?'

'It was sent to Lord Ashley,' says Arlington. 'His Majesty's Chancellor of the Exchequer.'

Chapter Four

In which I discuss politics with my wife

'So Lord Arlington's idea of helping us find Kitty is to send you to Paris to produce evidence that he may use against his old enemy, Lord Ashley?'

'Officially, Lord Ashley is an esteemed friend and colleague. And Arlington proposed sending us both. He thought that your acquaintance with the aristocracy was better than mine.'

'That is true, because your own claims to gentility are tenuous and entirely on your mother's side of the family. But I certainly wouldn't travel to Paris with the intention of betraying Clarendon. He's a family friend.'

'Clarendon wanted to have me shot when he discovered I worked for Cromwell. Now I think about it, I'm probably slightly less grateful than you are.'

'But I persuaded the King you weren't worth shooting. So, that was all right.'

'I told Arlington we wouldn't go, anyway, so issues of relative gratitude don't really arise.'

'Did Arlington say why Ashley is plotting with Clarendon?'

'I think Ashley, as one of the few completely unabashed Protestants in the King's council, finds himself increasingly isolated,' I say. 'He suspects, rightly, that things happen which the religiously flexible Arlington gets told about and he doesn't. Ashley is also in a minority over the problem of succession. With no legitimate child of the King's to succeed him, the crown passes to the King's brother, the undoubtedly Catholic Duke of York. Whereas Ashley would like Parliament to declare the King's eldest bastard son, Duke of Monmouth, as the legal heir.'

'As many others in the country would,' says Aminta. 'Ashley is, in that respect, a man of the people.'

'All of which has made him unpopular with both the King, who won't have royal succession interfered with by mere commoners, and the Duke of York, who must already be planning how many cardinals he'll have at court after the King's death.'

'Monmouth may not be quite the King's bastard people believe him to be,' says Aminta. 'There were many rumours that the King was secretly married to Monmouth's mother. That would make him the legitimate heir.'

'If there was ever proof of that, it has long since been destroyed,' I say. 'And Monmouth will not move against the King, who one way or another is most certainly his father. Monmouth is Ashley's only card at the moment, and he can't play it. Nor will the King oblige Ashley by divorcing the Queen and remarrying so that he can have a legitimate Protestant child to add to the growing army of bastard children by his various mistresses. No, sooner or later, the Duke of York will succeed, we shall have an openly Catholic king and Ashley will need to ride very fast to Dover and join Clarendon in exile – Amsterdam, rather than Montpellier, in his case.'

'But in the meantime Ashley and Clarendon plot together,' says Aminta. 'Strange bedfellows, except that both must feel they have fewer throws of the dice left than they had once hoped. I also remember people talking about Lady Byron back then. She was a little older than the King. I think he had great affection for her, but she was merely one of many mistresses and bore him no children.'

'Did she bear anyone else any children?'

'I think not.'

'Well, whoever the Byron girl was, it would seem that she is dead anyway. And we shall not be travelling to Paris to find out more. It's Arlington's problem, not mine. But we do need to find Kitty. I doubt she's far from London. It's a shame we don't know whose carriage she has been travelling in.'

'I did return to the theatre this morning to discuss money with Betterton. While I was there, I thought I might as well see if Neville had any better recollection than he had before about the coat of arms on the coach. The best he could come up with was that he thought it might have been cows.'

'I'm not sure cows have ever appeared as heraldic beasts. They lack the necessary gravitas. Plenty of lions. Plenty of eagles. A few stags, wild boar and serpents. But nothing that will allow itself to be tamely milked or herded. Heralds value ferocity and unpredictability over usefulness.'

'Perhaps we should simply take some comfort in the King's interest – everyone at the Duke's Company is now convinced that the King was about to or already had made Kitty his mistress. If Kitty was abducted, then it was by somebody who could afford to keep a coach and six, and anyone of that rank in society would have been aware that an attack on a mistress of the King's, even a potential one, would be seen as an attack on the King himself. We have a King who will laugh off most things, but never a slight against kingship.'

'That is what I am hoping too,' I say. 'That is her main protection.'

But, a few days later, as we are preparing to leave London for Essex, a messenger arrives.

'He just asked if this was where Lady Grey lived and thrust this thing into my hands,' says our maid, holding out a letter. She feels that no good will come from such a weather-stained missive, conveyed by such a grubby messenger.

Aminta seems to share this fear and opens it carefully. She reads quickly, as if hoping the end will be better than the beginning, but it isn't.

'It's from the coroner in Bishop's Stortford,' she says. 'They seem to have found a woman's body. With a copy of my play clutched in her hands. It was a bit late, but maybe Kitty finally decided to learn her lines?'

Chapter Five

In which we discuss the theatre with a coroner

'It is helpful to know the identity of the deceased,' says the coroner. 'From what you tell me, there can be little doubt that it is Mistress Burgess. But there was no need for you to travel all the way out to Hertfordshire. A brief letter from you, confirming the facts, would have sufficed. The inquest is done.'

'We were returning to Essex anyway,' I say. 'This diversion to Bishop's Stortford adds an hour or two to our journey at the most.'

'I am afraid you are also too late for the funeral,' says the coroner. 'We buried her three days ago. I was there. And the vicar, naturally. And the women who dressed the body. It was all done decently, in the pious hope of resurrection and that her friends might pay the necessary burial fees in due course.'

I nod. Kitty was kin of a sort.

'And the cost of the coffin, if at all possible, Sir John. Wood is so expensive nowadays.'

'We would obviously wish to do that too,' I say.

'I shall tell the vicar to send you the bill, unless you prefer to visit him while you are here? He lives close by.'

'We'll call in at the vicarage,' I say. 'I can settle matters there.'

'Thank you. That is very kind of you.'

'And the verdict of your inquest was what, exactly?' I ask.

'Her body was found by the side of the road, just outside town. She had been very badly beaten about the head.'

'Was there any attempt at concealment?'

'None at all. But I think she had been dead for a day or two when she was left there. Though her wounds were grievous, there was no sign of blood on the grass around her.'

'So, she died somewhere else?'

'Without doubt. In the evening, she was not there. Everyone is agreed on that. Then, the following morning, she was. Lying as if asleep, they said. But, when they tried to rouse her, it was clear at once that she was doing no such thing. We had, of course, no idea who she might be. Fortunately there was, about her person, the script of a play entitled *The Summer Birdcage*. I made some enquiries and it transpired that the piece had been newly written by Lady Grey. Very amusing, my Lady, though some of the scenes caused the vicar to raise his eyebrows when I showed it to him. Anyway, I sent a message post-haste addressed to Lady Grey in London – though I did not know exactly where to find you and it would seem that my messenger had some difficulty in locating the house.'

'Well,' I say, 'it would seem that, very sadly, it is Kitty. But, since we are here, I assume you will raise the coffin so that we can identify her properly.'

The coroner gives me a grim smile. 'It would do you no good, Sir John. She had been bludgeoned so that her best friends might not have recognised her. Nose, cheeks, jaw, all fractured. Scarcely a single tooth left in her head.'

'Is there any clue as to why she might have been attacked so viciously?' I ask.

'From the evidence we have – none at all. But there was one other thing of note – she had given birth to a child at about the time of her demise.'

'There was no sign of a baby?' Aminta asks.

'I would have said at once if there had been. If dead, further enquiries would have been needed. If alive, there would have been the question of who would take care of it. I should have been reluctant to foist it on this rather impoverished parish, if she had friends to whom the infant might go.'

'It should have occurred to me that she might be pregnant,' says Aminta. 'Several people commented on her figure. But nobody said that they thought she could be with child.'

'If the child was born before its time,' says the coroner, 'it may be that her condition was less advanced – less obvious – than it might have been.'

'Was there anything else to identify her?' asks Aminta. 'Apart from my script.'

'Two things,' says the coroner. 'There is the dress she was wearing, which I still have and can show you. It is a very fine one. Silk. Pale blue. London made, if I am any judge. Strictly speaking it now belongs to the women who prepared her body for burial, and I have told them that they shall have it – or a guinea in its place, which I hope you will be so good as to pay if you wish to take the dress with you. There was also a ring, with a crest upon it. I shall fetch them both.'

He returns half hidden by a voluminous blue silk dress with much gold lacing, around which he wraps his arms with some difficulty. He disencumbers himself and drapes it over his dining table, which it covers almost completely.

'Yes,' says Aminta. 'That is hers. Or at least it is the very twin of one that I have seen her wearing and which I was told she was dressed in when she left the theatre. There seems to be almost no blood on it.'

'Almost none, as you say – just a little round the neck. Had she been beaten to death while wearing it, then it should by rights be covered with blood. So we must assume she was not wearing it at the time, but was dressed in it after death. Of course, if she had taken to her bed before the baby was born, then she would obviously not have been wearing the dress at that time, or just afterwards when she was killed. But perhaps a little blood got onto it when she was dressed in it later.'

'Was there blood on her linen under the dress?'

'Yes, slightly more – already well dried when they found her. The clothes under the dress were old and poor quality though. Clean enough, but not what you would have expected a gentlewoman to wear. Still, she was an actress and, I suppose, more concerned with outward show than inner purity. Do you wish to take the dress? A guinea for it is cheap.'

'No. Please give it to the women, as you proposed,' says Aminta. 'I have as little use for it as Kitty does.'

'Thank you, my Lady. They would prefer ready money, I think . . . but, no, of course, the dress if you prefer.'

'She was wearing a black cloak when she left London, according to the only witness we have. Was there any sign of that?'

The coroner shakes his head. 'No, my Lady. Perhaps her killers thought they could sell that at least? Here, however, is the manuscript,' he says, removing a roll of paper from a drawer. He hands it to Aminta, who quickly glances at it.

'I'll take that anyway. Copyists aren't cheap and Betterton will be able to use it, especially if they have a long run. I'm assuming it is not already promised to the curate or the church cat?'

'I think it would be of no great value to either,' says the coroner. 'Odd that it should be there at all, really. When you think about it.'

'I have thought about it, and it is,' says Aminta. 'Very odd indeed.'

'I agree,' I say. 'If her body was carried there, then this must have been carried there too, and placed quite deliberately, and slightly improbably, in her hands. It is not there by chance. Could it be that whoever left her there, with her face disfigured as it was, wanted her identified?'

'I truly cannot say. Anyway, the meaning of the script could have easily been overlooked. It was only by a lucky chance that we knew to contact you. Well, if that is all . . .'

'You also mentioned a ring,' I say.

'Thank you for reminding me,' he says. 'I must give you that to return to her family or whoever you think best.' He looks again in the drawer and produces a small gold signet ring. He hands it to Aminta, who squints at the coat of arms in the half-light of the coroner's parlour.

'Cattle?' I ask.

She shakes her head and passes the ring to me. I also examine it and nod thoughtfully.

'You recognise the crest?' asks the coroner.

'Samuel Pepys,' I say.

'The Navy Board man?' he says.

'The crest is slightly unusual, or I would not be so certain. I have seen it on his finger many times. And, when we last met, I noted that his signet ring was missing.'

'How very odd,' says the coroner. 'I wonder how she got that? Well, it must be his then, if you say so. I'm sure he'll be pleased when you return it to him.'

Chapter Six

In which my wife and I have a small difference of opinion

'I am most grateful to you for the prompt payment,' says the vicar. 'We are not a rich parish, at least for this part of the world, and there is always work to be done about the church. Or the vicarage. Not to mention the poor, who impose unreasonable demands upon us by having children they cannot afford and then dying in the most careless and inconsiderate manner. To have burial fees paid, for once, in a timely and gentlemanly manner is very welcome. Would you require change or are you happy to donate the very trifling balance to church funds?'

'I would not wish to trouble you for a few shillings if it was inconvenient,' I say.

'That is very kind. I do worry of course about the child.'

'The child?'

'The infant that the lady was delivered of before her death. What became of it? From what you tell me, she was abducted. Whoever abducted her must now have it — boy or girl. But to what end? I mean, I am grateful they did not leave us with another hungry mouth to suck at the meagre resources of the parish. And yet, as a Christian, I do worry.'

'The child could be anywhere by now,' I say. 'Assuming it was not stillborn.'

'Stillborn? I think not. Surely they would have left it with its mother, to be buried together in a seemly manner? Why take it, unless it is alive? What use could a poor dead child be to anyone?'

'I don't know,' I say. I dismiss the disturbing thought of witchcraft, though it must have occurred to the vicar as well.

'Well, at least we have a name for the mother,' he says. 'Something to put on the gravestone. I suppose you wouldn't like to pay for the stone? Since she was your friend?'

'No,' says Aminta. 'I don't think we would.'

'But you are her closest family?' asks the vicar.

'She has a guardian,' says Aminta. 'A clergyman in Hampshire.'

'He has a good living there?'

'I think not. The parish is pretty but not rich. My cousin's income is in proportion to its wealth, not its beauty.'

'Ah,' he says. 'Then a simple wooden cross may have to suffice. I suppose it's all the same on Judgement Day, though stone is considered more genteel.'

Our coach rattles along over the hard summer roads, sending up a cloud of ochre-coloured dust behind us.

'I'm surprised you didn't want to pay for the headstone,' I say. 'It would have been a small thing to do – to ensure Kitty was buried under her own name.'

'I'm not paying for a stone for a total stranger,' says Aminta.

'What do you mean?'

'That wasn't Kitty.'

'But the coroner identified the body as hers,' I say.

'On the flimsiest of evidence. We didn't see her face. All we know is that it was her dress, my manuscript and Pepys's ring.'

'We've discovered a little more than that and it all fits in very well with what we already knew. To begin with there is the timing of the discovery, so soon after Kitty vanished under such worrying circumstances. And we should also have considered, in view of the comments about her noticeably gaining weight, that she might be with child. That, together with the three items found with her, is strongly suggestive that the body is hers. I think Kitty must have given birth as she was being driven north from London. The jolting of the coach on these roads, especially if it was being driven at speed, might have been enough to bring about premature labour. After the baby was born, she tried to escape her captors, seemingly in nothing but her shift. They caught her again and brutally killed her. That explains the disfigurement. That also explains the blood on the underclothing and the lack of blood on the dress.'

'So, what happened to the child? And why leave so much evidence as to who she was? Why not just leave her in a plain white shift? Come to think of it, why not bury her remains in a dark wood or on a deserted heath? Both must be freely available round here. They wanted us to find the body and identify it as Kitty. You said so yourself. That's why it was dressed in blue silk, left on the grass verge in plain sight, and the manuscript and the ring left with it. And that's why they had to make her face unrecognisable. They didn't want us digging up her body, as you would have done if you could, and discovering it was another woman entirely. No, Kitty is still alive somewhere, having made her escape wrapped in the missing cloak, while some poor woman, who had probably died in childbirth, has been left in a silk dress by the roadside and then buried in her place.'

'Look, Aminta, I can understand why you may have doubts, but you must agree that everything you've said is somewhat speculative. And nothing you've said really rules out the body being Kitty's. I concede that the child's disappearance is unexplained – but perhaps it was always the child they wished to abduct and had to kill the mother to do it? Or the child was simply buried decently elsewhere. As for leaving the script with her, perhaps, having killed Kitty, the murderers were overcome with remorse and wanted her friends to know what had become of her? There are many possible explanations for how and why she might have been found as she was. I am sorry for your loss and your cousin's loss, but I think you have to accept that Kitty is dead. She was seen walking into a trap some days before. We feared something like this would happen. And so it has. The alternative, as you say, is that somebody has obtained a dead woman from somewhere, dressed her as Kitty, given her your script and Pepys's ring – and then caused us to be summoned from London to identify her. But which is more likely? Women are sadly murdered all the time, often for no very good reason. Few are spirited away as a result of some overly elaborate plot.'

'She isn't dead,' says Aminta stubbornly. 'As for the overly elaborate plot, we are going to find out exactly what it is.'

I look out of the window at the sunny and gently rolling hills of Hertfordshire. The pale green of spring has long since given way to the rich, deep green of summer. The grass is long and lush in the fields. The unheraldic cattle are fattening up.

There is honeysuckle in the hedgerows and, here and there, a last dog rose or two. Whenever we have to slow down, to navigate a bend or edge round some pothole in the road, and the constant rattling of our great wheels is reduced to a low rumble, I can hear the song of the larks high above us.

I admit there is much that I do not understand. Whoever killed Kitty, why was she brought to Hertfordshire to die? Why was she not killed in London, in some dark alley a few yards from the theatre? Because she had to live long enough to give birth to the child she was carrying? Because her kidnapper had a house out here, where she could be conveniently lodged until then? Because, whatever the reason for her abduction, her death was simply an unfortunate mistake, which just happened to occur in Hertfordshire? But, whatever Aminta may wish to believe, she is dead. Dead and buried. And the child has gone.

'I think there's an inn just ahead,' I say. 'We could stop there to eat. I can order a roast chicken and some bread and perhaps wine if it can be obtained in this part of the world. I think we deserve some refreshment, don't you?'

'I've already told you, John. Don't try to change the subject and assume I'll just forget it all once we get home to our own house and our own son and the half-completed manuscript of my next play. Kitty is still out there somewhere. And I'm not giving up until I find her.'

'Of course not,' I say.

'I would strongly advise you, John, not to use that patronising tone.'

'Of course,' I say.

'I mean it, John.'

I do not doubt that she means it. Not for one moment. I shall say nothing further for the moment that might imply that I doubt her. But she is still wrong for all that. Kitty is dead. Dead and buried.

Little Charles runs, slightly unsteadily, to greet us as we descend from the coach, and throws himself at Aminta's stiff, gold-laced petticoats before she has even placed two feet on the ground. She lifts our son, complaining loudly and happily at the weight he has put on during the few days we were away. He laughs and puts his arms round her neck. I wonder what somebody who wished to steal him from us would have to do to Aminta before she let him go. Only repeated blows, of the sort that Kitty apparently suffered, would make her finally release her grip on his tiny hand.

Aminta's father, Sir Felix, appears at the door and somewhat theatrically hobbles down the steps and on to the gravel drive. I think that, deep down, he enjoys being old. Being young was all about riding at a gallop, in a buff coat and steel helmet, into the massed ranks of Cromwell's cavalry. Middle age was all about trying to pay off debts incurred during the war and eventually enduring penniless exile in Brussels with the King. Only recently has he experienced, as our guest, complete peace, modest prosperity and an unlocked cellar entirely at his disposal.

'I hope *The Summer Birdcage* enjoyed the success it deserved?' he says.

'It was magnificent,' I say. 'Very sadly, however, we have lost a talented actress from the cast.'

'A pretty one?' he asks, instinctively curling the ends of his grey moustache. 'Defected to the King's Company, no doubt? Or found herself a rich husband?'

'I wish either was the case. I'm very sorry to have to tell you that it was Kitty Burgess – the ward of Aminta's cousin. She was abducted from the theatre and we have just come from Bishop's Stortford, to where we had been called to identify her body.'

'Identify her body?' For a moment Sir Felix just stares at us. 'What are you saying? She was murdered?'

'I fear so,' I say.

He shakes his head. 'Reginald is my kinsman – I mean my late wife's cousin's son. That makes Kitty almost kin too. And she was how old? Not yet twenty, by my calculation. That is very sad indeed.'

'Except that the body wasn't hers and she hasn't been murdered,' says Aminta. 'I'm not saying it isn't very sad for the family of the dead woman, whoever she was, but that is another matter entirely.'

'I'm getting confused,' says Sir Felix. 'Was it or wasn't it Kitty who was killed?'

'Aminta thinks not,' I say. 'But I fear it must be. We shall need to tell her guardian.'

'Will you inform Reginald?' he asks Aminta. 'Or shall I? I think you may find the right words and tone more easily than an old soldier like me.'

'It's not her, father,' she says. 'There is no need to trouble my cousin in any way, either with simple prose or in the form of a Petrarchan sonnet.'

'John seems to think it was Kitty,' says Sir Felix, nodding in my direction. 'He knows quite a lot about dead bodies.'

'Not this one. He hasn't even had the chance to inspect it, much though he would have liked to dig it up. On what grounds, father, are you saying my husband might be right and I might be wrong?'

Sir Felix looks first at his daughter and then at his son-in-law, considers his position in our household very carefully and says: 'Well, one of you is doubtless correct. Either it's her or it's somebody else. Very sad, either way, of course. For somebody. Has Betterton paid you what you're owed, Aminta?'

'Most of it,' says my wife.

'And you spent it all on new silk gowns, I suppose, while John wasn't watching?'

'I find that question objectionable in so many ways,' says Aminta, 'that I am tempted not to give you the present I bought you.'

Sir Felix, unable to see anything wrong with his remark, looks at me and smiles apologetically. He genuinely thought that he'd brought Aminta up as a dutiful daughter and obedient spouse. He probably blames his own long-absent wife. 'There's a letter for you, by the way,' he says. 'A rather scruffy letter, to be honest. It's on the table in the drawing room.'

We need to wash the dust of the road from our faces and brush it from our clothes before we can contemplate sitting on clean tapestried chairs. It is therefore half an hour later that we are presented with a roughly folded and quickly sealed sheet of paper addressed to My Lady Grey at the manor house in Clavershall West, Essex.

'It arrived a day or two ago,' says Sir Felix. 'I can't remember exactly when. It was delivered by a boy who claimed to have ridden up from Epping. He demanded five shillings for his trouble, which I paid him. I hope it's worth the money.'

Aminta opens it. She reads it twice, smiles, then frowns, then smiles again. On balance she feels that the contents are to her advantage rather than mine. She hands the letter to me. 'It's from Kitty,' she says. 'She's asking for our help.'

Chapter Seven

In which my wife and I discuss a course of action

'I write to you, my Lady,' I read from the paper in front of me, 'to request your most urgent assistance. I should have listened to Meg's advice. I have been duped into leaving London and am being taken I know not whither in a coach and six. We have stopped at Epping, since it is too dark to drive further tonight and the horses are tired. I am to be ready to leave early tomorrow morning, travelling towards Bishop's Stortford, and have been warned that I will be watched constantly and that escape is impossible. I shall give this to the stable boy at the inn and ask him to ride to Clavershall West, where I understand you have a house. I have had to promise him five shillings, which I have told him he will receive on delivering this and which I will repay you as soon as I can. My abductors say we are to travel northwards to meet with their master. I cannot be certain, but I think that they may be Lord Arlington's men, for they have whispered his name to each other several times. Please help me. Really, I know nobody else to whom I can turn. May God bless you for your kindness. Your most unfortunate Kitty.'

'What did I tell you?' says Aminta. 'She is still alive enough to write letters. And do you still think it can't be a Byzantine plot – with Arlington involved in some way?'

'It proves nothing,' I say. 'She merely thinks she overheard Arlington's name. That's hardly proof beyond reasonable doubt. As for her still being alive, the letter is undated. Everything points to its having been written over a week ago, probably the same evening that she fled the theatre and well before she reached Bishop's Stortford, which she says quite clearly is where they are going next.'

'If she had written it the night she vanished, then surely she would have sent it to me in London, where I was then, not here? But she knew I would be travelling back to Essex later. It makes more sense that this was written in the last day or two – long after the burial of the woman you claim is Kitty. But I can see you have got it into your head that she is dead, and nothing will change your mind.'

'The letter certainly reads to me as if she has only just left the theatre on the night she was taken.'

'Really? If you will be kind enough to look at it properly, I think you will find that it says nothing about the theatre at all – it merely tells us she has been duped into leaving London at some unspecified time.'

'Very well,' I say. 'I shall get some maps from the library. Then perhaps we can settle this.'

I have returned. The maps are spread across the table, like the clear indisputable facts they are. I am about to prove my point.

'So, the theatre she was taken from would be about here in London,' I say, indicating the approximate spot in the northern part of the city. 'She wrote from Epping, which you will see is here. Then Bishop's Stortford, where she'd been told they were going, is further north . . . So was that intended to be their final destination, or were they on their way to another place to meet with the abductors' master?' My finger follows the road on which they must have been travelling, northeastwards from Bishop's Stortford, winding across the gentle hills of north Essex, skirting this very village that we are in and then on into Suffolk. Eventually my hand hovers above the town of Bury St Edmunds.

Sir Felix peers at the map. 'Very pleasant countryside round there,' he says. 'Good and fertile. But why would they stop in Bury St Edmunds?'

'Euston Hall,' I say.

'Yes, it's marked,' says Sir Felix. 'Who owns it?'

'Lord Arlington,' I say. 'It's Lord Arlington's country residence.'

'That's a coincidence,' he says. 'I mean in view of what Kitty overheard and all that.'

'What is Arlington's coat of arms?' asks Aminta.

'It can be blazoned as follows: gules, between three demi-lions rampant argent, a bezant,' I say.

'Meaning what exactly?' says Aminta.

'It's a red shield, on which we have three upright silver lions depicted only from the waist up, with a small gold disc in the very middle.'

'So, animals, as Neville said?' she asks.

'Half the coats of arms in England must have animals of some sort,' I say. 'And, as I've said, lions – whole and in part – are especially common.'

'Tricky animal to identify, though, a demi-lion,' says Sir Felix. 'You rarely meet them in the street. And seen from a distance, at dusk, they might be anything. You'd struggle, a day or so later, to describe what you'd seen on the side of a coach – just a mass of claws and teeth.'

'Yes,' I say. 'Neville probably would be at a loss to describe one, if he hadn't seen them before. It might explain why he couldn't make out a neck in an animal that was only half there.'

The three of us stare at the words 'Euston Hall' on the map. The mapmaker has included a small drawing of a very stylised mansion, with four pillars and many chimneys.

'Is there anything Arlington would not do for the King?' asks Aminta.

'Nothing at all,' I say.

'And is he capable of the basest sort of deceit?' asks Aminta, though she does know the answer.

'It's his job.'

'And what did Arlington say when you told him you were trying to find out what happened to Kitty?'

'He tried to send me to France,' I say. 'First by bribing me with an interesting puzzle, then by trying to blackmail me, then, as a last resort, appealing to my better nature.'

But Sir Felix is tapping his finger on Bishop's Stortford. 'If John is right,' he says, 'and the body is Kitty's, then things do begin to fall into place. You say the King was interested in Kitty? What if she was already secretly the King's mistress and pregnant? What if the King, for reasons we do not yet understand, wished to gain possession of the child, as he did back in the 1650s with his son by Lucy Walter, the Duke of Monmouth? Then, Daniel O'Neill, one of the King's most trusted servants, was sent to capture the young Duke. Perhaps this time Arlington obligingly offered to abduct the unborn child and, out of necessity, the mother. But Kitty inconveniently gave birth before she reached Euston Hall. She refused to give the child up. She tried to escape, at the dead of night, with the baby in her arms. Arlington's men beat her to death, left her by the road and took the child, exactly as requested. But they wanted Kitty, as the King's mistress, to at least have a decent burial under her own name. Hence the script and the rest of it being carefully left with her. Doesn't that explain everything?'

It is not unlike the theory that I put to Aminta earlier. But there is one objection that I should, in all fairness, point out.

'But Monmouth's attempted abduction was a long time ago,' I say. 'All of the King's other bastards – and they are many – have been allowed to remain where they were, unless they were put out to be nursed. Lucy Walter was considered mad and unsuitable to bring him up. Kitty may have been vain and demanding, but I know of nothing that would have made her a bad mother – or no worse than my Lady Castlemaine, who is often vague about where her children are.'

Sir Felix taps Euston Hall again with his finger. 'Even so,' he says. 'The theatre, Epping, Bishop's Stortford and Euston lie in as near a straight line as you could wish. She said the kidnappers were taking her north to their master. And Arlington's name was mentioned by them.'

'Very well. I think I should speak to Arlington,' I say. 'If it wasn't his work, somebody certainly wants us to think it is. And Pepys's work too, in view of the ring we were given. I shall need to stay here a few days to see what jobs need doing on the estate, and Charles may be more than a little disappointed if Aminta leaves at once. But I think we must return to London as soon as we reasonably can. I'll write to Betterton to tell him and also let him know what we have discovered, even if it is inconclusive.'

'You will not go on to Euston Hall now?' says Sir Felix. 'You could be there and back in a day from here, I think, if you ride rather than travel by coach.'

I consider this. I'm certainly not going to find her in Suffolk if she's buried in Hertfordshire.

'Even if she is still living, as Aminta thinks, they'll have hidden her well. I could search Euston – the house and all its outlying farms and cottages – for a week and find nothing. That's assuming they'll let me search at all, which is unlikely. Whether she's dead or alive, we'll have a better chance of picking up the trail in London.'

'We'll leave for London the day after tomorrow at the latest,' says Aminta. 'Kitty *is* alive and I cannot bear to think of her caged up somewhere.'

'Better imprisoned than dead,' I say. 'There are worse places than a cage, when you think about it.'

Chapter Eight

In which I annoy Lord Arlington, but less than I usually do

'Why should I wish to kidnap a pregnant actress?' asks Arlington. He is red in the face and I have been in his office for scarcely more than five minutes. It usually takes me ten at least to enrage him this much.

'The letter refers to you by name, my Lord,' I say.

'The letter merely says that my name was mentioned. I don't think I am being unduly conceited if I say that I am reasonably well known, even in Epping. You can scarcely believe that every time the name "Arlington" passes somebody's lips I am obliged to go and abduct an actress. The theatres would be empty very soon, sir.'

Arlington has many minutely graded degrees of indignation. This is neither the nicely judged false indignation that he would deploy routinely during a meeting with the French Ambassador, nor is it the wary and resentful indignation of an Arlington caught in his own web of deceit. This is the near apoplexy of a Secretary of State accused of a piece of duplicity that he had not even thought of. Already I am convinced that he knows nothing of the purported stopover in Epping. Of course, that doesn't mean there aren't things he hasn't yet told me.

'How then, my Lord, do you account for what Kitty Burgess overheard?' I say.

'It is perfectly clear to me, Sir John, as it should be to you, that the whole thing is a fabrication by one of my many enemies to discredit me.'

Lord Arlington believes that he has enemies who labour night and day to bring him down. Fortunately he can see the evidence for this everywhere he looks, even if I can't. That, as he would explain to me if he thought it was worth the effort, is why he is the King's closest advisor and I am merely a country magistrate.

'But which of your many enemies, my Lord?'

'Ashley,' says Arlington.

'Ah,' I say.

But of course. At the moment, in my Lord's view, Ashley is behind everything. Paris or London – if anything odd is going on, Ashley is the cause of it. In establishing who killed Kitty Burgess my two main stumbling blocks will be Aminta's conviction that Kitty is still alive and Arlington's that the Chancellor of the Exchequer murdered her simply to annoy him.

'Can you even be sure that this letter is in Kitty Burgess's hand? Of course you can't.'

'Neither Aminta nor I are familiar enough with her writing to be certain,' I say. 'But my wife thinks it is not unlike a letter that she received from Kitty some months ago, but sadly did not keep. On balance it looks genuine enough.'

'Ha! Do you think I – and Ashley for that matter – don't have people who can imitate a woman's handwriting? If you are happy to wait here for a quarter of an hour, Sir John, I shall obtain for you a second letter that will inform you Mistress Burgess was quite mistaken that she was in danger and that she is now at her guardian's house in Hampshire, safe and sound, begging you to forgive her for having troubled you in any way. And if I can do it, so can others. Even that dried-up little turd, Ashley. I'd say you have been duped, Sir John. It is a clever trick to have fooled you – a very clever trick indeed, sir – but my enemies do not lack guile. And I suspect this has been planted by one of the worst of them.'

I nod and wonder why he has paid me the compliment of acknowledging that only his most bitter and determined enemies would have the skill to deceive me. It is a grudging piece of flattery, but it is flattery nonetheless.

'It seems likely she was the King's mistress.'

Arlington shakes his head. 'Not yet. I'd have heard of it.'

'She was pregnant.'

'Not necessarily by the King. But let's agree she might have caught the King's eye. She was young and female and pretty. Her pregnancy wasn't obvious yet. And actresses have an unfortunate reputation for being compliant. So, I'm not saying that His Majesty had no interest in her. But I can assure you she wasn't his mistress yet and, whoever kidnapped the woman, it wasn't me.'

'Could somebody else have done it to oblige the King? Not Rochester, who has an alibi, but perhaps one of the other rake-hells who surround the King? Herbert or Sackville or Sedley. Would it not be the sort of thing that would amuse them? They took her without intending any harm, but then it somehow all went wrong. Both Sackville and Herbert have killed people – or nearly killed them – apparently on a whim. And Herbert was at the theatre that night, offering Kitty his advice from Wits' Row. Advice that she seems to have ignored.'

Arlington nods. Now I am accusing people he dislikes, he is much more inclined to be helpful. Still, he would wish to be fair, or at least give the appearance of fairness. He weighs things up carefully before he speaks.

'Young Herbert is mad and unpredictable, like his grand-father,' says Arlington. 'He might do anything. Sackville claimed he killed that man in mistake for somebody else entirely and begged the court's forgiveness, which of course they extended to him in view of the fact that the dead man was merely a tradesman and in recognition of Sackville's noble birth and the ancient titles he would inherit in due course. Perhaps, as you say, it began as an innocent joke. Then, maybe, they discovered she was already pregnant by somebody other than the King. Perhaps she had already reminded them how she had disdained Herbert's helpful advice from Wits' Row. Perhaps she made it clear, furthermore, that she thought they were a pack of young idiots. You mentioned in passing that the three demi-lions on my coat of arms went against me. Herbert has three whole lions on his.'

Arlington smiles, having turned my only hard evidence into a piece of heraldic nonsense.

'Unless Neville's memory improves, that may not help us much,' I say.

'Exactly. What we have discussed is quite possible but we have no proof at all. Nothing we could set before a magistrate. I would certainly be careful who you accuse on the basis of heraldry alone. You handle a sword well, but you'd be no match for Herbert.'

'I suspect I'd be no match for Sackville either,' I say.

'You underestimate yourself. I think you could kill Sackville quite easily, if you set your mind to it – just not Philip Herbert. But if Herbert was involved you shouldn't expect anything to make sense – he wouldn't need a reason to attack her or know when to stop – and after the woman was dead, it might seem funny to him to try to pin the blame on me, or you or anyone else. Yes, the whole thing: the abduction of a pretty woman who had briefly caught the King's eye, the senseless brutality of her killing and the carefully staged discovery of the body – you'd say it couldn't happen, until you consider people like Herbert.'

I nod. Abduction by one of the King's friends is beginning to look very likely. And, though Aminta was right that the King's interest would have offered Kitty a great deal of protection, she'd forgotten Philip Herbert.

'I could talk to Herbert,' I say.

Arlington shrugs. If I want to take the risk of accusing him of murder, that's my affair, not his. And since I won't oblige in the small matter of Ashley's guilt, he's losing interest again. I have nobody to blame but myself.

'You haven't thought further about our proposal that you should go to Paris, I suppose?' Arlington adds.

Well, at least I now know why he paid me that compliment. Any question of diverting me from my investigation to one side, he'd really like me to trepan Clarendon for him.

'No, I haven't. My wife says she is a good friend of Clarendon's – a non-corresponding one, of course. She'd rather not betray whatever secrets he has left.'

'He's no friend of yours. He threatened to pistol you to death.'

'It was a long time ago. He may have meant no harm by it.'

'Aren't you at least slightly intrigued as to who the Byron girl is? And what Clarendon and Ashley are plotting?'

'Not intrigued enough to travel to Paris. But do tell me if you find out.'

Arlington smiles. For some reason, he still thinks I won't be able to resist going to Paris. But I can resist it very well. I have more important things to do here.

'Yes, that is my ring,' says Pepys, as I hand it to him. 'Thank you for returning it to me. I am much obliged to you, Sir John. You will doubtless be curious to know how Mistress Burgess came by it?'

He hopes, as a friend and a fellow graduate of Magdalene College, I'll say 'no'.

'Yes,' I say.

Pepys swallows hard. A story can be told many ways, and Pepys is a good storyteller, but he's still not sure which way he's going to tell this one.

'I gave it to her,' he says. 'In a manner of speaking. I had engaged her in conversation. She made a pretence of admiring my ring. She asked if she could examine it more closely. I took it off, purely to oblige her, whereupon she laughed and marched away with it. She made me look a fool, sir! In front of many friends who were present at the time. People whose goodwill I count on to do the King's business efficiently and profitably. She was a minx, lacking in manners or respect for her betters. My own ring, Sir John, with my family's ancient crest upon it – a camel's head erased, bridled and lined.'

'You could have simply followed her and requested its return,' I say.

'I would not have humiliated myself in that way,' he says. 'To beg a saucy young harlot of her sort . . .'

If what Aminta tells me is true, Mister Pepys is not above begging young women for a range of services that he requires. But the ring, even with the Pepys crest, was perhaps not worth enough.

He goes to put it back on his finger, pauses, and drops it into a pocket. Well, it has been on a corpse since he wore it last. Or perhaps he prefers not to be reminded, every time he looks at his right hand, of what must have been an embarrassing trick by a woman of little or no account. That must have angered him quite a lot.

'I am very sorry, of course, that Mistress Burgess met her end in the way she did,' he says. 'I would not have wished that upon her, whatever her moral character.'

'I was discussing her death with Lord Arlington,' I say.

Pepys opens his mouth in horror. 'You did not mention my ring, I trust?'

'Not in any way. It was not relevant.'

'Thank you, Sir John,' he says. 'I am very grateful for your tact and understanding.'

'We wondered if her death was in fact a result of some buffoonery on the part of the King's companions that went badly wrong. Herbert was in the audience the night she vanished.'

'I can believe almost anything of this court, Sir John. Herbert is nasty and ungovernable. He knows only how to strut, drink and swear foul oaths. It does the King no credit, sir, to have men like that about him. But you will need to cast your net wider than Herbert. He is but one of the many young fools who hang around the King.'

'Oh, I agree – it could be any of them. Sackville and Sedley spring to mind for their lack of regard for what anyone thinks of them. Philip Herbert for his brutality and unpredictability.'

Pepys nods. 'You may recall that Sedley and Sackville were tried back in 1663 for a gross breach of public decency, cavorting naked in Covent Garden, Sedley drinking the King's health from a wine glass that he had previously washed his prick in.'

'I was in Amsterdam and Brussels that year,' I say. 'The King had work for me there. It would seem that I missed nothing of any importance by being away.'

I wait to see if Pepys will add anything else on the subject of the King's companions, but he doesn't. He could of course abjure the royal court himself, but he has to steer a careful course between his conscience and his pocket.

'Well,' says the rightful owner of the ring, 'I must return to the perusal of my accounts. Unless I can do anything for you in exchange for your kindness and understanding?'

I consider. Perhaps there is one thing. 'Arlington mentioned somebody to me – the Byron girl. Does that name mean anything to you? She would seem to have lived in France.'

'Is she connected in some way with Kitty Burgess?'

'I don't think so,' I say. 'Quite the reverse. Arlington is almost using her as a way to divert me from investigating Kitty's murder. He dangles her in front of me, as a mystery I should not be able to resist. I am not sufficiently curious to wish to go to Paris, but I'd like to know why he has chosen to tell me about that rather than something else.'

'I certainly know of Eleanor, Lady Byron, of no good repute. She was, sir, the King's seventeenth whore abroad. And she made him pay for it. After she returned to England, she would not let him be until she had got him to give her an order for four thousand pounds-worth of plate. But by delays, thanks be to God! she died before she had it.'

'That's a lot of money,' I say.

'For poor men such as ourselves,' says Pepys, who never misses the opportunity to emphasise how little he makes from his transactions on behalf of the King. 'The King is of course also generous to Lady Castlemaine and the other mothers of his children.'

For a moment we are both left to our various thoughts. Then I say: 'Could the Byron girl be the King's daughter, then? Both Arlington and my wife thought not.'

'But even if she were,' says Pepys, 'it would be of no great importance for Lord Arlington or anyone else. Not now. At the time – back in the 1650s – it would have been very different. The King's reputation mattered a great deal to Clarendon – or Sir Edward Hyde as he was then. He needed to gain support for the exiled King and form alliances on his behalf. That His Majesty should become known publicly as a penniless, drunken philanderer was not in any way desirable, however true it was. Clarendon would have been punctilious in keeping many things quiet. Since his exile, his views may have changed. He may not mind embarrassing the King, though another child laid at the royal door would make very little difference now. Even the Queen is inured to it. Of all of them, only the Duke of Monmouth is of any political significance. And even Ashley despairs of making any capital out of it.'

We look at each other for a long time. I wonder if we are thinking the same thing. Had Ashley discovered a new card to play? A royal bastard, probably Protestant and of adequately mature years, who might prove more malleable than Monmouth? But she would have only been one of many and not even the most senior. Moreover, sadly for Ashley, she is already dead. As dead as Kitty Burgess.

'Thank you,' I say.

'I'd be grateful, Sir John, if you would tell nobody about the ring. Nobody at all. It is not just my own reputation that I am thinking of – what touches me, touches my master, the Duke of York. The King's heir. Your next King.'

'I can't see why I should need to say anything to anyone,' I say.

Still, it's a good point that Pepys has just made. I'd thought the ring was there to embarrass him. Maybe it's to embarrass the Duke of York. In the constantly changing pattern of alliances and rivalries at court, almost anything is possible.

I arrive home to find that Aminta rather than our maid opens the door to me.

'At last!' she says. 'I hope your meeting with Lord Arlington went well. And now, though you don't have time to change your clothes, there's a duchess waiting for you in the drawing room.'

'Ah,' I say.

'Don't worry,' says my wife. 'I'll stay within calling distance.'

'Why don't you join us?' I say.

Chapter Nine

In which I am not in fact seduced

'Good morning, my Lady . . . I mean, your Grace,' I say, because our visitor has been given a new title since we last saw her. She is no longer merely Lady Castlemaine. She is now, by the King's command, Duchess of Cleveland.

I wonder briefly how many thousands of silkworms had to die in order to produce the magnificent outfit she is wearing – these small, insignificant creatures have become a vast, glowing, rose-coloured cloud that shimmers and hisses every time she moves. Every inch of her costume speaks to other women and informs them that their husbands could never afford to dress them in the manner in which the King dresses his new Duchess. And yet, in a way, the dress shows great economy. No silk covers her shoulders, which are bare. The extravagantly ruffled sleeves reach only her elbows, allowing white linen and long white gloves to complete the job. The waist is as narrow and tight as can be managed. And the skirts do not meet in the middle but are fashionably swept back to reveal the stiff, gold-laced petticoats beneath. I think her petticoats carry enough bullion to pay for a small house. Not that she needs another house, if the rumours I have heard are true.

'Good morning, John,' she says. 'You don't need to call me "your Grace". We are old friends. I have said to Aminta that you should address me as Barbara, as my very closest companions do. You and your beautiful, talented wife are in London too little. The ladies of the court are so dull, John. They think only of their costumes and their hair and their lovers. It sends me to sleep just thinking of them. That orange-selling girl – Nellie – how the King stays awake when he is with her, I do not know. *She* will never be made a duchess, I can promise you that.'

I nod. 'Duchess of Cleveland,' I say. 'It is a noble title. I congratulate you, your Grace.'

'*Barbara*,' she says. 'But yes, I was quite pleased to find myself elevated to the very highest rank of the peerage. I am also now Countess of Southampton and Baroness Nonsuch.'

'I had heard that the King had presented you with Nonsuch Palace,' I say.

She smiles. I think she likes having her own palace. 'Harry the Eighth built it. Did you know that? It was his favourite residence. All fantastical towers and grand gateways and plaster figures of gods and goddesses, most of which I'm sure the sculptor made up, because I'd never heard of them. But still, a place fit for a fairy queen. Nonsuch. A place with no equal. And I am Baroness Nonsuch. It is a hard title to live up to, don't you think? Actually, more than Cleveland, wherever that is. I shall go and visit Nonsuch at the first opportunity. Of course, I may have to make a few small changes to be truly comfortable there – Henry the Eighth lived a very long time ago. But once the work is done, I shall give a ball so that everyone may come and admire my . . . palace.'

This final word is an entire chorus of pride and delight. The King may have other mistresses, but none of them has her own palace nor ever shall. Nonsuch is, of course, a little way out of London and the King may be hoping that she goes there and stays there and doesn't bother him again. That must have occurred to her. But today is no day for suggesting such things.

'A ball would be lovely, wouldn't it, John?' says Aminta.

'Possibly,' I say.

'And I shall insist, John, that you dance the very first dance with me. You won't mind, will you, Aminta? You will allow me to borrow your husband? Whenever I require him?'

'I am very happy,' says Aminta, 'that he treads on your feet rather than mine.'

'Ah! It is sad that so many handsome men of action do not take the time to study dancing,' says my good friend Barbara, looking me up and down. 'I could give you lessons, John, if you wished. You could come to me, every afternoon, until I was entirely satisfied.'

'I fear he is too old a dog to learn new tricks,' says Aminta.

'It depends who the trainer is,' says the Duchess. 'You would be surprised what I can get an old dog to do, when I have a mind to it. Sit. Roll over. Beg. Anyway, John, you must practise a few steps for Lord Ashley's ball. It's only a few days away now.'

'We are not going,' I say.

'Not going?'

'To be honest, I was unaware there was one. Certainly we are not invited. Not to any ball.'

'But the whole town will be there! You really must go. I could not bear it if you didn't! I shall speak to Ashley myself. Invitations will be with you before suppertime.'

There is a pause. I think we may finally be about to discover why the Duchess is here.

'Betterton says that you have been out to Bishop's Stortford,' she says as if commenting on the weather.

'Yes. Kitty Burgess, one of his actresses, vanished on the opening night of Aminta's new play. We heard that a body had been found there and went to see if it was her.'

'And?'

'It was . . . inconclusive. On balance, I believed that it was Kitty. Aminta did not. That was what I told Betterton in my letter.'

'But you think differently now? Aminta says that you have been talking to Lord Arlington?'

'And Mister Pepys. The circumstances are very odd. When she vanished, I could think of no good reason why anyone would abduct her – let alone kill her. But I now think the King may have been planning to take her as his . . .'

'Mistress, were you going to say? You do not need to be coy about these things. I am well aware that other women try to ensnare him. Let them. He always returns to me in the end, leaving them to go back to selling over-ripe fruit or whatever they did before.'

'Indeed, your Grace. Anyway, perhaps Kitty was wisely proving resistant to the idea. Perhaps she had another lover – she was certainly pregnant when she died. In which case, her abduction may have been some prank of the merry gang that surrounds His Majesty.'

'Which of the merry gang?'

'Rochester, who wouldn't hesitate, has an alibi. But there are plenty of others: Sedley, Sackville and Philip Herbert, for example.'

'It wasn't Sir Charles Sedley,' says the Duchess with a smile. 'I can vouch for him, all night. Don't look so shocked, John. If the King can have other women, then I too must be allowed a little harmless fun. And a few hours of Sedley is, frankly, no more than that.'

'It is helpful to know that Sedley also has an alibi, your Grace,' I say. 'I shall of course not reveal who he was with.'

'*Barbara*,' says Barbara. 'And I care not a fig if you tell everyone where he was. The King makes no secret of his liaisons. At court, after midnight, you never know who you'll find in anyone's bed. It is awkward only when a gentleman forgetfully invites two ladies to join him. And even then most ladies can reach some sort of accommodation between them. Don't raise your eyebrows like that, John. You know what goes on at court as well as I do.'

'A little less well,' I say.

'I hope she didn't fall into Philip Herbert's hands, though. That young man frightens me. I would not want to be alone with him in any room, ever. He says so little, but stares and scowls under those thick dark eyebrows and takes offence at the slightest thing. And he is very strong. His grandfather was much the same. He should be sent away from the court before he kills somebody.'

'My fear is that he has already,' I say.

'You mean this Burgess woman?'

'Yes,' I say.

'But, Aminta, you disagree with you husband?'

'Precisely, my dear Barbara,' says Aminta. 'And with Pepys

and with my Lord Arlington, who for some reason both think as he does. The only evidence we have for it being Kitty are three objects found with her. They were clearly planted there. Why plant them if not to deceive us?'

The Duchess considers this. 'So if it is not Kitty, somebody wished us to think it was?'

'Yes,' says Aminta. 'If it is not Kitty, somebody went out of their way to gather items that would connect her to the body found in Hertfordshire. In short, the whole murder is a subterfuge.'

'It is a plot!' exclaims the Duchess.

'Arlington said much the same thing,' I say. 'That his enemies had left clues that would lay the blame at his door.'

'Arlington? Why should anyone plot against Arlington? His days are numbered anyway. He is losing the King's favour. He'll be joining Clarendon in Montpellier before he knows it. It is pure pride and conceit on his part to believe that anyone would even think it worth conspiring against him. It is self-evidently a plot against me. You can see that, surely? Idle tongues have been wagging. Everyone in Whitehall now seems to believe that the King was about to take Kitty as his next mistress. And, since the body was discovered, the whole court is whispering that I have killed her – or paid somebody to have her killed. I am openly accused, almost, of seeing off a new and very slightly younger rival. Rochester is said to be penning a satire, even as we speak, about "the murdering nonsuch". How dare he! That man wishes to take the very gloss of my new title and my beautiful new palace and drag it all through the common mud of Hertfordshire. It is too bad.'

'I am sorry to hear that,' I say.

'I should hope you are. Well, you are going to get me proof either that the body isn't Kitty's, as your wife thinks, or that somebody else killed her, as you think. Either is acceptable. And in good time for me to rub their snotty noses in it at Lord Ashley's ball.'

'That may be difficult,' I say. 'We have little evidence other than a brief sighting of a coat of arms on a coach door by somebody who knows nothing about heraldry. The arms seem slightly unusual – possibly cows – but that's as much as I can say.'

'Then I would suggest you get straight out there again and question Herbert. Or anyone else with a suspect coat of arms. Indeed, I must insist that it is the very next thing you do.'

'The second thing,' says Aminta firmly. 'If you've no objection, Barbara.'

'What's the first?' I ask. I am not convinced that this new thing, whatever it is, will prove easier than the Duchess's thing.

'We're going shopping,' says Aminta. 'If we are attending Lord Ashley's ball, then I shall need some new clothes.'

From my Lady Grey's celebrated comedy, *The Summer Birdcage*

Act 1 Scene 2, A garden full of birdsong
Enter Livia and Snarkly

LIVIA: Marriage, Mister Snarkly, is but a gilded cage that tarnishes a little more each year. A foolish bird is she that enters it. I cannot think what would induce her to do so.

SNARKLY: Perhaps she hopes to find a cock inside.

LIVIA: You speak of birds, I hope, sir?

SNARKLY: I speak of birds, madam.

LIVIA: Then, it would be a poor cage with but one cock to keep her amused. Why, if she remains outside, she might have any in the garden!

SNARKLY: It is true that gardens are full of 'em. I am told that, every night, St James's Park has many a noble cock in't and that they flit there from bush to bush.

LIVIA: Your cock, Mister Snarkly, should take great care which bush he flies into. Some are traps for the unwary and he may find himself clapped up. That, methinks, will make his proud head droop.

SNARKLY: You speak of birds, I hope, madam?

LIVIA: I cannot imagine what else you think I mean, sir.

SNARKLY: *(Aside)* Upon my oath, I think this one wishes to ruffle my feathers. I have not blushed so much since I was last in a box in Drury Lane.

Chapter Ten

In which I go shopping

We have come to the New Exchange. The much older Royal Exchange has reopened after the Fire, but so far only for the merchants to store their goods. The shops are not yet set up and customers are still not welcome. But the New Exchange just escaped the flames in 1666 and has been doubly busy ever since. In the vast hall, well-dressed men and women have come to admire the goods on display at the stalls and to be admired by the other shoppers. There is a smell of new cloth and of bright, soft leather and fresh linen. Every luxury that London could desire is on display under one high roof. Merely by wandering up and down the aisles, you can buy Venetian crystal and the latest books, lace collars and fans made of ostrich feathers, coloured ribbon by the yard and cards of sharp, gleaming pins.

'What are we here to purchase?' I ask. I have to raise my voice above the sound of buying and selling.

'I'm not sure, but I cannot see Lady Castlemaine – I'm sorry, I mean her Grace the Duchess of Cleveland – without feeling the need to buy *something*,' says Aminta. 'Anyway, my father believes that no woman can earn money without running off and frittering it away on silks and satins. Filial duty dictates that I should conform to his principles. And, having endured his unwarranted disdain, I may as well have a few yards of Brussels lace in compensation.'

'You mean Barbara,' I say. 'We are to call her Barbara.'

I look around and wonder whether I am permitted to view the book stalls or whether my only function is to advise on Aminta's purchases. Then she stops abruptly.

'Kitty!' she calls out.

Several people turn and stare at us, but, looking now where Aminta is looking, I see a figure retreating rapidly into the crowd, skirts swishing behind her – two figures perhaps, because the woman seems to be accompanied by a servant dressed in black and carrying several parcels.

'The woman ahead?' I say.

'Yes – that was Kitty. I'm certain of it. Go after her, John. You can move quicker than I can in these stupid skirts.'

I start to push through the throng, but it is a hopeless task. Whereas a moment ago everyone was moving purposefully to a known objective, now the whole world seems intent on stopping to admire some trifle or greet an acquaintance that they have not seen since Candlemas Eve. The woman, of whom I caught only the briefest glance, has already gone, possibly out of one of the wide-open doors on the far side of the hall. Nevertheless, I keep going until I too am in the midday glare of the hot, dry, bustling street. I think I see a man in black disappear round a corner and into a lane, but I cannot be sure that it was the servant we saw and, even if it was, that he was ever in the presence of Kitty Burgess. I turn to find that Aminta has caught up with me.

'Why have you stopped? Which way did she go?'

'I don't know. I think the servant went that way, but I wasn't certain enough to follow. She must have heard you shout – if it really was Kitty, wouldn't she at least have turned to see who was calling her?'

'Are you saying it wasn't Kitty?'

'I really don't think it was her. Mainly because she is dead.'

'Kitty is alive, John, and I just saw her.'

I say nothing.

'That was Kitty Burgess,' Aminta repeats. 'I couldn't be mistaken.'

'We caught no more than a glimpse of her. How can you be so sure?'

'I just am. I'm as certain that it was her as I am that it is you standing in front of me.'

'Look, Aminta,' I say. 'I realise that you *want* Kitty to still be alive but—'

'Don't,' she says, narrowing her eyes.

'Very well,' I say. 'There's nothing to be done about it now. Shall we go back in and buy some lace? The collar that you saw was very fine indeed and not too dear.'

'No, my old lace will do very well, after all. And I fear lace collars are going out of fashion. Let us go home, John. I am suddenly very weary.'

She takes my arm and we walk home, in silence, through crowds of people who neither know nor care whether Kitty Burgess is dead.

*

'Thank you for writing to let me know what you'd discovered in Hertfordshire,' says Betterton, 'but you say Lady Grey doubts that the body was Kitty's?'

'Aminta has taken it all very badly. She refuses to believe Kitty is dead. She now even has visions of her in the New Exchange.'

'If Kitty had a ghost, then the New Exchange would be what she haunted. She always had a taste for finery. Remarkably so, coming as she did from a vicarage in Hampshire. Obviously, I hope she is alive. But, from what you've told me, Sir John, I agree that it does seem more likely she's dead. As for her being carried off by some aristocratic thugs, Herbert and his friends singled her out for a lot of abuse that last evening. The fact she made no response, and frankly didn't seem to care, just enraged them even more. They'd have thought it funny to carry her off somewhere – they wouldn't need a reason to do it. Those idiots imagine that they are immune from punishment, and up to a point they're right.'

'Even so, I don't think it was simply that they felt insulted by her that evening and decided on the spur of the moment to get their revenge. Both Meg and Mister Neville seemed convinced Kitty had been expecting the coach – that suggests a little forward planning and even cooperation on her part.'

'Perhaps she expected somebody else in the coach and found herself face to face with Herbert?'

Aminta and I have dined, and I am now back at the Duke's Company and seated on the stage with the company's manager. Thomas Betterton is, when standing, above average height. He is solidly built but there is an athleticism to him. He could leap from the stage to stop a fight in the pit, as he has had to do more than once. His voice is not the most mellifluous I have heard, but it is strong and clear. He is a man who has studied his profession and who can play Lear or Hamlet or Falstaff or Oberon equally well. They say that kings should watch him, to see how a monarch should carry himself. But at the same time he is a practical man of business, who runs his company much better than Killigrew runs his. Aminta has to correct his adding up much less than she has to correct Killigrew's. Nor, unlike Killigrew, does he spend his evenings drinking with the King. He has the stamina to stay the course, and can play the rake on the stage as well as any, but he would not enjoy it in real life. And by ten o'clock he would want to get home to his wife, Mary, who is his partner on stage and off.

'However it was done, her abduction was a cruel thing,' I say, 'even for that crowd. They may not have known she was with child, of course.'

'I certainly didn't,' says Betterton. 'Mary says the same. So does Meg. We all thought Kitty was getting a little plump, but no more than that. There was no sign of the infant?'

'No,' I say.

'An odd business altogether,' says Betterton. 'I don't regret the King's return – we couldn't even keep the theatre open in Cromwell's day. I know which side my bread's buttered on and who owns the royal butter knife. But things have changed very much in the last ten years, since the good order of the old Republic broke down. It frightens me sometimes what these young gentlemen think they are allowed to get up to. And how reluctant His Majesty's judges are to bring them to book.'

I nod. 'I may as well return this to you,' I say. 'It's Kitty's copy of the script. It was with her body.'

Betterton looks puzzled. 'No, we have Kitty's script, with her annotations, here at the theatre. She was leaving us for good, remember. She would have had no reason to take it with her, when she planned never to act the role again. That's the prompt copy. We noticed it was missing on the third night and had to find another one quickly.'

'Why would Kitty have taken that?'

'She wouldn't. It was of no use to her. It's as simple as that. Anyway, we had it on the second night, so she couldn't have done. It was later we noticed it had gone.'

'Where would it have been kept?'

'In a chest, in my office. It would have been returned there immediately after the performance. We wouldn't have risked leaving it lying around.'

'A locked chest?'

'Locked? Not most of the time, no. Anyone who knew, or guessed, where it was could have taken it that night. And many of the aristocratic gang come backstage after a performance, as you will have noticed. With the King visiting that day and everyone fawning round him as he left – yes, it would have been easy for somebody who was familiar with the theatre to creep into my office, open the chest and take it.'

'Was Herbert there that evening too?'

'I remember him the first night. Not the second. But even he might have had the sense not to draw attention to himself if he planned to steal something. I take it, from your question, that you didn't see him?'

'I've no idea what he looks like,' I say, 'so I wouldn't have remarked on his presence or absence. And we stayed only a short time after the performance ended. Do you still have Kitty's script?'

'Yes, of course. It is probably in my office. In the very same chest. Unlocked. I'll fetch it.'

He comes back with another roll of paper, a little grubbier than the first, and places it in front of me. I take from my pocket the letter that Kitty wrote from Epping and compare the two documents, side by side.

'The annotations on the script,' I say. 'Are they in the same hand as this letter? What do you think, Mister Betterton?'

Betterton looks over my shoulder. 'You think the letter may be a forgery?'

'Arlington thought so, but it suited him that it should be. Aminta thinks it's the real thing.'

'The annotations to the script are done quickly – during rehearsals. The letter is written with greater care – the author wanted no doubt as to their meaning. But whether the two are the same person . . . I truly couldn't say.'

'Nor I,' I say. 'But I know somebody who may.'

Chapter Eleven

In which I learn my letters

I am, so I am told, fortunate to find Sir Samuel Morland at his desk at the Post Office. He has many concerns and, only yesterday, was at Hampton Court to investigate building a new water pump there for the King, who desires a fountain greater and more magnificent than those at Versailles, but at a reasonable price. The King trusts Morland to build a cheap water pump. He does not trust Morland in most other respects. Nobody trusts Morland if there is somebody else they could trust. But Arlington knows how useful Morland was to Cromwell. This is a man who can crack any code the enemies of the King have yet devised. This is a man who can open and reseal any letter without the recipient guessing for one moment that they are not the first to read the information it contains. This is a man who can tell whether the letter was written by one person or another, regardless of the lying signature at the end. This is a man who is a master of, and an active practitioner in, all known forms of duplicity. I'd rather not do business with Sir Samuel Morland either but, like the King, I have a job that needs doing quickly and cheaply.

Morland rises, smiling, from his desk as I enter his gloomy and rather cramped domain. He was allocated more floorspace and more daylight in Cromwell's time. His face is still as smooth and his hair is still as sleek as it was when I first met him, a dozen years ago. Of course, the hair is now a periwig – a mass of golden curls that flow over the shoulders of his green silk suit. Like Pepys, this year he wears a broad fringed sash diagonally across his chest, with a neat little sword dangling slightly lower than you might wish if you needed to draw it quickly. Unlike Pepys, I think he does know how to use the sword. He has been a spy of one sort or another for a very long time, sometimes for this side and sometimes for that, drawing a salary from one or both. Such was his honest zeal for every cause that he is now universally regarded as a traitor, though not one worth troubling the executioner with. The executioner too is a busy man.

'Sir John!' he exclaims. 'It gives me so much pleasure to see you again. It is fortunate that you called today. Yesterday I was with the King in one place, tomorrow I shall be with him in another. He is a demanding master! But those of us without great fortunes must work. I am newly married – again. Life as the head of a household is not cheap.'

'I congratulate you, Sir Samuel,' I say.

'Your own family are well?'

'Our son is thriving back home in Essex. My wife's latest play has been well received.'

'And yourself?'

'I am kept busy enough as a magistrate and lord of the manor. I have given up my legal practice. The old wound in my leg is less troublesome than it was.'

'But you are clearly working for Lord Arlington again?'

'No. Not really. But I hoped you would help me with a small problem that I have. An actress from the Duke of York's Company has vanished.'

He nods. 'Kitty Burgess,' he says.

'A body has been found.'

He nods. 'Bishop's Stortford,' he says. 'Seemingly battered to death. Perhaps by Herbert and his friends. And a missing child. An interesting case, is it not?'

'You are well informed,' I say.

He smiles. That is the greatest compliment I could have paid him. He has no intention of telling me how he knows. The source is almost certainly Arlington or Williamson, but that isn't the point. He knows.

'The question is whether somebody is trying to deceive us as to the time and manner of her death,' I say. I take out of my pocket Kitty's script and the letter written from Epping. 'Was this note written by the same person who annotated the script?'

Morland examines the two documents carefully. 'You can never be certain. Most things can be forged and one day somebody will do it well enough to deceive even me. But, as near as I can tell, the writer of the two was the same. See in the letter how the R is formed in the word "Really". It has many unnecessary flourishes, does it not? And here in the script there is an annotation "enter R". Look, we see the very same thing! And here we have two rather pretentious loops in the L in "Lady", which match the loops in "exit L" in the script. The Ws in both documents conversely are formed with very straight lines − not graceful but forthright, confident and unyielding. The K of "King" in the script also matches the K of "Kitty" at the end of the letter, though the curls she produces when writing her own name are far more enthusiastic than any others that we see here. Yes, truly, I think these are the same hand. Or some forger has finally got the better of me.' He flutters his lashes, not doubting which I shall think is true.

'Then the letter is probably genuine,' I say. 'At least to the extent of its having been written by Kitty herself, though we still have no idea when it was written. Some firm ground in the shifting sands. I had begun to wonder if anything was as it seemed.'

'There is some oddness about the letter nonetheless,' says Morland. He looks unreasonably pleased with himself.

'Really?' I say.

Morland nods. 'For example, we both know that the King may have been enamoured of Mistress Burgess.'

'Again, you are well informed,' I say.

He waves away my compliment, though not very far. 'Is it not therefore passing strange, Sir John, that she does not ask you to go to the King for help?' he says.

'She might wish not to embarrass him, if she thought that the liaison was still secret.'

'Even when threatened as she was? She may not have known she was about to be killed, but she must have suspected it. We would, of course, all die for the King if we had to. What greater honour is there than to give our lives for such an upright and pious ruler? But few of us would wish to trouble the King's conscience by dying for him in a wholly unnecessary manner. That would be inconsiderate. So, why does Kitty not ask you to tell the one person who might have the power to stop whatever nonsense his courtiers were getting up to? To stop them with a single word, almost. But she just appeals to you and your wife.'

'True,' I say.

'And there is no mention of the child,' says Morland.

'No,' I say. 'There isn't.'

'Does that not likewise seem odd? She appeals to you to save her. Wouldn't an appeal to save her and her unborn child be even more urgent? Especially if it might have been the King's. Or the child of some other powerful protector?'

'I agree,' I say.

'Nor is there any mention of Herbert, if he was indeed her abductor.'

'Perhaps she didn't recognise him? It seems generally agreed that she ignored the Wits and treated them as if they were not there.'

'Did she? Even so, do you not think that there is something a little inelegant about the story we are being told? Something unsatisfactory? Too many missing pieces? Too many strange things that people should have noticed but didn't? I mean, Kitty Burgess being the King's mistress, for example. The King is rarely reticent about having a new companion. Matters might hang in the balance for a day or two, but to keep everything a secret – perhaps for as long as nine months? At this court? I think not. And, if Herbert was responsible, why do we have no reports of rake-hells driving across Hertfordshire, giving a well-deserved thrashing to any watchman who tried to stop them and question them? No, Sir John, it will not do at all. And when a story is as inharmonious as that, it is also probably false. I do think the letter is in Mistress Burgess's hand. It is everything else that should arouse your suspicions. Perhaps I should tell you, as a friend, that your account has intrigued my Lord more than a little.'

He smiles at me. He is my friend. Of course, he is also Lord Arlington's friend. That is how he operates. I can expect everything I say to be reported back to Arlington. Perhaps I should say nothing else about Kitty, but I'm curious about one other thing. There's a good chance that Morland knows and a small chance that he will tell me.

'My Lord wants me to go to Paris,' I say.

I watch his expression carefully. Though he tries to give nothing away, I think this is news to him. That's a surprise. Arlington has told him all about Kitty Burgess but not about this.

'Do you know who the Byron girl might be?' I ask.

'She is in France, then?'

'If she is still alive. Which she does not currently seem to be.'

He considers. 'When I was working for Mister Thurloe, during the tyrant Cromwell's unlamented days, our agents in Paris reported that the Pretender Charles Stuart, as we then foolishly referred to him, was much enamoured of the widowed Lady Byron.'

'Yes, I know. Was there a child?'

'There were rumours of one. From an old woman who claimed to have assisted at the birth and had urgent need of money to buy gin. That would have been in 1652 or 1653. But the child, if there was one, died before 1660. When Lady Byron returned to England in that year, she was alone. She could have safely brought the girl, had she been alive, but she didn't. I would have produced a memorandum on it at the time, of course, for Mister Thurloe. But I have not recently had access to the papers that I possessed when he was Secretary of State and I worked for him. They were taken from me ten years ago, when the old Republic was overthrown, and have never been returned. They say that the King rewarded Lady Byron well, however. Surprisingly well. That is all I can tell you unless you wished to take me further into your confidence? I could spare you a few more minutes.'

I'm sure he could. But I think he has told me all he intends to tell me. And I've already given him more than enough in exchange. Maybe a little too much.

'I wouldn't wish to trouble you, Sir Samuel. The King has, I am sure, given you a great deal to do.'

'Indeed,' he says. 'The King places much trust in me. It is a great honour.'

He looks around his little office with its single, tiny window and its piles of papers, and he sighs deeply.

It is the following day when Williamson calls on me.

'You need to be more careful,' he says.

'I tell myself that all the time,' I say. 'Perhaps I should listen to my own advice. It's often quite good.'

'I mean Morland,' he says.

'He has reported back every word I told him?'

'No. He wouldn't do that. Just most of it. Enough so that we don't blame him if things go wrong.'

'That's very wise of him.'

'Not really. He'd be better keeping quiet and building reasonably priced fountains.'

'Old habits die hard,' I say. 'I think that he wishes to be liked by the people he tells things to. That, above all, has prevented his rise to the heights that he believes he should have reached. A very talented man with a fatal flaw. And also slightly ridiculous. If he was the hero of a play, I think Aminta would place it firmly in the realms of tragicomedy.'

'He's always tried to hedge his bets. He might have come

94

over to the King in 1658, but he didn't quite dare to. So he continued to work for Cromwell and Thurloe while betraying their lesser secrets to the exiled royalists. That's why nobody trusts him.'

'So, Lord Arlington asked you to pass on a warning not to rely too much on Morland? I learned all that in 1658, or was it 1659?'

'My Lord does not know I am here. I tell you as a friend. Don't trust Sir Samuel Morland. And don't mention the Byron girl to him again. You've made him much too curious. He is demanding access to his old papers.'

'Does it matter what he knows about her?'

'He could tell all sorts of people. Morland has been seen with the Duke of Monmouth.'

'Is that so bad?'

'We don't know yet. We thought Ashley had broken off with Monmouth entirely but now we're not so sure. They're both people who like to keep their options open. So does Morland.'

'Yes, I know. Has Lord Arlington spoken to Ashley – I mean if he's curious to know these things?'

'Ashley has vanished. Nobody has seen him for over a week. We think he may have gone to his estate in Dorset – Wimborne St Giles.'

'He'll need to be back for the ball he is giving. It will be quite inconvenient for everyone if he is not.'

'Yes, my wife and I have been invited to that. Are you and Lady Grey going?'

'My Lady Castlemaine – I'm sorry, Cleveland, I keep forgetting for some reason – is anxious I should attend. Invitations are apparently to be issued to us.'

'You know there are rumours that she was the murderer of Kitty Burgess?'

'She told me so.'

'A lot of people believe it's true.'

'On very little evidence. She wishes me to disprove it anyway. It seems to make her life at court uncomfortable.'

'Perhaps you should be careful there too.'

'Really? Do you believe it yourself?'

'Of course not. But it might suit the King if she was at court a lot less than she is. He has one mistress too many at the moment.'

'He's just made her Duchess of Cleveland,' I say.

'Henry the Eighth made Thomas Cromwell Earl of Essex,' says Williamson. 'Three months later, he had him executed.'

'And he's given her Nonsuch Palace.'

'If I were her, I'd go there and stay there,' he says. 'It's what the King wants her to do.'

'I'm seeing her tonight,' I say. 'At the theatre. But I doubt she'll listen to my advice. Good though we've agreed it usually is.'

From my Lady Grey's celebrated comedy, *The Summer Birdcage*

Act 1 Scene 6, The Palace

Enter the Queen and Snarkly

SNARKLY: You do not dance tonight, Your Majesty?

QUEEN: The King intends to dance with Lady Fortinbras. I am superfluous, Mister Snarkly. A pair of dusty, outmoded petticoat breeches in a fop's chest. Truly, I begin to fear the moth. Had I but known the King kept a wench, I should never have agreed to come to this country and my father would never have given me to him in marriage – not even for the treaty against Spain. You shall see the jewel she wears on her breast tonight. It was part of my dowry. But the King can hold onto nothing of value.

SNARKLY: That is untrue, madam, for he holds on to you.

QUEEN: Yes, having snared me, he will not allow me to flutter from his grasp the way he allows his gold to fly away. His alliance with my father depends on't.

Enter the King with Lady Fortinbras and members of the Court.

SNARKLY: *(Aside)* My Lady Fortinbras is like the moon. To sparkle she must steal another's light. *(To the Queen)* Madam, what the King has lost, you can regain.

QUEEN: What is your meaning, sir?

SNARKLY: Lady Fortinbras is no better than the King at guarding her storehouse. Once the dancing has ceased, she will go to the gaming table without doubt. As her losses mount, she must look to her breast.

QUEEN: You think to win back my diamond at cards? Fie! You will need to stake all you possess.

SNARKLY: A great deal more than that, I promise you. But there is a gentleman I know who can lend me what I need.

QUEEN: I cannot let you be so foolish. Not another word, sir!

Music.

SNARKLY: See, they begin the dance – 'Cuckolds All in a Row'.

QUEEN: How many men here fear they will be made cuckolds tonight? If you present me with a diamond, Mister Snarkly, my husband will suspect I have given you something in return.

SNARKLY: Like the thieving magpie, madam, I shall seize my prize in plain sight, but none will see where I let it fall.

QUEEN: Enough, Mister Snarkly. Like everyone else in the room, I simply wish to watch Lady Fortinbras. She glitters as I never shall, nor wish to.

Chapter Twelve

In which Her Grace the Duchess of Cleveland makes some observations on the conventions of storytelling

'I think,' says my good friend Barbara, 'that everyone in the theatre is looking at us, wondering who is that handsome man who has accompanied me here this evening.'

'I hope,' I say, 'that they will be too enrapt by my wife's play to notice even who they are themselves sitting next to. And I think they will gain little pleasure or instruction by staring at me all evening.'

'Well, even if you do not wish to be stared at for your own sake, you will at least oblige me by being stared at for mine. The day people pay more attention to the play than they do to what I'm wearing and who I'm with, I shall retire to a nunnery.'

'Would you like living in a nunnery, your Grace?'

'Of course. Religion is very, very important to me, John. I am already a saint twice over – did you know that? Peter Lely painted me as St Catherine of Alexandria, holding some sort of palm-leaf thing and a sword. And then he painted me and my bastard son Charles as the Virgin Mary and Infant Jesus. The father is understandably absent.'

'You have a palace to retire to,' I say. 'That must be more comfortable than a convent.'

'I have just visited Nonsuch and I can assure you that it leaves much to be desired. It is so *old*, John. Older even than the Earl of Clarendon, I should think. I shall have to make so many changes to it. And they will cost a lot of money. John, you don't know where I could get a lot of money, do you? I really need some for my palace.'

'From the King?' I say.

'No, he has become dreadfully stingy – apart from giving me that old crumbling ruin. You always seem quite rich. Where do you get your money?'

'Aminta and I are not at all rich,' I say. 'Or not as rich as Samuel Pepys has managed to make himself. But, with the help of our steward, the estate now makes a small profit. And, of course, my wife earns money writing plays.'

'Ah yes, her wonderful plays.' She finally turns towards the stage. 'This one seems to have started. Where are we now?'

'We are in the middle of act one, scene six,' I say.

'The music is very fine, what is it?'

'"Cuckolds All in a Row",' I say. 'It's a very old melody, so I'm told, but now fashionable again.'

'And who is that dreadful woman dancing with the King?'

'Lady Fortinbras,' I say.

'She seems most unpleasant. Very much like Nell Gwynne. I, for one, hope she hazards the diamond and loses it. Who is the gentleman she was talking to?'

'Snarkly,' I say. 'Initially he appears to be a useless fop, but later reveals himself as a true friend to the Prince and the Queen.'

'Why isn't that made obvious from the beginning?'

'Because writers like to deceive their audience as to the true nature of things. Then later they reveal the truth, mainly to demonstrate their own cleverness.'

'That is most disobliging of them. They would do better to make the audience feel clever. Then they might come back and watch other plays of theirs. So, does Snarkly marry Livia later? They seem to dislike each other so much that I assumed that it must end well for them.'

'Yes, I fear that convention fools nobody any more,' I say. 'Their initial hostility is too obvious a trick.'

'The King loved me from the moment he first saw me,' says the Duchess. 'But less so now. He is bewitched by that orange-selling Gwynne woman. Just as the king on the stage there is bewitched by the vile Lady Fortinbras. Your wife writes very perceptively. How much longer does this act last?'

'Only a few minutes more, my Lady,' I say. 'Just one more scene after this one – quite a short one.'

'Good. Then we can get some refreshments. *Not* oranges. I do so enjoy the theatre, don't you, John?'

But our attention is drawn away from the stage by a commotion in the pits. A rowdy group of young bucks has arrived and pushed its way to the front. For a minute or so the actors' voices are drowned out by oaths and threats, swords are drawn and flourished, then things settle down again, people move seats, and, on stage, a new scene begins in front of us. The court has progressed to a game of cards for very high stakes.

'Who are the gentlemen who have just arrived?' I whisper.

'It is as I promised you – that is Philip Herbert, Charles Sackville and some of their friends. They have ejected the citizens that they did not like and have taken over Wits' Row, at the very front of the pit, so that they may better criticise the action. Shall you arrest Herbert now and clear my name?'

'I have no powers of arrest here, my Lady, nor any proof against him. But thank you for introducing me to him. Now I know Herbert, I shall seek him out after the play and question him. I think perhaps you should remain safely in my coach outside. He looks a brute.'

'He is. You have brought your sword?'

'I won't need it,' I say. 'I'm not planning to pick a fight.'

'That doesn't mean he isn't,' says the Duchess. 'I just hope he doesn't hurt you too badly. You wouldn't want blood on your new leather seats. And now, John, I really must ask you to be quiet so that I can concentrate on your wife's wonderful play. Lady Fortinbras is starting to finger the jewel she is wearing. I want to know what happens next.'

Finally the play is over, and those with any pretensions to wit or gentility are backstage, as the actors and actresses all desperately attempt to change out of their costumes and remove their make-up. Everyone is trying to talk over everyone else. The cheap candle flames flare and sway to and fro, sending long streams of tallow-scented smoke towards the high ceiling. Whenever a face turns towards me, it seems to be wearing a hideous red and black mask. Hell must be a bit like this, only slightly less pleased with itself.

Betterton passes me, still in his scarlet plush robe.

'A second visit, Sir John? And Lady Grey not with you? I thought I saw you in a box with the Duchess.'

'I was. But I have come to talk to Philip Herbert. Have you seen him? It's time I asked him a few questions about Kitty.'

'Over there,' says Betterton, pointing into the hot, sweaty, constantly shifting throng. 'But he's very drunk. I doubt you'll get much sense out of him tonight.'

'But perhaps some truth,' I say.

'*In vino veritas*, eh?' says Betterton. 'The problem is that he's at his most difficult when in his cups. You don't have a sword?'

'No.'

'Do you want to borrow mine? It's the real thing – not a cheap prop.'

'No. But thank you for the offer. You couldn't use a sword safely in here.'

'That won't bother him, of course,' says Betterton.

'I imagine it wouldn't,' I say.

I make my way, slowly and with difficulty, over towards the man that the Duchess of Cleveland identified for me. He is quite tall – a good two or three inches taller than I am. His face, in this light at least, is very dark. His black periwig is dishevelled and askew. There are stains on the mustard-coloured velvet of his suit. The scabbard of his dress sword sticks out at a rakish angle, regardless of the risk to anyone behind him. He laughs loudly at something he has just said and then, perhaps sensing my presence, turns suddenly. My first impression is that he is very cross with me, then I realise that this is his natural expression. He is waiting eagerly, like a snake with its head raised, in the hope of an insult he can respond to. He prefers to have a good reason for killing somebody.

'Mister Herbert?' I ask as politely as I can.

His eyes narrow to slits. 'Do I know you?' he says.

'My name is John Grey,' I say. 'My wife wrote the play you've just watched.'

'Wait! I recognise you! You were in a box tonight with that damned Catholic whore Cleveland?'

'Yes,' I say. I decide not to add anything about her pious hopes to enter a nunnery.

He claps me on the shoulder hard enough to bruise it. 'Good man!' he says. 'I'd take a turn with her too, if I had time.'

'I'll let her know that,' I say. 'She will be most gratified. Did you enjoy the play?'

'Yes, once we'd ejected the cits who had usurped our places in Wits' Row. Those seats are for true wits, Mister Grey – not half-wits.'

I smile encouragingly. 'You were here on the first night too. When Kitty Burgess performed the role of Queen?'

'Was I?' He frowns, then his face clears. 'Yes, so I was. The wits gave her some good advice that evening! We sent her off with a flea in her pretty little ear.'

'You were displeased with some aspects of her performance, Mister Herbert?'

'She has a fine voice, I grant you. And she bears herself like a queen. But she spoke her lines as if she had received the script an hour before she came on stage. We wits, sir, expect better for our money. The new girl – Charlotte – was more to our liking. I must tell her that. I shall take her to some inn, sir, and thank her as an actress should be thanked. Eh? Ha!' He looks round uncertainly. I hope, for her sake, Charlotte has already changed and left, though Betterton is unlikely to stand for any nonsense from Herbert here at the theatre.

'Did you see Kitty Burgess after the play?' I ask.

'Who?'

'Kitty Burgess. The lady to whom you gave such good advice.'

'I looked for her. But Sackville was spewing his guts by then. By the time he'd emptied himself, the actresses had gone, damn them – and damn him too, I say. Damn everybody, Grey, except you and me.'

'Did you know that the King was enamoured of Kitty Burgess?'

'No. Is he?'

'I'm told he was.'

'He's bedding Nell Gwynne. I do know that. Wouldn't mind a turn with her myself, eh?'

'Indeed. But that wouldn't stop him looking elsewhere for entertainment.'

'Ha! You're right, Grey! Having one mistress doesn't stop the King from bedding another! It doesn't stop men like you and me either, does it? We could have any actress here that we wanted. Which one do you wish to try, Grey? I'll give you first pick. Because I like you.'

He leans forward in a companionable way, with his arm on my already bruised shoulder. His breath smells very strongly of wine. He is heavy. I'm not sure he could even locate his sword, but I'd definitely prefer not to have to fight him. Arlington hasn't authorised me to kill anybody. And my family tree, as Aminta often tells me, wouldn't stand scrutiny in court if I did.

'If some of the young bucks at court thought the King was about to take Kitty Burgess as a mistress,' I say, 'would it amuse them to abduct her and hide her from him? I mean as a joke. Perhaps at a house in the country.'

His face lights up. 'Where is she? Let's do it now! Do you have a coach, Grey? We'll hide her at Sedley's house. He won't mind. Game for anything, Sedley.'

'I wasn't suggesting we did it tonight.'

'Weren't you?'

'She's not here.'

'Ah! Good plan, but it wouldn't work if she's not here. Still, there are other actresses. We could take one of them. Let's take two. One each. Take them to Sedley's house. Hide them, like you say.'

'If,' I say, 'somebody had abducted Kitty Burgess in the way I've described, would you have heard about it?'

'But you said, she's not here?'

'I mean, if they'd done it on the opening night ...'

'When she was here, you mean?'

'That's it ... would you have heard about it then?'

'A good thing like that? Yes, of course. Nothing that clever could stay a secret for long at court.'

He's right, of course. It's obvious, really. Nothing stays a secret at court and certainly not something as funny as kidnapping an actress and killing her. And, as Morland said, Herbert and his friends wouldn't be able to travel from London to Bishop's Stortford without beating up an officious watchman or two. They probably couldn't get beyond the end of the lane at the back of the theatre without picking a fight with somebody. The planning, the ingenuity of Kitty's abduction, would be utterly beyond the man in front of me.

'Thank you, Mister Herbert,' I say. 'You've been most helpful.'

'Have I? Let's go whoring then. I'll pay for both of us, if you don't mind a cheap one.'

'I must return to my Lady Castlemaine,' I say. 'She awaits me in my coach.'

'Of course you must. Tell her I'm next in the queue! The King will have to wait his turn!'

'I shall certainly try to impress that upon her,' I say. 'And fortunately the King has other distractions.'

'Well,' says Aminta, 'I'm flattered you turned down an evening of whoring with your new friend so that you could report back to me as quickly as possible.'

'It would have been a short evening,' I say. 'A moment after I left Herbert, he was vomiting over the gentleman he'd just been speaking to. I had a lucky escape tonight in so many ways. Escorting *your* new friend Barbara back to Whitehall took me a few extra minutes, of course. I'm sorry about that.'

'She didn't suggest ways in which you might like to spend the rest of the evening? She didn't want to give you those dancing lessons straight away?'

'You shouldn't judge her too harshly. She says things without meaning them. She says them to everyone.'

'Does she? I doubt she risks saying them to Samuel Pepys. Anyway, you don't think Herbert and his friends had anything to do with Kitty's disappearance?'

'He didn't even know she was dead. And I don't think he is good at deceit. He's like the Duchess in that he doesn't know what he's saying half the time. Things just come into his head and go straight out of his mouth. If anyone had abducted Kitty as a joke, I'm sure he's right that word would have got out. Morland also pointed out to me that Kitty's letter fails to mention Herbert in any way. I wondered if she simply didn't recognise him, but her abductors sound far too efficient and businesslike. It doesn't mean that somebody more sober than Herbert and his friends didn't kidnap her, of course, and for some better thought-out reason. But I don't think it was one or two of the younger courtiers simply looking to amuse themselves. Maybe Arlington's right. The whole thing is a plot against him. It's just that Arlington wants the plotter to be Ashley and I don't think Ashley is cruel enough to have had her killed if there was no need – less still would he have killed the child.'

'Since the body wasn't Kitty's, she isn't dead and hasn't given birth,' she says. 'So Ashley is guilty of many things but not those two. Did the Duchess enjoy the play?'

'I think she enjoyed the parts she actually watched. She regards the theatre primarily as one of many places to be seen. But, in the coach on the way back to Whitehall, she was very complimentary about it all.'

'She wasn't offended by Lady Fortinbras?'

'I don't think she saw herself in that at all.'

'No, I thought she might not. People so often don't.'

'She rather thought the character was based on Nell Gwynne.'

'Oh dear. Does that make me a complete failure as a satirist?'

'The play was an enormous success,' I say. 'The applause was tremendous. And Charlotte was quite good as the Queen. For once, Wits' Row was silenced.'

'And you weren't offended by how I portrayed you as Snarkly?'

'Snarkly?' I say. 'Me?'

'I'm only joking,' says Aminta kindly. 'Actually I based the idiot footman on you. Did you manage to eat, or would you like some supper? There's cold ham and cold chicken. As long as you promise not to spew it up later, like your new best friend Philip Herbert.'

Chapter Thirteen

In which the King dances

The following day, I find Aminta reading a letter.

'It's from my cousin in Hampshire,' she says.

'You wrote to him about Kitty's disappearance?'

'No, my father did. He seems to feel that, even if I am right and she is alive, my cousin should at least know that Kitty is missing. I didn't want to worry Reginald unnecessarily but, on reflection, I suppose that was the right thing to do. My father also wanted to check that she hadn't simply gone back to Hampshire, which is also reasonable.'

'I had assumed we would have already heard from one source or another if she'd done that.'

'So had I. Anyway, she's not there. Reginald is mildly concerned, suggesting to me that my father did not discuss any of the more troubling options with him. He suggests that we wait patiently for news. Strangely he does not say he is praying for her safe return. I think that is rather remiss of him, as a clergyman.'

'Only mildly concerned?' I say. 'However tactfully your father phrased his letter, surely what we know already should trouble your cousin quite a lot.'

'Unless she's done something like this before, and he recalls that prayer didn't work last time round? I think he has always regarded the guardianship as an unreasonable burden imposed on him by his late wife and, more recently, an embarrassment to him in his duties as a parish priest. Her influence on the young men of Hampshire was seemingly not good, though she had a high enough opinion of herself that she always kept them at arm's length. According to Reginald, at least. But in truth I know so little about her. I don't even know who her parents were.'

'Perhaps we should ask,' I say.

'Yes. I'll write back, thanking him for letting us know, and ask in passing whether she might have sought out some distant member of her father's family, or her mother's. That may help us track her down, wherever she is now.'

'Or discover who killed her,' I say.

'You don't seem to be making much progress in showing that anyone killed her at all. Not even Philip Herbert. Which would lead any reasonable person to conclude that you are wrong and I am right.'

'Look, Aminta, I agree that we probably have to rule out Herbert and his friends. They wouldn't have been able to keep it a secret. And Arlington. There was no political advantage to be gained from her death. And the Duchess. My Lady has seen off so many other mistresses – Moll Davis, for example – without resorting to violence of any kind. She really doesn't need to kill them. She just waits for the King to get bored with them. And we know she was with Sedley that night anyway. But, just because nobody seems to have had a reason for killing her, and some people had no opportunity, it doesn't mean Kitty's alive. As a magistrate I've had to sit on a number of cases where we were unable to convict anyone. The victim was indisputably dead for all that.'

'She's alive. You'll see. In the meantime, we are invited out to dinner the day after tomorrow – friends of my father's who have regrettably learned we are in town. I can't refuse. And the invitation to Lord Ashley's ball at Exeter House, the following evening, has arrived.'

'Then we can't leave London for another three or four days,' I say. 'But after that we should return to Essex. There's nothing more to be done here for Kitty. Not unless some new evidence appears out of nowhere. If we keep trying, there's a danger we shall just make fools of ourselves.'

'I'm not giving up, John.'

'No,' I say. 'I can see that. You're definitely not giving up.'

Exeter House is already a blaze of light, though the sun has scarcely set. No tallow candles here, as there were behind the scenes at the theatre and will be in most London homes tonight. Just the purest, creamiest wax. Our coach has taken us to the door and we have ascended a wide staircase to the first floor. I am pleased that the music has already begun, because that may mean that I have avoided the first two or three dances.

'Now don't you wish you had accepted the Duchess's offer of lessons?' asks Aminta.

'I imagine that most people are here simply to be seen,' I say. 'And to discover who is plotting against them this week. Nobody will think it odd if I don't take to the floor.'

'Nobody will notice in this throng, certainly. I am surprised that, even with the Duchess's help, we managed to get invitations. That is the Duke of Buckingham over there, with a large crowd of admirers and hangers-on. That's the Duke and Duchess of Ormonde with a slightly smaller one. And there's Arlington and his lady.'

'And Williamson,' I say, 'though he seems a bit lost without his code books and his lists of agents. Mistress Williamson is enjoying herself, though. I don't think she gets out as much as she'd like. The Duchess of Cleveland will of course make her entrance later. She can make it only once and won't want to waste it on a half-empty room. I suppose, at the moment, most people are speculating on who the King will bring with him – the Queen or Nell Gwynne.'

'Or some other lady,' says Aminta. 'I wonder if it would have been Kitty – had she not vanished. Whatever else we're wrong about, there is a general agreement that the King did wish to make Kitty his mistress.'

Lord Ashley comes over to greet us, his thin face wreathed in pinched smiles. Would he welcome me like that if he knew that I had read the message to him from his good friend, the exiled Earl of Clarendon? And does he recall that, the last time we met, he was the sworn enemy of Clarendon and that he had just instructed his men to drown me in the Thames if at all possible? Probably not. I'm not that important. He looks ill because he always is, though it would be a brave disease that actually tried to kill him.

'Welcome to Exeter House,' he says. 'I'm honoured, Lady Grey, to have London's most celebrated playwright here.'

'So, you've invited Dryden this evening?' says Aminta.

Ashley gives a dry, crackling laugh. 'You put Dryden in the shade, my Lady, where he belongs.'

'I think that, as our new Poet Laureate, he has been elevated to heights that I shall not attain. And he can write both tragedy and comedy. I merely seek to amuse the Town with puns and allusions that are as close to indecency as I dare. No, my Lord, we play-scribblers all live in the shadow of the author of "Astraea Redux".'

'"Astraea Redux" was written simply to flatter the King.'

'But Dryden had the good sense to write it and I didn't. That is the difference, my Lord. It is one of two good reasons why I shall never be Poet Laureate myself.'

'You think that sycophancy counts for more than talent?'

'Yes, of course. If you want to make money. But Dryden is the better writer anyway.'

'And you, Sir John – who do you consider the greater playwright? Dryden or your wife?'

'Well . . .' I say. 'I think . . .'

But I never discover what I think. The babble of many conversations has ceased. Suddenly all eyes have turned towards the door. The King is here and he has Mistress Gwynne with him. Ashley does not wait for my critical judgement. He is already halfway across the room, his coat-tails flying behind him, his arms wide open in welcome. I think he may approve of sycophancy after all.

'That was lucky for you,' says Aminta. 'Just so that you know, if you'd said I was better than Dryden, I would have despised your lack of good taste for ever. If you'd said Dryden was better, I'd have poisoned your food.'

'Thank you for clarifying that,' I say.

'My pleasure,' says Aminta. She waves across the room. 'Nell Gwynne,' she adds. 'She was quite good in my last play, wasn't she? The King wants her to give up the stage. That would be a shame. But some men are reluctant to let their women outshine them in any way. Oh sorry – I don't mean you, John.'

'Working for Arlington,' I say, 'it would have been dangerous to shine more than I had to.'

The room has fallen silent again. Hard on the heels of the King, almost as if she might have planned it that way, is the Duchess of Cleveland. She is dressed all in white, the glistening silk merging effortlessly into crisp virginal lace in a vast tidal wave of irrefutable purity. There are pearls in her hair. There are even larger pearls round her neck. In her hand is a fan of creamy ostrich feathers. To provide a little contrast, however, she has obtained from somewhere a young infantry officer. She hesitates shamelessly at the entrance to the room for just long enough to be seen by everyone, then sweeps onwards, scarcely glancing at the King and seeming not to notice Mistress Gwynne at all. Every now and then she pauses briefly to acknowledge the homage of the lesser nobility and their wives, progressing by degrees into a safe haven, on the far side of the room from the King. She drops anchor close to the Duke of Albemarle, much to the consternation of her young escort, who suddenly finds himself outranked many times over by everyone in the group.

'She should hand him to a servant to look after until she needs him again,' I say.

'Or to a nursemaid,' says Aminta. 'Is that Arabella's little brother, John Churchill? I heard the Duchess had taken up with him.'

'No, John Churchill is serving under Allin somewhere in the Mediterranean,' I say. 'I've no idea what this one's name is.'

'I doubt if the Duchess does either,' says Aminta. 'She can't have known him long. At his age, nobody can have known him very long, when you think about it.'

Then I am aware we have been joined by a man in a nose patch. I think there is only one of those here tonight. His coat is of glossy black velvet – expensive but unobtrusively so – entirely appropriate for a man who has spent a lifetime feigning honesty and respectability.

'Good evening, Lady Grey,' he says. 'Good evening, Sir John. I hope you are both well?' Then, having done his duty to polite conversation, he adds: 'Ashley is up to something. But what?'

'Good evening, my Lord,' I say to Arlington. 'Now that I have retired from espionage, I know no better than the next man what the Chancellor is thinking.'

'He is going to announce something or to do something this evening. Ashley never organises dances just to please his wife and her friends. I don't think he even knows how to dance.'

'The Duchess of Cleveland gives dancing lessons quite freely,' says Aminta.

We look across the room to where Ashley is. He appears unpromising material for the most optimistic instructor. He is small and so thin and brittle that too vigorous a dance might snap him in two. He is talking very earnestly to a man at least a head taller than he is, dressed in a plain brown coat and black periwig. I am about to ask Aminta if she knows who the other gentleman is, when the two of them are joined by somebody capable of attracting much more attention than either: a young lady in a dress of red watered silk. Her hair is done in the latest Paris fashion that many of the women of London have adopted this summer – pulled flat from a centre parting across the top of the head, with a cloud of tightly formed curls on each side. A small, neat fan of printed Chinese silk dangles from her wrist. Ashley seems to make some sort of apology to his male companion then, with a hand lightly on her shoulder, he guides the lady in the red dress over towards the Duke of Buckingham.

'So who is she, then?' asks Arlington.

'He's very familiar with her,' says Aminta. 'Almost as if she was his daughter.'

'As if she was his next candidate for the King's mistress,' says Arlington.

'Then he wouldn't show her to Buckingham,' says Aminta. 'He wouldn't risk alerting him to the danger she posed. Not until she was established in her post.'

'He's up to something, though,' says Arlington.

We watch as Buckingham, still smiling, asks a question, head on one side. She replies. He frowns. He looks quite worried, in fact. Ashley places his hand on the young lady's shoulder again and leads her away. Whatever the purpose of the short discussion with Buckingham, Ashley has succeeded in achieving the effect he desired.

'That was interesting,' says Aminta. 'Whatever she said to the Duke put the fear of God into him. Where will they go next?'

We watch Ashley's progress round the room. He seems to be introducing the lady to the more important guests, though not to us. Finally he reaches the little circle surrounding the King.

'See,' says Arlington. '*Exactly* as I told you. He approaches stealthily, but it is the King who is his real target. He seeks to ensnare His Majesty in red silk.'

We still cannot see the lady's face clearly but can watch the King's dark features. Like Buckingham, he greets her with a smile – cynical, world-weary, but not unwelcoming. She curtseys very elegantly. The King makes her, to judge by the expression of contempt on Nell Gwynne's face, a most graceful compliment. The lady replies. The King is enchanted. Then he asks a question and his mouth falls open at the reply. Ashley turns to look directly at us and grins. He leads his charge onwards round the room towards another group of distinguished and unsuspecting guests. Nell Gwynne tries to engage the King in conversation, but he is staring after the lady in the red silk dress. He doesn't even notice that his current chief mistress is by his side or that she is furious with him. She stamps her foot and marches away across the room. He doesn't notice that she's gone.

'The King is less merry than he was. Not a good beginning for the lady in the red dress, not if she hoped to occupy the King's bed,' I say.

'The course of true love never did run smooth,' says Aminta. 'And sometimes initial impressions can be wrong. There was a time when you thought I was an annoyingly precocious little girl – do you remember? As for the lady in red, we are only at Act One of her drama. It's a shame that Ashley didn't choose to make an aside to the audience. Something along the lines of: my evil plan has met with wholly undeserved success.'

'A Prologue would have been helpful,' I say. 'Who on earth is she? She's clearly worth introducing to everyone of importance in the room – though not to us.'

'There's something familiar about her,' says Aminta. 'I shall ask Mistress Gwynne, who will probably be willing to tell me all she knows, judging by the expression on her face. I don't think Ashley will bring her over here, anyway. He seems to be avoiding this part of the room.'

For a moment I am left alone, then I am tapped on the shoulder with a fan of ostrich feathers.

'Well,' says the Duchess of Cleveland, 'that was interesting, wasn't it? Mistress Gwynne has most certainly had her nose put out of joint. I rather enjoyed that. It should happen more often. It's no fun to have your successor introduced to you, with no warning. Especially when she is younger and so very much prettier.'

'But who is she?' I ask.

'Some are saying Ashley's bastard daughter,' says the Duchess.

'Would Ashley propose his own daughter as the King's mistress?'

'He'd propose his grandmother if he thought he could gain some small advantage by it.'

'She clearly did not impress the King in any way.' I say.

'I wouldn't say that. The King hasn't been able to take his eyes off her,' says the Duchess. 'Look – he's still staring at her now. There's more than one way to capture a King. He'll ask her to dance in a moment. You'll see. Have you made any further progress as to who killed Kitty Burgess?'

'I am afraid not,' I say. 'Except to rule people out – including you, of course.'

'I should hope so. It could have been that Gwynne woman, though, could it not? That would be very funny. As an actress she could have met Kitty before and formed a strong dislike. She has her own coach, and no coat of arms could be more appropriate for her than a herd of fat cows. You saw how she behaved when presented with a rival. Pure hatred. Never have I seen a more obvious murderess.'

'I merely saw her walk away across the room,' I say.

'She stormed off, like the common orange girl she is. Her mother was no better than she should have been either.'

'I didn't know her mother, but Mistress Gwynne was a noted actress before she became a royal mistress,' says a voice beside us. 'At least, that is what my father tells me.'

The Duchess and I turn to look at her young infantry officer. I think we had both forgotten he was there.

'Oh, go away, George. What do you know about actresses? Go and play with some of the maids of honour,' says the Duchess.

He bows and departs, slightly uncertainly. I am not sure he knows which ladies the maids of honour might be, though a few enquiries would clarify that for him. They will probably prove more agreeable playmates this evening than the Duchess of Cleveland.

'So his name is George?' I say.

'I've really no idea. It might be.'

'You should have kept him to dance with,' I say. 'Just in case.'

'But I am dancing with you,' she says. 'You promised faithfully that we should have the first dance.'

'No,' I say. 'That is at the ball you will give at Nonsuch. Tonight I shall tread on Aminta's toes and nobody else's.'

'That is very tiresome of you, John. Then I may have to dance with the King, *faute de mieux*. I don't think the orange seller is going to oblige him in *any way whatsoever* tonight. I shall catch the King now, before Ashley's woman ensnares him. Don't go anywhere. I shall be back to talk to you and your lovely wife very soon.'

'The Duchess has deserted you,' says Aminta. 'I saw her assault you with her fan, then march off.'

'The King is a better dancer than I am.'

'And the child she brought with her?'

'Sent to dance, much to his relief probably, with the maids of honour. What did Mistress Gwynne tell you? I assume she was well informed?'

'Actually,' says Aminta, 'Nell knew almost nothing about her. The woman did however introduce herself to the King as Elizabeth Needham.'

'Barbara thinks that she is Ashley's daughter,' I say.

'Not at all. Some distant kinswoman of Lord Ashley's, who has been residing in France. He wishes to launch her into London society.'

'The ball is in her honour?'

'Something on this scale? For a distant kinswoman on a visit? I wouldn't have thought so.'

'Why did the King react so badly to meeting her?'

'Nell didn't know. One minute all was well, even if the King was paying Mistress Needham a little too much attention. The next the King was staring at her with horror and wouldn't speak to anyone.'

'And she said nothing more than her name?' I ask.

'Nothing to cause alarm, certainly. Ashley had just intro-duced her as Mistress Elizabeth, his kinswoman from Paris. So they were just talking about this and that. The King had asked her about France and King Louis. She had said that His Majesty was both taller and more handsome than the French King, and better loved by his subjects. That was very well received, as you may imagine. Then His Majesty, realising he only knew her Christian name, belatedly asked about her family and it all went very wrong.'

The music has begun. A lively English country dance. The King has taken to the floor and has led Elizabeth Needham out with him. Our friend Barbara has been too slow. Or the King too quick.

'She dances well enough,' I say.

'Yes, well enough. I don't think that she is used to events such as this, but she has a natural, youthful elegance that makes up for any lack of experience.'

'Ah, the Duchess of Cleveland is now joining them. She has retrieved George, if that is his name, and made him dance with her.'

'He also dances competently,' says Aminta. 'For an ensign in a foot regiment, anyway.'

'I am sure a knowledge of country dances is very helpful to him in his military duties.'

'He really is very young. Even for the maids of honour, who are quite worldly and experienced for their age.'

'It will do him no harm. He is smiling. At some stage in the distant future – around 1720, say – a gouty old general will be telling his grandchildren how in the days of Good King Charles he danced a country dance with the famous Barbara, Duchess of Cleveland. The Duchess, however, does not look happy.'

'Don't flatter yourself that it is because she is not dancing with you.'

'I'm not,' I say.

'The King and Mistress Needham are talking very earnestly. But I don't think they are speaking of love.'

'Perhaps they are discussing the fountains at Versailles,' I say. 'Coming from Paris, Mistress Needham may have studied how they work.'

'Ah,' says Aminta. 'Perhaps it is that. She doesn't look like an expert on plumbing, but I've never thought you looked like a country gentleman and magistrate. Much too dashing. We really must get you a sober and respectable periwig to deny all of the exciting implications of that scar. Shall we take the floor for the next dance? Otherwise the Duchess of Cleveland will come and carry you off, even though you are twice the age of her current partner and have never held any military rank of any sort.'

We do in fact dance three dances, then the King relinquishes Mistress Needham and we are allowed to disperse to the edges of the hall, where the ladies compete for the small number of chairs available.

I notice Ashley whispering to his kinswoman following her dance. They both look towards us, as if we, rather than the King, were the subject of their discussion, though that is unlikely. She shakes her head quickly but vigorously. Ashley smiles at me, then starts to push Mistress Needham in our direction. I think she would rather not join us, but joining us is in some way part of Ashley's plan for tonight. Her face suggests that she will make the best of it.

'Elizabeth wishes to meet the distinguished Lady Grey,' he says. 'She is somewhat in awe of you, my Lady, but I told her you would not bite. She attended your latest play recently and much admired it.'

'It was the wittiest thing I have seen in a very long time,' Elizabeth Needham says. 'But we have few English plays in Paris. They are very different from the French ones. More . . . I have forgotten the right word . . . daring? I am sorry – I lived abroad so long that I probably speak English like a Frenchwoman.'

She in fact speaks English fluently with only the slightest French accent.

'How long have you lived in Paris, Mistress Needham?' I ask.

'All my life, really. We were exiled under Cromwell. Later, my mother returned to England and sadly died here. I was left in the care of some English nuns just outside Paris, but with strict instructions that I was to be allowed to practise my own religion and lead a reasonably normal life. Sadly that did not extend to dancing. I have had to take lessons in order not to embarrass Lord Ashley this evening.'

'They permitted you to remain a Protestant?'

'They were paid to permit it, Sir John. The English chaplain in Paris visited me regularly to see that they kept their side of the bargain.'

'And you never came back until now?' I ask.

'Only in secret. The circumstances were difficult. I would rather not speak of it. *Pardon, madame. Je regrette* . . . Forgive me for mentioning it at all.'

'So we have never met before?' asks Aminta.

'Not unless you have been to Paris, *madame*. No, I fear not.'

'My father and I lived in Bruges and later in Brussels. We never visited any of our fellow exiles in Paris.'

'Brussels? I did not know that.'

'Why should you?' asks Aminta. 'Since we've only just met.'

'But Lord Ashley told me all about you,' says Elizabeth. 'He too is a great admirer of yours, my Lady.'

Ashley smiles and nods but, to my relief, does not mention Dryden.

'You had a long conversation with the King, Mistress Needham,' says Aminta.

'He remembers Paris very well,' says Elizabeth. 'But it is changing so quickly. So much building. *Le Roi* . . . King Louis wanted to pull down the Palace of Versailles and build it again from the ground up, but he has been persuaded by his finance minister to envelop the old structure in a new façade. It is cheaper and money is needed for the next war, whoever it proves to be against.'

'And King Louis is happy with that? I mean the plans for Versailles?'

'*Content? Moi, je pense que non. Mais* . . . I told King Charles that he should demolish Whitehall Palace and build something even grander than Versailles. Not in smoky London but in the country. Winchester, perhaps. Lord Ashley showed me Whitehall yesterday. It is a pitiful collection of buildings, isn't it? Except for the sublime banqueting hall, of course, and the King hates that because his father was executed there. *C'est triste, ça.*'

Ashley, who has been looking across the room, not really listening to this last exchange, taps her gently on the arm and whispers something to her.

'I am so honoured to have met you, Lady Grey,' she says. 'And you, Sir John. A great pleasure. I hope we may meet again soon.'

'You plan to stay long in London?' I ask.

'Oh yes, I think so. If all goes well. Which happily seems to be the case.' She glances at Ashley who gives her in return a crooked smile, like a crocodile who has fed unexpectedly well.

Aminta stares after her as she departs. Then she says suddenly: 'Bloody hell! That was Kitty Burgess!'

'But Aminta—'

'I know what you are going to say, John: that I can't accept that Kitty Burgess has been killed and that I am seeing her everywhere.'

'Yes,' I say, 'that is exactly what I was about to tell you. First, the woman at the New Exchange and now this lady. Everyone in London can't be Kitty Burgess. Anyway, I don't think it did look like her.'

'She's lost weight and she's dyed her hair black and done it differently and she's dressed herself – or rather she's been dressed – in the latest Paris fashion and she's rouged her cheeks and she's acquired a silly, affected French way of speaking, but that's her. Brought up by nuns! Wait till I tell my cousin Reginald that!'

'You think her accent is affected? It sounds authentic enough. At least she wasn't constantly exclaiming "*tête non!*" and "*ventre bleu!*" as some of our dramatists believe the French do.'

'She had me fooled for a few minutes, but truly, that is Kitty. I may or may not have been mistaken at the New Exchange, but this time I'm certain. It's the finest part she's ever played, but it's her all right.'

I can, of course, state the obvious yet again: that Kitty Burgess cannot be both here at the ball and buried in a churchyard in Hertfordshire. But Arlington arrives before I can say it.

'I think Ashley is determined I shall not get to speak to that lady,' he says. 'Well, I now know who she is – Elizabeth Needham. Or so she claims anyway.'

'That is what she told us,' I say. 'But Aminta is convinced she is Kitty Burgess in a new dress.'

Arlington smiles triumphantly.

'Impossible,' he says. 'With the greatest respect, Lady Grey, you are much mistaken. I have just had a message, delivered to me here only a few minutes ago, from one of my agents in Paris. That is, without any doubt whatsoever, the Byron girl. Far from being dead, as Clarendon claimed, she is very much alive. Since we intercepted Clarendon's traitorous letter, we have been watching half the convents in Paris, in case the Earl visited again. Three weeks ago a young girl, very fashionably dressed, was observed leaving the English convent and returning again after a few hours. She clearly lived there even though she wasn't a nun. My agents thought that odd. So we set a watch to observe her comings and goings, which were many. Then they stopped seeing her. Nothing for over a week. After a while, they made enquiries and were told that the young lady had been collected, at the dead of night, by somebody on behalf of Lord Ashley.' He waves a paper at us. 'It's all here in black and white. And the one thing I've learned about Mistress Needham this evening is that she freely admits she was brought up by nuns in Paris.'

'But, as you say, she's Needham,' I say. 'Not Byron.'

'Needham was Lady Byron's maiden name, before she married Sir John Byron,' says Arlington.

'No wonder the King's face fell when she was introduced to him,' I say. 'He hoped he'd met his next mistress, only to discover she was his long-lost daughter.'

'Lady Byron was able to persuade the King to pay her well for whatever it was she had done or knew,' says Arlington. 'Perhaps she passed on her secrets to Elizabeth – a steady income for her daughter in an uncertain world. Now the King fears the worst.'

'She is, for all that, Kitty Burgess,' says Aminta. 'Mistress Needham is merely the part she is playing tonight.'

'But it is less than a week since your actress disappeared?' says Arlington.

'Yes,' says Aminta.

'Then, as I explained, it simply cannot be her. My agents have been watching this woman for much longer than that. She could not have been in Paris at the very same time as she was appearing on the stage at the Duke's Company. I am sorry, my Lady. Much though I have come to respect your judgement, this time you are wrong. And your husband clearly agrees with me.'

Aminta purses her lips. She has now been doubted by one too many men.

'I'm not going to be taken for an idiot,' she says. 'Not by Kitty Burgess. How dare she? I'm going to settle this now.'

'I wouldn't,' I say. 'I really wouldn't.'

But my wife has turned sharply on her heel and set off towards the group that Elizabeth Needham has now joined. I follow on, as quickly as I can. This could be awkward.

Aminta stops just short of her target. 'Kitty!' she exclaims.

One or two people look at her, but the woman in the red dress does not appear to notice. Aminta taps her on the shoulder.

'Lady Grey!' she says, turning. 'Did you want me? I was just speaking to Mister May here, but I can join you again in a moment.'

Bab May, a close friend of the King's and an acquaintance of mine, gives me a friendly nod. Our interruption of his conversation does not trouble him unduly, but he doesn't know what is likely to follow. I, on the other hand, do.

'No more of this nonsense, Kitty,' says Aminta. 'I don't know what you are up to, but the curtain is about to fall on your little comedy.'

'I don't understand,' says the woman in red. She is clearly puzzled but no more than that.

'I know you are Kitty Burgess,' says Aminta. 'Neville saw you getting into the coach. Idiot that he is, he did nothing. But he told us you didn't want to go. I received your letter from Epping, asking for help. You don't have to pretend any more. I don't know what mess you've got yourself into but you can come home with us now. We shall make sure you are perfectly safe.'

'My name is Elizabeth Needham,' says the woman very patiently. 'I am in no mess at all. I have no idea who Kitty Burgess is. And I don't know why it matters that this Neville person saw me get into a coach. It is, surely, a perfectly normal thing for a gentlewoman to do?'

Bab May gives me a sympathetic smile. My wife has obviously been drinking more of Ashley's wine than is good for her. That's writers for you.

'I'm trying to help you, Kitty,' says Aminta. 'Whoever abducted you, we can just walk out of this room together, now. Nobody will stop us.'

I haven't counted exactly, but I'd say about a third of the people in the room are now listening to Aminta and the woman in red. One or two may be uncertain who the idiot Neville is, but otherwise the overall nature of Aminta's accusations is very clear.

'*Je suis desolée mais* . . . I fear you have made a mistake, *madame*,' says the woman. Her French accent seems a little stronger than it was before. Or perhaps that's my imagination. She turns back to May, as if nothing is amiss, and begins to discuss the balance of power in the House of Commons: the supporters of the King and those who are proving less cooperative. She's well informed for somebody who has only just arrived in London. But then she is, it would seem, the

King's daughter and a good friend of the Chancellor of the Exchequer.

Over her shoulder I see Lord Ashley. I would say that he is rather enjoying this exchange. Of course, he hadn't forgotten that we were previously enemies. Not for a moment. It isn't something he does. That my wife is making a fool of herself – and of me – is the second-best thing that has happened this evening.

'Aminta, we need to speak,' I say, pulling at her arm.

She finally turns and looks at me. 'Very well, John,' she says.

She is silent as we cross the room, perhaps aware that a lot of people are looking at her.

'So, did Mistress Needham obligingly confess to being an actress?' asks Arlington when we find him again.

'The lady denies being anyone other than who she said she was,' I say.

'Precisely,' he says. 'I told you. That is most certainly the woman we saw in Paris. My agents' description of her matches Mistress Needham as closely as it could – her height, her hair, her somewhat aristocratic bearing. And she has appeared here shortly after she left the French capital with Lord Ashley's servants.'

'She is nevertheless Kitty Burgess,' says Aminta. 'However she has done it, that's who she is.'

The three of us turn again to Ashley. He raises his glass.

'He certainly thinks he has won something,' says Arlington. 'That's how he would look if he thought that he had fooled everyone in the room, including us.'

'What if Ashley employed somebody else to impersonate her at the convent?' says Aminta. 'Two false Elizabeths. That's how she was, if only briefly, in two places at once.'

'My agents are not that stupid,' says Arlington, though he does not sound very convinced. He has quite a low opinion of most of the people he employs.

'No?' says Aminta. 'I give you in evidence my Lord Ashley's smile.'

We look at it for quite a long time. Not quite evidence beyond reasonable doubt, but certainly convincing on the balance of probability.

'Very well,' I say. 'Let us suppose, just for the moment, that Ashley and Clarendon had some scheme that involved the Byron girl, whom Clarendon knew about from his own time in Paris. When Clarendon travelled there from Montpellier, however, he discovered, from the convent records, that the real Byron girl was long dead, exactly as the note that you intercepted said. But, for the plot to work, Ashley and Clarendon needed Elizabeth Needham to be alive. So, first, her death had to be covered up.'

Arlington nods. 'As you say, Ashley first got somebody to impersonate her in Paris to fool my agents into reporting to me that somebody very much like Elizabeth Needham was, contrary to any reports we might have had, still very much alive.'

'Of course,' I say, 'this first Elizabeth was never intended as anything other than a temporary stand-in. Though the French version was the right age and plausible in most respects, she was not capable of sustaining the role of Elizabeth Needham under close scrutiny. On a visit to the theatre, however, Ashley had already seen Kitty Burgess, who could act any part, who could change her voice and appearance better than anyone else currently on the stage. Ashley therefore did a deal with her. She would cease to be the ward of a Hampshire vicar and would get to play the part of her life – the part of anyone's life.'

'At which point the first impersonator could be paid off and returned to wherever she came from,' says Arlington. 'The convent was doubtless bribed to keep quiet – other than to tell my men that Ashley had taken her.'

'So Kitty Burgess was not killed in Bishop's Stortford. She may have never left London, except to go into hiding at Lord Ashley's country house. I don't know how Ashley obtained the body of some poor woman who had died in childbirth, but everything can be done at a price. Then all he required to complete the deception was the dress Kitty had been seen leaving the theatre in, a copy of the script stolen from Betterton's chest and a ring that Kitty had decided to keep as a joke. Just in case nobody worked it all out and summoned us to Hertfordshire, Kitty was told, as a back-up, to write you a letter saying that she had been abducted and was heading in that direction. That would have sent us all to Bishop's Stortford if nothing else did. Kitty lost a little weight and got herself a new hairstyle. Finally, Ashley gave a ball at which she could be launched on the town and her story tested on the sort of people she would need to convince – including Aminta and me, since the Duchess had unexpectedly pressed him for invitations for us.'

'Thank you, gentlemen,' says Aminta. 'I'm delighted that, now Kitty's being alive is your idea rather than mine, you are so much more comfortable with it. At least we are finally agreed that the body in Hertfordshire could never have been my actress. Neville may have been right that Kitty had last-minute doubts but, since then, she has clearly come round to the idea that she'd rather work for Ashley than Betterton. It was a good performance tonight. One of her very best. I hope Ashley's paying her well for it.'

'But to what end?' I say. 'I agree you are right. I can see how it was done. But I can't see why. It's a lot of effort to go to, just to give the King a fright. Whatever information Elizabeth Needham had, Kitty Burgess can know nothing that would embarrass the King.'

'Unless Clarendon has always known the secret and has passed everything on to Kitty via Ashley,' says Arlington.

'If Clarendon knows something,' I say, 'he doesn't need to go to these lengths. He can just tell the world himself.'

'It's Ashley's influence. He's being too clever, as always,' says Arlington. 'He'd never do anything in a straightforward way if he could find something more twisted and devious. But my Lord has made one mistake. He hadn't counted on Neville seeing Kitty get into his coach.'

'We don't know it was Ashley's coach. Unless Ashley's coat of arms—'

'Look!' says Aminta. 'The silver punchbowl!'

We turn and stare at the vast bowl that two servants have carried into the room and placed on a nearby table.

'So, that's Ashley's coat of arms on it?' I ask.

'It certainly is,' says Arlington. 'Argent, three bulls passant sable, armed and unguled or.'

'Those would seem to be the cows that I mocked Neville for having claimed to see,' I say. 'Bulls should have occurred to me. Easily dangerous and bad-tempered enough. I'll ask Neville tomorrow. It was a small error on Ashley's part, but we can get a statement from Neville, under oath, that it was Ashley's coach she got into. He'll have difficulty explaining that away.'

I take a notebook and pencil from my pocket and quickly sketch the arms to present to our witness.

'Good,' says Arlington. 'Let's see what your Mister Neville has to say, and what he may be prepared to swear before the City magistrates. Ashley isn't going to get away with this. We'll show he abducted Kitty Burgess against her will and has made her impersonate the King's daughter – much to the King's dismay. Which I for one shall decry as a scurvy trick. Then let's see how much in favour my Lord Ashley is at Whitehall Palace!'

'It's not only Ashley who will suffer. Kitty will too,' I say.

'If it leads to Ashley's downfall and exile,' says Arlington, 'that really shouldn't bother any of us. Look at Mistress Burgess now, strutting around in her red dress! She may have been reluctant to begin with but she is clearly complicit now. She deserves no sympathy at all. Well done to all of us, I'd say, on a good evening's work.'

The following morning Aminta and I are at breakfast when we find we have an early visitor. It is Betterton and he looks pretty tired, as if he's been up all night.

'I've bad news,' he says. 'We have sadly lost another member of the cast, my Lady. Neville was found dead in his lodgings last night. His landlady heard a scuffle in his room then some footsteps descending the stairs. When she plucked up the courage to pull on a shawl over her nightdress and go and investigate, she discovered the poor man bleeding to death from a chest wound.'

'Was he able to speak?'

'No. He was conscious, she says, when she found him, but he died almost at once. She sent for me straight away, but there was clearly nothing to be done for him. All I could do was inform the watch and then send for the coroner this morning. And now I have to find another footman for this afternoon's performance. But nobody could play the idiot as Neville could. He was the king of foolishness.'

'I told Kitty that Neville saw her,' says Aminta.

'And Ashley was close by,' I say. 'That was fast work. Poor Neville. I think that it may have been his knowledge, not his foolishness, that killed him.'

Chapter Fourteen

In which I interview a landlady

'I've already told the watchman and the coroner everything an honest woman might be expected to know,' says Mistress McCrum. 'Who did you say you were?'

'Sir John Grey,' I say. 'I'm a magistrate.'

Her narrowed eyes still look doubtful, but this may be one of the few occasions on which my knighthood proves to be of some practical use. An untitled magistrate probably wouldn't get beyond where I am, standing on the doorstep in the shadows of the scrofulous, soot-stained houses opposite; but one whom the King has knighted, however undeservedly, might be allowed into the oak-panelled hallway at least.

'I've nothing for you,' she says, nevertheless standing back so that I can enter the dark, narrow, cabbage-smelling interior. 'You'd best come into the parlour. This is no business for the common ears and noses of the street. I run a respectable house.'

'Thank you, Mistress McCrum,' I say. 'I'm very grateful to you.'

I have to duck to pass through the low doorway into her inner chamber, a spacious room also panelled in oak so old it is almost black. The light from the narrow leaded window reveals a canopied bed in one corner, a table and several uphol-stered chairs, built by a craftsman of another era. A small fire, unneeded for warmth but essential for cooking, smoulders away on the hearth, sending smoke impartially up the chim-ney and into our lungs. At least it helps hide the fragrance of long-unwashed bedlinen.

'Had Mister Neville rented a room from you for long?' I ask.

'Fifteen months, come full moon next Sunday,' she said with the accuracy of one used to calculating how many shillings are due and when. 'He was a good tenant, for an actor. Polite when he said anything. Sober whenever he could be. He owed me ten and sixpence, when he died . . .'

'Doubtless his executors will take care of it,' I say.

'You think so?' she says.

'If he made a will.'

'Then it sounds as if I am to be the loser again,' she says, her face falling. 'And who's to pay for the funeral? I can't rent that room out until he's gone from it and buried. No tenant wants to share a room with a dead body. And if I store him in the cellar, the beer will just turn sour, as it does with corpses. People who get themselves murdered should stop and think of the consequences for others.'

'I'll speak to Mister Betterton,' I say. 'Neville was probably owed some wages.'

'At how many shillings and sixpences a day?'

'I don't know,' I say.

'Well . . .' she says.

'What do you recall of yesterday evening?' I ask. 'I understand that a group of men walked into the house and stabbed him?'

'Walked in? Do you think I offer my tenants no locks on the doors, Sir John? No, after I was already abed, a little before midnight, I heard a frightful knocking and somebody calling out Neville's name. Well, I wasn't getting up to allow in a greasy crowd of players. They could stay where they were in the street.'

'They sounded like actors?' I ask.

She considers this. 'They sounded as if they spoke with authority. Men of education. Men who could declaim. Men who could hold a pen without awkwardness.'

'What next?' I ask.

'I heard Neville come down the stairs and pull back the great night-bolt and then the ordinary day one. They spoke in whispers, as if it was not my right and my duty to know what they said. All I heard clearly was Mister Neville insisting that he would do and say whatever they wished him to do or say. Then several pairs of feet ascended to his chamber.'

'What next?' I ask.

'For a while I could make out nothing more,' she says. 'Even with my ear pressed hard to the door. But then Mister Neville cried in a loud voice: "You have deceived me! You villains would slay me in my own chamber!" Then: "I die, I die!"'

Well, those last words at least fit my knowledge of how Neville thought things should be played out. It would seem he expired, in some respects at least, exactly as he would have wished.

'What next?' I ask.

'There was a chattering of feet, running down the stairs. The door opened and slammed again. I heard their shoes slide on the moon-shiny cobbles outside.'

'You saw their faces?'

'Not I. Nor would I wish to have done. Had they seen my curtain twitch just half an inch, they would have been back in an instant to cut my throat.'

I nod. There is every chance that is true.

'What next?'

'I went up to Mister Neville's chamber. He was bleeding all over the bed. I can wash the sheets and blankets, but who's to pay for a new mattress, I ask you?'

'I don't know,' I say. 'But I shall see what Betterton tells me about any money due to him.'

'I suppose I'll just have to turn it,' she says.

'He was unable to speak before he died?'

'He tried to say something, but there were just bubbles of blood. Pink froth. Then there was nothing at all. It was a peaceful death, if you don't count the stabbing and the shouting.'

'Had he said to you that he was in any sort of danger?'

'He told me about the actress friend of his who was kidnapped. He feared they might come for him too. He was worried that he had said too much to somebody. He said he should never have told anyone about the cows, though who he meant by that is anyone's guess.'

'I suppose he didn't say who he feared would come after him? He didn't mention Lord Ashley's name?'

She shakes her head. 'Satan, he said. But surely he would not have ushered Satan up into his chamber? He knew I would never permit such a thing.'

'The body is still upstairs?'

'You wish to view it?'

'If you please, Mistress McCrum.'

I am led up the narrow wooden stairs. The door to the room in question is ajar because, decency apart, what would be the point in closing it? Who would willingly enter and who would leave?

I push the door open slowly. It is a fine chamber in a house that was once much grander than it is now. Two hundred years ago, some rich merchant would have lived here at his ease, just inside the City wall. Now many people have a room or half a room each. And underneath the floorboards is an army of rats, for ever gnawing away. Perhaps it would have been kinder if the Great Fire, which destroyed so much of London, had not capriciously spared it. Neville is lying on his back, his eyes wide open as if in amazement at the rich plaster mouldings of the ceiling. The mattress is, as Mistress McCrum feared, ruined. Blood has soaked into the canvas and through the straw stuffing and on to the floor. She will turn it in vain. I examine his body. There are several deep wounds. One has pierced his throat very neatly. Two of the other thrusts, when I study the matter further, have penetrated his back and another three his front. There are cuts on the palms of his hands, where he tried to fend off the blows. The attack must have been sudden and coordinated – no chance brawl after an argument but a well-planned assassination by experienced swordsmen, who first talked their way in.

'The coroner examined the body?' I ask.

'Of course. He didn't take long. He said the cause of death was obvious to any fool, but he must needs convene a jury tomorrow for the sake of the fools who employ him.'

My eyes scan the bed and then the floor. Then I look under the bed. There is a sheet of paper there. I kneel, avoiding the congealing blood as much as I can, and retrieve it. It is a little stained but now dry and still legible. 'Lord Arlington commands you to go to the third house on the right in Bell Yard and do as instructed. The man you want has a chamber on the first floor.'

'Who's Lord Arlington?' she asks.

'One of the King's ministers,' I say.

'You'd think he'd have something better to do,' says Mistress McCrum.

Chapter Fifteen

In which I decide, uninfluenced by anyone else, to visit France

'Have others seen this note?' asks Arlington, holding up the blood-stained sheet of paper that would implicate the Secretary of State in a murder, if only it could.

'The two of us and Mistress McCrum,' I say.

'Does she know you work for me?'

'I think her world is limited by the four wooden walls of her room. What happens beyond is of little concern to her, unless it affects the timeliness of rent payments.'

'So she'll keep quiet about it, then?'

'She will not speak against either of us in any way, so long as she believes I am interceding with Betterton for the cost of Neville's funeral and a new straw mattress.'

'Well, we now have the letter and she doesn't, so let her say whatever she wishes. Nobody will believe her. This killing is Ashley's work, without question. Your wife should not have told Kitty that Neville saw the coach.'

For once I do not deny that Ashley may have been involved.

'Everyone in the Duke's Company knew that Neville had seen the coach,' I say. 'It wasn't a secret. Ashley would have found out sooner or later. He may have known already.'

'We might have kept the actor alive for another day. Just long enough to sign a statement. That's all we needed.'

'The timing of Neville's death is certainly very convenient for Lord Ashley,' I say. 'Though I doubt a coroner's jury would dare to suggest his lordship played any role in the killing. I should go and see Betterton, I suppose, and enquire how much Neville was owed.'

'You have more important things to do than act as a middle man in the purchase of mattresses.'

'Such as?'

'I still need you to go to Paris and talk to Clarendon. Whatever you thought before, you must agree now that it's all connected – Kitty Burgess's abduction, the fate of the real Byron girl and whatever Ashley and Clarendon are plotting. We know that, with Kitty's help, they've resurrected a dead daughter of the King's. But we don't know why. Clarendon is willing to swear to something – so is Father Christopher. But we don't know what. Clarendon trusts you in a way that he would never trust either of my agents in France, which is wise of him bearing in mind the ease with which he and Ashley duped them. But you can get the Earl to tell you the whole story in the strictest confidence. You can swear on your honour that you will not betray his secrets.'

'And – forgive me for asking – will I betray him?'

'Yes, of course.'

'My wife is reluctant to trepan such an old friend.'

'He's an old friend of mine too. He's an old friend of a lot of people. I don't see that makes any difference to anything.

He has to be tricked or bribed or frightened into giving away Ashley's secrets. We have to stop Ashley doing whatever he's doing.'

'Aminta disagrees.'

'You cannot be dictated to by your wife, Sir John.'

Shall I point out to Arlington that his wife is Dutch and that he has long favoured an alliance with the Netherlands? Of course, it may just be a coincidence.

'The problem is, my Lord, that my wife is often right,' I say. 'For example that Kitty Burgess is alive and well.'

'Presumably she'd like to keep her alive and well? You said she felt responsible for her. As things stand, Mistress Burgess is, as you've observed yourself, in the greatest danger.'

'I'll speak to Aminta. She likes being proved right. If my wife thinks that a visit to Paris would rub salt into my wounds, she'll probably be willing to reconsider her previous opposition to it.'

When I arrive home, Aminta has a sheet of paper of her own.

'It's from my clerical cousin in Hampshire,' she says. 'He says that he knows nothing of Kitty's family. She came to them as an orphan. Her parents were a Colonel and Mistress Burgess, who were related in some way to his wife, but she is now dead and cannot be further interrogated on the matter. He thinks the family came from the west country – Bath, perhaps – but the girl would not have been sent to them if she had anyone more closely related to her. He does now suggest prayer as a practical way forward, which means that he may be a little more concerned than he was before. He says he gave Kitty much advice, which was always ignored. Apparently she listened to his late wife in a way that she did not listen to him. He hopes no harm has come to her, but it clearly wouldn't surprise him if it had. In short, his views are not unlike Betterton's, except that they are endorsed in some way by God.'

'Will you write back and say that Kitty is safe and impersonating one the King's bastards, possibly to extract money from the King, as Lady Byron did before her?'

'I fear he may not be surprised. I'm furious with Kitty, of course – the way she just stood there and allowed me to make a fool of myself. But she had Ashley watching her the whole time. It may not be entirely her fault. If only there was some way to talk to her on her own.'

Our maid enters the room. 'There is a lady at the door. She says she's Mistress Needham. Shall I show her in?'

The lady now calling herself Elizabeth Needham settles into an upholstered chair, carefully rearranging her skirts – figured green satin today in place of the striking red silk. She wears a little lace cap most becomingly on her undoubtedly fashionable black hair. Ashley has invested in her quite heavily.

Our visitor and my wife eye each other up, like two cats who have chanced to meet in an alleyway that they both consider belongs to them. Mistress Needham does not seem to be noticeably repentant. I fear that Aminta may already be feeling less charitable than she was a couple of minutes ago.

'Last night,' says our visitor, slowly removing a glove, 'you seemed to mistake me for a lady called Kitty-something?'

'Kitty Burgess,' says my wife.

'Burgess . . . yes, of course. I had forgotten the lady's family name.'

'For which you may be forgiven – she was not that well known.'

'Indeed? Lord Ashley thought otherwise. But last night, being newly arrived, I myself had no idea who this Kitty might be or why you might think that I was she. My Lord has since kindly explained to me that a most promising actress of that name disappeared and was, very sadly, later found murdered. In Bedfordshire or Hertfordshire, I believe. He said that she was related to you in some way. Though it had not struck him before, he realised that I bore some very slight resemblance to her. I can see that, in your understandable distress at losing a friend, and a most valued colleague, you might momentarily have thought you saw her across the room – indeed, that you might have hoped that the reports of her death were false, for such things do happen. I am sorry if I inadvertently caused you any embarrassment in front of so many of your friends.'

Aminta has been icily silent throughout this careful explanation. Now she smiles. 'And I apologise unreservedly for my silly mistake, Mistress Needham,' she says. 'I can see now that you are indeed somewhat shorter than Kitty. And your hair is much darker. And your nose perhaps not quite so fine. And your eyes a less attractive colour than those I remembered.'

'Ah, she must have been a beauty indeed! And so very talented, I hear.'

'But nothing like as clever as she thought she was. I cannot stress that too much, Mistress Needham. You will stay and take tea with us? My maid is preparing some at this moment.'

The lady in green satin glances for a moment at the door. 'Regrettably I do have a number of people to visit . . .'

'I should be honoured if you would stay for a short while. And tell us a little more about yourself. I would take it as a sign that you have forgiven my ridiculous error.'

'Perhaps just one cup . . .'

'Thank you, Mistress Needham. I shall call our maid and let her know you are staying.'

The maid arrives and departs. Shortly after, the tray is brought in. The teapot, the delicate little cups, the fine golden colour of the tea are admired and commented on and our maid departs once more.

'So you grew up in Paris?' asks Aminta.

'Indeed,' says Elizabeth Needham.

'You must speak French very well.'

'*Un peu.* But I was brought up by English nuns. I spoke English most of the time.'

'How very convenient for you in all respects. And why did you grow up in a convent? An unusual choice for a young girl to make.'

'I should say at once, my Lady, that the circumstances of my birth were somewhat of an embarrassment to my mother, who was then a widow and known to be a friend of the King's. People made assumptions. Assumptions that I have lately discovered were correct in all of the important details. My mother visited me often, but not so often as to arouse suspicion. She died six years ago, leaving me penniless but with a good knowledge of languages and history and music. And religion, of course. A great deal of religion. The nuns taught me less of physics and chemistry and thought that novels and plays were the work of the Devil. The path to hell, they warned me, is paved with romantic comedy.'

'Did anyone there speak of your father?' asks Aminta.

'Not at first. I was in a convent and, though I was aware that most girls had fathers, the absolute necessity for one had not been explained to me. It was the whispering of the nuns, when they thought I was asleep, that first made me wonder if

I was not quite like the other girls there. That and a grudging respect from the Abbess, which I could not easily explain. Then, more recently, Lord Ashley confirmed various matters and all fell into place. He does not doubt my parentage. Nor, I think, does the King.'

'Your hair is as dark as his Majesty's,' says Aminta.

'But not my skin. I have my mother's colouring – hair almost black and skin very white. Sir Peter Lely painted her as Saint Catherine.'

'Did he? He also painted the Duchess of Cleveland in the same guise.'

'Saint Catherine must be deeply honoured by so much condescension from the very highest members of society.'

'Your hair is certainly a very fine colour.'

'For which I must thank God.'

'You are too modest,' says Aminta. 'More tea, Mistress Needham? If you refuse, I shall have to think I am only partly forgiven.'

Elizabeth Needham gives us a thin smile and proffers her cup. It would seem that she has more time to spare than she first thought.

'And how do you know Lord Ashley?' I ask, as the still steaming tea is being poured, its colour now slightly darker than before.

'He is related in some way to the Byrons. He heard of me and took pity on an orphan, whose only future seemed to be to remain at the convent and teach generations of young girls like herself.'

'The fact that he believed you to be the King's daughter influenced his actions in no way?'

'He has not said that it did.'

'He is such a kind man,' says Aminta. 'Whenever I see him, I think that. A saint, of sorts.'

'I agree. A deeply religious man, though I am not sure of which religion.'

'And what do you intend to do now? How will you live, with no inheritance?'

'Lord Ashley says that he will provide for me.'

'Would that not, strictly speaking, be the duty of your father?'

'The King has many calls upon the money that he is able to extract from Parliament – the navy, his mistresses' gambling debts, his other children, his yachts, his dogs. Lord Ashley says the King would welcome my being taken under his lordship's wing, so to speak, for the time being. But I'm sure His Majesty will do what he can. In the fullness of time. Once he is more used to the idea of me as his daughter. The King is a kind man too, though nobody would perhaps confuse him with a saint.'

'That,' says Aminta, 'is the last straw. It is one thing to be humiliated in front of Ashley's guests. That he should send Kitty Burgess into my own home to try to humiliate me in front of my own servants is one insult too far. Kitty always overestimated her ability and she's about to land on her face again.'

'I agree,' I say, 'that Ashley's confidence is remarkable. But you have to concede that was an impressive performance on Kitty's part. Even knowing what we know, I could have sworn she had been born and brought up in a convent in Paris. She included a lot of detail – the grudging respect from the Abbess, for example, and the whispering of the nuns – that was very nicely judged.'

'Kitty always had that skill,' says Aminta. 'Don't forget that even for a moment. And Ashley clearly knows how to tell a story. But she is not, and never has been, Elizabeth Needham. And she is most certainly not the King's bastard daughter, even if the late Elizabeth Needham was.'

'So, what was she doing here this afternoon, other than having fun at our expense?'

'Ashley, having observed my very visible and well-justified doubts, clearly sent her as a final test before he does with her whatever he's planning to do.'

'Which is what exactly? Perhaps Ashley has discovered some secret known by Lady Byron and hopes to blackmail the King with it. But I still can't see why he has to dress Kitty up in green satin to make it work.'

'Nor can I,' says Aminta. 'I wonder what she'll report back to Ashley. I doubt that she'll play down her success. She'll probably claim she ran rings round us. I can just hear that tinkling little laugh of hers as she tells the story. Most of me hopes she does end up looking like an idiot. But a small bit of me fears for her all the same. And, in a slightly less concerned way, I fear for Ashley when the King finds out the truth. His Majesty will not forgive them.'

'It's more of a risk for her than for him. However wrong it goes, at the worst Ashley can expect a few months shut up in the Tower or skulking in Amsterdam before he is pardoned. But Kitty, as a commoner without friends at court, could face execution for trying to defraud the King, if that's the plan.'

'Not that Ashley will care,' says Aminta.

'Well, there's nothing more we can do about it,' I say. 'Not if Kitty won't help herself.'

'Oh, we're going to do something, John. We're going to do

exactly as Arlington proposes. We'll go to Paris and find out what that old rogue Clarendon is up to. Then we'll denounce Ashley, as he deserves, and send Kitty back to Betterton to learn her lines, preferably before she does anything that she can lose her head for.'

'I thought Clarendon was your friend?'

'He's my father's friend. If we need to trepan him, I can live with it.'

'I'll go and see Williamson, then. He'll arrange passports, under our own names or somebody else's.'

'I'd be happier to be myself. But, if I must be somebody else, tell Williamson that I want to be a fake countess at the very least. I've been a real viscountess, don't forget, and always thought that it would be fun to be one rank higher.'

'You'll probably be a haberdasher's wife. We need to excite as little attention as we can. I'd like to get in and out as safely as possible. Arlington never overestimates the danger of one of his schemes – at least for other people.'

From my Lady Grey's celebrated comedy, *The Summer Birdcage*

Act 2 Scene 1, The Palace gardens – early morning – birdsong

Enter Livia and Emilia

EMILIA: Is this corner of the garden sufficiently obscure for your purposes, my dear sister? I declare that I am nervous what secret you wish to disclose, if we have to hide away like this for you to do it. I hope you are not about to offend my puritan sensibilities?

LIVIA: Tush! No fashionable lady has allowed herself the luxury of puritan sensibilities since the King came to the throne. And anyway, I think I will make you laugh rather than tremble. Mister Snarkly took me aside this morning in a place not unlike this.

EMILIA: I hope you looked to your honour, sister, however Anglican your convictions!

LIVIA: My honour is ever in my mind. I permitted him to take me into the garden but to take me no further. *(Aside)* At least for the moment. *(To Emilia)* A man may lose his honour many times and buy himself a new one, as bright and shiny as the last. We women may lose it only once, then all is over with us. There is a gentle staircase, sister, that runs downwards from virtuous to wanton to whore. It is easy to descend and men will kindly offer you whatever help you need on your descent. But it is almost impossible to climb back up, and the same men who were once your friends will have unaccountably vanished. And yet I think Snarkly is an honourable man and I trust him.

EMILIA: He is still a man, sister.

LIVIA: That is a deficiency which he cannot help. Do but hear what he said to me. I fear we may not remain undetected for long, even in this corner. He asked me, my dear Emilia, what you most desired!

EMILIA: What I desire! Then I have cause to tremble, indeed! I am nothing to Mister Snarkly. Tell him plainly I require nothing from him.

LIVIA: You misunderstand me. He asks in secret – a secret I have sworn not to disclose even to you, my dearest friend – and on behalf of Prince Bellair, who is much cast down by your rejection of him. What could Prince Bellair do that would win him your favour?

EMILIA: I shall never marry Bellair! I have seen how his father treats the Queen. The apple does not fall far from the tree – or at least it does not in this garden.

LIVIA: You do not need to marry him, sister. You need only take his gifts, which would please him mightily. What shall I tell Mister Snarkly? Will it be gold? Or pearls? Or diamonds?

Or a fine house? Bellair has been granted the revenues from the Post Office for life and is rich enough for all that, if you do but wish it. Why refuse him the exquisite pleasure of your taking his money?

EMILIA: I would scorn to deceive him thus. I wish him only to be faithful to me, if he wants truly to win my hand.

LIVIA: Faithful? What wife wants a faithful husband? That means she has a husband that no other woman desires. And, if we women want a man badly enough, we can always find a way to snare him. A faithful husband? Who would let such a poor, ill-favoured creature into her nest?

EMILIA: And yet that is what I most desire. I do not want gold or jewels.

LIVIA: Then bespeak them for me. For I am clearly the more easily pleased of the two of us.

EMILIA: No, I must discover for myself whether Bellair can be faithful.

LIVIA: How, sister? Bellair will not tell you. And men are annoyingly loyal to each other in matters such as that, until they fall out and will tell you anything, in which case they are not to be trusted either.

EMILIA: I shall ask his friends, but I shall do so in disguise. I shall don breeches and a fine periwig. If they think I am a man like them, they will at least be honest with me.

LIVIA: You will need to learn how to drink hard, belch and swear strange oaths, sister, and to boast of your many conquests, both true and false.

EMILIA: Is that so hard to do?

LIVIA: It must be easy indeed since all men do it. But I fear for your safety if you are found out. Men may be fools, but they do not like to appear fools, for all that. Have a care, sister. If worst comes to worst, then turn papist and pray to some plaster statue for help.

EMILIA: That may be more dangerous still.

LIVIA: Pshaw! All the court are papists now, or wish to be thought so. Nobody will notice one more.

Chapter Sixteen

In which my wife does not become a countess as she desired

Williamson hands me two passports and a sheet of paper with addresses on it. 'You are Mister John White, a clerk at the Office of Works, taking your wife to see Paris and Rheims – a visit that you promised some years ago, but have only just arranged. Do you have any questions?'

'My wife wondered whether she might be a countess – albeit one married to a clerk at the Office of Works. Or, failing that, whether we could at least travel under our own names.'

'Lord Ashley, if he realised the nature of your mission, might try to stop you. We're now as sure as we can be that he ordered Neville's death. He may well have agents in Dover looking out for Sir John and Lady Grey. It would be best to be obscure.'

'I shall be careful to be somebody else then until I am in France.'

'The French authorities may be looking out for you too, if Ashley has tipped them off. They have promised to help us by arresting and questioning any Englishman who attempts to visit the Earl of Clarendon. You should avoid falling into their hands if at all possible. We could of course try to alert them to the fact that you are working for us, but that would mean telling them where Clarendon now is. The King doesn't want him arrested and sent back to England.'

'If it's so dangerous for him, and possibly for us, why is Clarendon still in Paris? Surely his work there is done. The false Byron girl is in England.'

'We don't understand that either, but our agents in France told us he was still there a couple of days ago, at the address I've given you. Perhaps he is waiting for confirmation all is well in London. Perhaps there is something he still has to do. Hopefully you'll find out what.'

'Can we call on Lord Arlington's agents for help, if all else fails?'

'Sadly not. They have been obliged to leave Paris. Somebody informed on them. Or they may have informed on each other. This will help you, though.' He hands me a sealed letter. 'It's from the Duke of York, Clarendon's son-in-law. It introduces you as friends, whom the Earl may trust.'

'The Duke is no friend of Lord Arlington's and he is, as you say, Clarendon's son-in-law. Why is he so willing to help us?'

'The Duke is, for reasons that I do not need to go into now, very much on our side. I think you will find the introduction helpful. If the Earl requires further evidence of your benign intent, you may like to warn him that his post is being intercepted. Quote to him from that letter of his that fell into our hands.'

'Doesn't that mean that you won't be able to intercept future correspondence?'

'I think he is already becoming more cautious. And the Duke's letter encourages him to give you any post he wants brought back to England. That will be helpful. You will find you also have the address of Father Christopher, the English chaplain.'

'In case I need spiritual guidance?'

'In case you can frighten him into telling you about his part in the plan.'

'Who else knows I am going to Paris?'

'Just Lord Arlington and ourselves. And the Duke of York. And I think you mentioned the Byron girl to Sir Samuel Morland?'

'Yes, so I did,' I say.

'That may prove to have been unwise. As unwise as telling Kitty Burgess that Neville observed her departure in Ashley's coach. But my Lord has every confidence in your ability. Have a pleasant and safe journey, Mister White. I hope that Mistress White enjoys her long-promised visit to Versailles.'

We are travelling in a carriage along the dusty Dover Road. It follows a remarkably straight line between London and the Kent coast. Once, Romans marched this way, though it was then much better maintained and the prices in inns were probably somewhat lower. The Kent countryside is green, like Essex but hillier, and there seem to be orchards everywhere, with apples that are starting to ripen.

Just three passengers have boarded the Dover coach this morning – myself and a somewhat resentful Mistress White, both dressed in our older and plainer clothes, and, opposite us, a gentleman in a shabby blue coat and breeches. For a while he looks displeased, as if we had met before and he hadn't liked us much then. Only after much consideration does he introduce himself as Mister Green.

'Are you also bound for France?' I ask.

He thinks about this for a moment.

'Indeed,' he says brightly, having decided where he is going. 'Calais, then onward to Paris. And you?'

'The same,' I say.

'Ah,' he says. 'A beautiful city, is it not?'

We agree that it is. He does not add that he looks forward in any way whatsoever to travelling with us. Perhaps he prefers to travel alone. Some people do.

'And what is your business there?' he adds.

'Pleasure,' I say.

'Ah,' he says.

'And yourself?' I ask.

'I'm a merchant,' he says. 'I have interests in France. Interests of various sorts and in various places. Including Paris, of course.'

He settles back in his seat and for the next hour he sleeps, or pretends to. Once or twice I think he is observing us through half-closed eyes.

When we stop at Bexley, Aminta and I take a short walk.

'Did you recognise our fellow passenger?' she asks.

'His face is familiar,' I say. 'And he seemed to think he recognised us, though with no great pleasure.'

'He's the man who was talking to Ashley at the ball, before the *soi-disant* Mistress Needham came and joined them. He was a lot better dressed then. Either he's come down in the world over the past few days, or he's as much in disguise as we are. We may take it for granted that Green is an assumed name.'

'You think he works for Ashley, then?' I say.

'Who knows?' says Aminta. 'At the very least, they're good friends. And if we've recognised him, then he will almost certainly have recognised us as being the man and woman who were talking so earnestly to Ashley's sworn enemy.'

'I think we should be very cautious of him. But I don't think he's a paid assassin who's been told to follow us to Dover and kill us anywhere that is convenient for him. In fact, I think he was as surprised to see us as we were to see him. It's more likely that he's just carrying a secret message from Ashley to Clarendon.'

'We must at least assume our friend knows for certain you are not a clerk at the Office of Works. And as for me . . . I do repent my becoming Mistress White. It would have been far less suspicious to travel under our own names.'

'Perhaps we shouldn't have said we were going to Paris either,' I say, 'but if he's travelling that way himself the chances are we'll run into him on the road or even end up sharing a coach again. There wouldn't have been much point in lying and saying we were travelling to Frankfurt or Bruges or Geneva. We'll just have to try to lose him as soon as we can. But there's no avoiding him until Dover.'

We reach Dover with a large sun low in a reddening sky. The great, shadowy chalk cliffs now tower behind us. In front of us, seagulls wheel and screech, swept across the harbour on the fresh breeze. Mister Green jumps from the coach with some agility and, making the briefest farewell that decency allows, vanishes with his bag into the crowd. Our box takes slightly longer to unload. I arrange for it to be carried to the nearest inn, where I obtain a chamber of modest size, suitable for the people Mister Williamson wishes us to be.

'I'll go down to the harbour while it's still daylight,' I say, 'and see what boats are due to sail to France tomorrow. Hopefully we can find one that doesn't contain Mister Green. Did you see where he went, by the way?'

'No,' says Aminta. 'He left us very abruptly. He'd gone before I could even get out of the carriage.'

'He wasn't very communicative on the journey,' I say.

'If he didn't wish to arouse our suspicions, he should have made himself more pleasant. Most people, thrown together on a long journey, will amuse themselves by asking after each other's families or telling stories of their previous travels.'

'He probably hopes he's lost us,' I say. 'And that's fine by me. But, if we can, we must try to beat him to Paris. As I say, I doubt he's preparing an ambush for us, but I'm sure he'd like to get to Clarendon before we do and warn him we are on our way.'

It isn't difficult to find out what boats are due to set sail for France tomorrow. Unfortunately there is just one, leaving at nine o'clock in the morning. Its captain can be found at the Anchor inn if we wish to reserve places on it, inevitably it would seem in the company of Mister Green.

'Places? I should think so,' says the captain. 'What's your name, my good sir?'

He's a large man with a leather coat, sea boots and a whiff of salt about him. His face is the same colour as his coat, but not as new or well-cared-for. Wisely, for one who must be on deck in all sorts of weather, he does not wear a periwig, but his broad hat is planted firmly on his sparse grey hair. The Anchor is his place of work when he's ashore and he now sits at his table with a battered pewter tankard on one side and a scuffed leatherbound ledger on the other. A quill pen and a pot of ink lie between them.

'I'm John White,' I say, without my conscience troubling me overmuch. 'And my wife will be travelling with me. We also have a small chest to transport.'

The captain opens his ledger a cautious inch, glances briefly into the shadowy void and closes it again.

'Unfortunately I'm full,' he says. 'I can't take another passenger – not for any money. With or without a chest.'

'Is that because I'm called John White?' I ask.

'Why should that be?'

'You discovered your boat was overloaded only when I mentioned my name.'

'Is that so? I don't need to give you a reason, Mister White. It's my ship and I'll take who I choose. If I say we've no more room, then we've no more room. If I say you should get out of my sight, then you'll get out of my sight. Good day to you, sir.'

'Is there a Mister Green travelling with you?' I ask.

'Still here, are you? Then I'd point out that's none of your business, since you won't be on the boat.'

I wonder how much Green has paid him to deny me passage to Calais. Well, he can't bribe every ship's captain in Dover, and I'll be, at worst, a day or so behind him. But whatever Green's plans are, delaying us must be worth quite a lot of money to him. He's won this round, even if I don't understand what game we're playing.

I raise my hat to the man at the table. 'I'll bid you good evening then, captain,' I say.

'Good evening, Mister White,' he says, without looking up.

'Please give my best wishes to your good lady. And to your luggage.'

'Ashley has doubtless provided his agent with more money than Arlington has provided you,' says Aminta.

'The advantage he has gained is hopefully small,' I say. 'Most days there must be two or three boats making the crossing. We've missed the only one I know of tomorrow, but we'll find another soon, if the tides are right and the wind doesn't change. I'll ask around in the morning. All is far from lost. Perhaps we can still overtake Green on the road. We'll see what another day brings.'

In the event, the next morning brings a surprise. At seven o'clock we hear a knocking on the door of our modest chamber. I open it to discover Mister Pepys, in travelling clothes.

'Thank goodness, Sir John,' he says. 'I am not too late.'

'You intend to accompany us?' I ask.

'I regret that would not be possible. The Duke of York requires my constant presence in London. The work of the Navy, sir, could not go forward without me. It is a burden to be so much needed, but it is a gratifying one for all that! No, I cannot leave England but I have to speak to you before you do so.'

'Take a seat,' I say, indicating the only chair.

He shakes his head. 'This will not take long. As you know, Lord Arlington alerted the Duke to the fact that he was sending you and Lady Grey to Paris.'

'And so the Duke requested that you should come to Dover and persuade me not to go?'

'On the contrary. His Highness is most concerned that

his father-in-law is getting into something that he would do well to stay out of. He fears that the Earl's plans may not work to the country's advantage – worse still, that they may be to the great detriment of the monarchy itself. He wants you to convey a message to the Earl that it would be best if he lived quietly where he was and that he, the Duke, will in return continue to press His Majesty that he, the Earl, should be permitted to return to England and to his family at some future date convenient for all concerned. I trust that is clear? Good. Any suspicion of a plot – especially one that involved one of the King's ministers – would mean that Clarendon's exile would be much prolonged – in effect, until the King died or Clarendon himself died. It is essential that you make this plain to him and that you ensure that you report back to me and nobody else whatever the Earl tells you – my master the Duke can then advise you how much, if anything, it is good for Lord Arlington to know. I rode down yesterday, hoping to overtake your coach, but I did not arrive in Dover until it was almost dark. It has taken me until now to find you. I understand the only ship due to sail today leaves in two hours. I could have caught you on board the ship, of course, but I could not have spoken to you as frankly as I needed.'

'Sadly we shall not be leaving on the ship in question,' I say. 'We were accompanied in the coach by a Mister Green, whom we saw a few days ago in the company of Lord Ashley. I think that he has bribed the captain not to take us, though he seems to be planning to cross the Channel himself. Could Ashley know of our mission?'

'Not from myself or the Duke,' says Pepys indignantly. 'The Duke detests Ashley above all men. I cannot answer for Mister Williamson's own clerks, however.'

I think again of Morland. He could have told anyone. Anyone at all. But when I mentioned the Byron girl to him, I had no idea I would be going to France.

'Well, I shall assume he is the creature of Ashley until I learn otherwise,' I say.

'What does he look like?'

'Fairly young. Medium height. Black periwig. At Ashley's ball he was wearing a brown suit. He seemed well acquainted with Ashley. Do you know him? It would be helpful to learn who he is, if you did.'

Pepys considers this. 'I think not,' he says. 'Not from that description anyway. But, whoever he is, we can settle matters very easily, and not to his advantage. There is one of our frigates lying in harbour. I shall inform the commander that he is to sail for Calais within the hour, with two very important passengers on board. In the meantime, I shall instruct the harbour master here that the ferry is to be detained, on the orders of the Admiralty, for a flagrant breach of quarantine regulations. That should give you a head start, I think.'

It would be good to be there to see the smile wiped off the face of the leathery captain. I don't think he'll like being in quarantine. But the more miles we can put between ourselves and Ashley's agent the better. And I think we'll now get to Clarendon before he does.

'Thank you,' I say. 'That would be very kind of you, Mister Pepys. We'll head straight down to the harbour, then.'

Chapter Seventeen

In which first we avoid Mister Green and then he avoids us

Though she briefly thought to trip us up at Dover, Dame Fortune has reconsidered the matter and decided she will favour us after all. The breeze is lively and the ship, lightly gunned and designed for speed, seems to slice through the water. A late summer sun shines on us and the beads of salt spray on my sleeve sparkle. I have crossed the Channel before under several names and in many different types of boat, but this is perhaps the pleasantest. Aboard the frigate I do not have to constantly watch my back in case one of the other passengers has been commissioned to ensure that I do not reach my destination. The only one who may have been ordered to impede me is hopefully now in resentful quarantine.

'What exactly is "haul down his clew lines" supposed to mean?' asks Aminta, as yet another order is barked and responded to.

'One of the many commands given at sea,' I say. 'It's worth noting if you plan to include any naval men in one of your plays. Shortly it will be followed by the captain ordering "in with the fore-topgallant" and "in with the main-topgallant".'

'All of that is as incomprehensible to any reasonable person as your bovine heraldry,' says Aminta.

'It means the captain is expecting a fresh wind for the next hour or so,' I say. 'We'll be in France in no time.'

We reach Calais before eleven o'clock, and are able to dine badly and expensively before taking our places on a coach bound for Paris. The vehicle has seen better days, but the horses are fresh and, most important, there are two places available. We could wait another day and do a lot worse. And we don't have time to spare. Mister Green's quarantine will not last for ever. The driver, when I question him, says confidently that he hopes to make Amiens tonight and Paris tomorrow afternoon; but, just as we are approaching the ancient walled town of Abbeville, we hit a pothole and there is an ominous cracking sound. The coach lurches to one side and we come to a halt, slewing across the road. The driver swears a great deal in French and descends from his box, sliding across the now tilted leather seat before dropping nimbly to the ground.

We disembark slightly more cautiously from the danger-ously inclined vehicle. We are unhurt, but it is clear that the coach has been less fortunate. One of the giant rear wheels has fractured in two places and its sudden collapse has caused damage to the axle. We cannot go further without repairs. Fortunately we are already in the suburbs, amongst thatched, half-timbered cottages with vegetable gardens behind well-maintained fences. From here, a proper cobbled street leads up to a great stone gateway and into the town. The horses are unharnessed and taken to a nearby inn. Enquiries are made and a wheelwright is sent for. There is much useful activity but I think we shall be in Abbeville for some time for all that. Our coach will not be ready until tomorrow and there are no other coaches leaving for Paris today.

'Mister Green is hopefully still on the wrong side of the English Channel,' I say.

'Wherever he is, I think we should follow our horses' good example and get something to eat,' says Aminta. 'There's nothing else that we can profitably do.'

The dining room of the inn is high-ceilinged, with white painted walls and an uneven flagged floor. The many-paned windows are long and narrow. The giant gothic fireplace, also painted white, is cold and swept clean for the summer, but there is steam emanating from the kitchen next door and an appetising smell. Our fellow passengers, and those from another coach parked in the courtyard, are already sitting on hard, narrow benches at the scrubbed pine tables, eating, talking and smoking their pipes. We take our places and are quickly served with two wooden bowls of mutton stew. But we have scarcely removed our knives and forks from our pockets before we hear the ring of horseshoes on the cobbles outside. A man, his face, hat and clothes powdered from the summer road, enters and surveys the room, his eyes slowly growing used to the interior gloom. He sees us, pauses uncertainly, then turns on his heel and leaves. A moment later there is a clatter of hooves and a small cloud of fine powder drifts in through the open door.

'I fear that was our travelling companion from the Dover Road,' I say.

Aminta nods. 'Mister Green is much dustier in France than

he was in Kent, but that was him. He must have talked or bribed his way round Mister Pepys's quarantine orders, which by the way I think Pepys may not have had the authority to make. Green has more influence than is good for him.'

'Well, he certainly didn't want to meet us again,' I say. 'Whatever he's planning, his main objective is most definitely to arrive in Paris before we do. With no transport, we'll just have to resign ourselves to the fact that he's won this round. It's his horse I feel sorry for. It was probably quite looking forward to joining our carriage horses in the stables until tomorrow morning. Now it has an uncalled-for hour or two of fast riding ahead of it.'

'By early tomorrow Clarendon will know all about us – our real names, our aliases, our likely intentions.'

'Green will certainly have worked out most of that.'

'Do you think he will also inform the police that we are spies, as a revenge for our quarantining him in Dover?'

'If the police want us, they'll have to find us first.'

'You think we can just vanish?' asks Aminta.

'It's what I usually do,' I say. 'Don't worry. Vanishing is not as uncomfortable as it sounds.'

I am not sure Aminta agrees about the lack of discomfort, now we are here. The repair to our wheel and axle took even longer than expected, but, since yesterday evening, we have been occupying a room above a butcher's shop, overlooking the Seine. On the far bank of the river, towering above the steeply sloping roofs of the houses, we can see the cathedral of Notre Dame. All night we heard the fitful tolling of bells through the damp air and the constant sound of slowly flowing water. But now, with the morning growing warmer, we also have the stink of meat, far from fresh, rising both up through the floorboards and in through the open window. The walls of the room are dotted with large flies that would like to feast on what we can smell, but have lost their way and merely found us. I swat one away from my face. Two others replace it at once.

'Why have you brought us here?' she demands. 'There must be places in Paris where we would be safe from insects as well as the police.'

'I've stayed in these rooms before. The owner is both venal and incurious – a helpful combination. And the flies will not try to eat you so long as you remain alive.'

'Your landlord is not worried that you have a different name each time you stay?'

'He finds it quite normal. I think most of his guests do the same.'

'His other guests must need strong stomachs.'

'So must the French police, if they wish to look for us here. They will try quite a few other places before they reluctantly search an establishment like this one. And, in such a poor district, our host has many customers for his suspiciously cheap mutton and pork. They tell him things that may be useful to us.'

'If it is all the same to you, John, I think we might pay Lord Clarendon a visit before it gets much warmer. Unless he is staying above a tannery or a slaughterhouse.'

'The information provided by Williamson suggests that it is a tailor's shop, which we should, by the way, assume Mister Green visited yesterday. But the letter from his son-in-law may trump whatever inconvenient truths Mister Green has already told him. In any case, I agree we should go as soon as we can. It is impolite to keep a Lord Chancellor, even a disgraced one, waiting – if he is expecting us.'

Clarendon seems as anxious as we are not to draw attention to himself. It is a shadowy location away from the river, close to the high, mossy, city walls and full of narrow plaster-covered houses and ateliers. It is, by several degrees, a less reputable district than our own, and recalls the more squalid parts of London before the Fire, ancient, grimy and long decaying. We approach the shop in the rue de Montagne-Sainte-Geneviève with caution. If anyone is hoping to attack us, this is probably where they wait, amongst these mean streets and twisting, garbage-filled lanes, where people know how advisable it is to keep themselves to themselves, step carefully over dead bodies and not ask too many questions.

We pause at the closest corner to our destination, as if discussing which way we should go, while I scan windows, doorways and alleyways for the slightest sign of movement – a partly visible boot that its owner believes is out of sight, a head that appears for a second and then retreats. But there is nothing amiss. Just early morning Paris, with the sun slanting along the street, dirty errand boys scurrying by and women with baskets on their hips, shopping for dinner. Nobody pays us much attention. Our shabby clothes are not noticeably English and Aminta's hair is impeccably French. If we seem lost, it is probably because we are from Tours or Lille or Dijon, and our confusion is nobody's fault but our own. Then the door of the tailor's shop opens and our friend Mister Green emerges. He is less cautious than I am and we are quick to step back into a doorway. His hurried glance both ways along the street therefore deceives him into believing he is unobserved.

If he is any sort of spy, I am surprised he has lived as long as he has. He smiles, pulls his hat down an inch or two and sets off, fortunately away from where we are hiding.

'The good news,' says Aminta, 'is that we can be certain that Clarendon is still at this address. The bad news is that he most certainly has been warned of our arrival. There was always a chance, until this moment, that Green's mission might have had nothing to do with our own. I begin to fear I have suffered the smell of decaying pig and a swarm of flies for nothing.'

'I agree,' I say, 'that Ashley has a temporary advantage. But let's see where we are after Clarendon has read the Duke's very flattering letter.'

Somewhat improbably, the tailor does not know his guest's name. He has not thought to ask him. A boy is dispatched to make enquiries, our letter of introduction in his hand, and we hear his feet thudding on the wooden stairs. He returns with an instruction to show us up three twisting flights to a garret room at the very top of the house, with views through two open windows over the sooty, tiled roofs, sharp gables and ancient stone turrets of Paris. Beyond them, the morning sky is very blue and hopeful.

Clarendon is, in many ways, exactly as I remember him. He has grown no taller and is still plump and irritable. But almost everything about him is now grey, except his black periwig, which sits on the rickety dressing table. His chin is unshaven so far today and there is much grey stubble in evidence. He wears a dressing gown of heavy grey silk with a soft, slate-coloured cap over his short hair. His stockingless feet are stuffed into slippers. His body seems very tired, but there remains a gleam of energy in his eyes. He has suffered much but he doesn't think he is entirely beaten. Not yet.

He squints at Aminta, though the light is good up here, and raises a questioning eyebrow.

'Lady Grey, I presume,' he says. 'The boy informed me that a Mister and Mistress White wished to see me. But the letter he handed me informed me that Sir John and Lady Grey enjoyed my son-in-law's confidence.'

'A small but necessary deception,' she says. 'It is of course illegal to see you, and there is no way of knowing who is in the pay of the French government or the English one. I had no wish to leave my real name lying around too many shops in Paris.'

'Did I not once know you as Lady Pole?'

'Yes, that was my name when we knew each other many years ago in Brussels. I am now Lady Grey, however, having remarried.'

He grunts economically and turns his gaze on me. 'And you, sir, must be Sir John Grey?'

'That's correct,' I say, before Aminta takes it into her head to introduce me as her footman or worse. She still resents the fact that I did not insist on a more prestigious alias than White.

'My son-in-law tells me you are to be trusted,' he says. 'Grey . . . Have I also met you before? There is something familiar about you.'

'You proposed to have me shot as a spy in Brussels some years ago. I was merely Mister Grey in those days.'

'And were you a spy?'

'Yes. I was working for Cromwell. But I have since been in the pay of Lord Arlington. At least, I was until recently.'

'You have no lasting sympathy with the Republic, then?'

'I have a great deal of sympathy for it. It was honest and decent. It tolerated more than it persecuted. It offered advancement to any man of talent, with relatively little regard for his birth. But I am now the loyal servant of His Majesty, who has been kind enough to knight me for my services to the Crown. You will find no visible traces of republicanism about me.'

'Once a nasty puritan, always a nasty puritan.'

'My wife says much the same.'

'So why are you here?'

'You still have friends in England,' says Aminta. 'People like us who remember you from our days of exile in Brussels. People who believe that the King treated you with little gratitude for your wisdom, your suffering and your loyalty. People who believe you deserve better.'

Clarendon grunts again. That much is self-evident to any blockhead. 'My son-in-law, the King's brother, seems to trust you. Why should I?'

'Though no longer in his employment, I still have the confidence of Lord Arlington,' I say. 'He tells me things that may be of use to you.'

'Such as?'

'Your letters are being intercepted – in particular the one to Lord Ashley concerning the Byron girl.'

'Thank you,' he says. 'I suspected that Arlington was still opening post – or getting that snake Morland to do it for him.'

'You feared that the Byron girl was dead, but happily she seems to be alive.'

'I was misinformed.'

'She has arrived in London. Lord Ashley is introducing her to everyone of any importance.'

Clarendon shows no surprise. He also shows no sign of being about to tell us she is Kitty Burgess. But it is impossible that he doesn't know. It's his plot, not mine.

'How has London received Mistress Needham?' he asks.

'The King is enchanted but disconcerted. As you might imagine,' says Aminta.

'And which of those things is Lord Arlington? Enchanted or disconcerted?'

'Arlington is not easily enchanted,' I say.

'And the Duchess of Cleveland?' he asks.

'She is most displeased.'

Clarendon smiles. He and she were never friends. He glances again at the letter in his hand. He asks nothing more about Ashley's ball, which would be odd if we were his only source of information. But Green, who was there, has already told Clarendon all about it. Perhaps including Aminta's discussion with the lady in red. 'So has the Duke sent you both to question me on the Byron girl? Is that it? Or is it your scheming master Arlington who wants to know, Sir John?'

'Arlington isn't my master,' I say. 'And I have no instructions from the Duke to interrogate you on anything. His advice, however, is that you should do nothing to make the King think you are plotting against him. He will ensure your return to England when he can, though that may not be soon.'

Clarendon laughs. 'I'm sure that is exactly what he'd like me to do. I'm well aware that he is perfectly happy to see me rot in France as long as I don't get in the way of his becoming king. Listen to me, Sir John Grey: my son-in-law could have prevented my fall and exile. He had only to argue my case to his brother, the King. But did he? Oh, he made a few protestations, but in the end he thought it better I should be exiled quickly than that he should be tainted by my fall from grace. Well, he has made his bed and must now lie in it. He will find things out soon enough, as will Lord Arlington, your master – or your former master, if that's what you want me to believe. And I think the Duchess of Cleveland will find herself exiled very soon – to Nonsuch Palace or somewhere even less pleasant.'

'You think Nonsuch is unpleasant?'

'A ramshackle old building like that? It is a pit into which she will have to throw thousands of pounds every year, just to stop it falling down around her. I told the King to demolish it years ago. I can see why he wishes to be rid of it, just as I can see why he wishes to be rid of her. I shall not live to see that painted harlot grow old, as I am now, but it will happen all the same. I can imagine it with great pleasure. One day she'll be an old forgotten woman in an old forgotten palace with a leaking roof, looking out of her window at a garden full of weeds. That thought gives me some comfort, even in lousy Montpellier.'

'I can tell her your views, if you wish.'

'I do wish, but I doubt you'll do it. Why should you? She still has a little influence at court. I have none. Or not at the moment.'

I nod. 'Of course,' I say. 'Let me offer, nonetheless, out of respect for the long friendship between my wife's family and yours, to take back any letters that you are happy to entrust to me, thus avoiding the routine inspection in the Post Office.'

'Thank you, that is kind. The Duke makes much the same offer on your behalf. But I shall decline it. I would not wish you to take such a risk, assuming of course that you are doing it without Arlington's authority, a ludicrous idea that you will permit me to doubt very much.'

'You have other routes for your letters?'

'You must forgive me if I don't tell you that.'

'Was that one of Ashley's men we saw leaving the building, just before we entered?' I ask.

I have finally managed to startle Clarendon. He must have hoped that Green had got clear before we arrived.

'Ashley has no agents in Paris,' he says eventually.

'We certainly saw somebody leave. Somebody whom we have seen in London with Lord Ashley.'

'I think you are mistaken,' he says. 'Ashley has no men here. He doesn't have Arlington's secret service budget to draw on. If he had, I'd have got them to do some things that I have had to do myself. I would not have travelled to Paris, at some considerable risk to life and liberty, if there was any alternative.'

Well, that makes sense. Why would he risk coming here unless he had to? And why is he still in this garret above a tailor's shop?

'You must have very pressing business here,' I say. 'Uncompleted business.'

'I thought you'd read my letters, Grey? It's all in there. If you've missed anything, ask Morland. I've told you all I'm going to.'

'Then we shall not take up any more of your time,' I say.

'Just out of interest, Lady Grey,' he says, 'what did *you* make of Mistress Needham? In the end, I mean.'

'A charming girl,' says Aminta. 'Very open and . . . genuine.'

Clarendon looks at her for a long time and then nods. 'I hope you both have a pleasant stay in Paris,' he says. 'But don't linger too long. London's much safer for you, just as Montpellier is for me.'

Chapter Eighteen

In which we discuss the laws of succession

'Arlington,' says Aminta, 'badly miscalculated if he thought that a letter of introduction from the Duke of York would persuade Clarendon to tell us anything.'

We are wandering along the banks of the Seine, admiring the fact that it has many fine bridges while London's Thames still has only one. The day is warm. Strangely, we have no wish to return to a room over a butcher's shop.

'Arlington rarely miscalculates,' I say. 'Not on things like that. The letter got us in there. After that, it was down to us to use our wits to trip Clarendon up. In the end, I think he tripped himself up. He said, for example, that the Duke of York had made his made his own bed and would have to lie in it – he'd find out what Elizabeth Needham was doing soon enough.'

'Meaning what?' asks Aminta.

'That the Duke will suffer more than anyone from the so-called Elizabeth Needham's arrival in London – a project that Clarendon's exile has somehow forced him to facilitate.'

'Hence the Duke sending Pepys hurrying down to Dover. Pepys may wish to be your friend, but the loan of a ship of the line, for our personal use, was a little too obliging. Whatever Clarendon and Ashley plan to do with Kitty Burgess, it worries the Duke very much indeed.'

'But, even if she were what she is claiming to be,' I say, 'Elizabeth Needham is just another royal bastard. No more than that. How does that harm the Duke? He has bastards of his own and he remains the King's heir presumptive. Unless the King produces a legitimate child somehow, the Duke's position is secure, as is that of his children.'

We stop suddenly, just short of the next bridge. The same idea has occurred to both of us at the same moment.

'Which means,' says Aminta, 'that the Duke must believe that Elizabeth Needham – the real one – was legitimate. Which would mean in turn that, if she miraculously appeared in London, he would no longer be heir to the throne.'

'The King married Lady Byron?' I say. 'It's possible. But it will be difficult to prove. We said there was the same suggestion regarding Lucy Walter, Monmouth's mother. But any evidence for that marriage, if it took place, has long since been destroyed. The King would have taken equal care to conceal any legal ties with Lady Byron. But the Duke, who was with his brother in France, may be one of the few who know Mistress Needham was legitimate – just as Clarendon does. But, even then, it can't harm him unless he strongly suspects there is proof.'

'So we should assume Clarendon has always had the evidence of the marriage and is now, in exile, willing to share it with the world. I'd wondered what justified the risk of travelling to Paris. Assisting Ashley didn't seem quite enough.

Gaining revenge on the King, while at the same time setting aside his disloyal son-in-law, might be.'

'The revenge could be quite comprehensive,' I say. 'If Lady Byron was legally the King's wife, then, whether Elizabeth Needham is currently dead or alive, the King's marriage to Queen Catherine was bigamous since it took place before Lady Byron's death.'

'I can see why the King's face fell when he met the apparent living proof of his past mistake. I can also see why Ashley looked so smug. He has got his hands on a Protestant heir to the throne – or at least a reliable facsimile of one. He doesn't need the beautiful but petulant Duke of Monmouth any more. So Monmouth is another big loser in this.'

'We no longer need to speculate on what Clarendon has offered to testify about. He's only a former Lord Chancellor, but his word would carry a great deal of weight.'

'According to the letter, he'll have Father Christopher testifying alongside him. I suspect the good father performed the marriage ceremony. And Lord Arlington has kindly given us Father Christopher's address.'

'Let us hope that Green has not already visited him,' I say, 'and tampered with our witness – or sent him to join the angels.'

Our next visit is therefore to a tall, emaciated dwelling, squeezed in between two much grander ones, close to the cathedral of Notre Dame on the Île de la Cité. We are no more than a couple of rows of houses and half a river away from our butcher's shop. Unless Green has also got here first, I am sure we shall not be turned away. Father Christopher is used to receiving English visitors. It's his job, after all.

He, unlike Clarendon and unlike his many royalist parishioners in the 1650s, is a wholly voluntary exile. He likes it here. It's comfortable. Nobody will criticise him if he seems a little more Catholic than the Church of England allows, even though it now allows a great deal. He will probably never leave. Not at his age. He's older than Clarendon by at least ten years, small, withered and with failing eyesight.

'How can I be of service to you, Sir John?' he asks.

I have given him our real names in case he has already been advised not to speak to anyone called 'White'. I could have said 'Smith' but you can trip yourself up with too many identities. I've seen it done regrettably often.

'We were visiting Paris. I thought we would call on you for advice as to what we should try to see in the short time we have here.'

'Of course,' he says. He seems relieved that is all we want, but wary all the same. 'A lifetime would scarcely suffice to take in all of the wonders of this city, my dear sir. There is Notre Dame, of course, right on my doorstep. You should go there at once on leaving here. And you must certainly travel out by coach to Versailles, where the King is building a palace that is unrivalled in the whole of Christendom – a nonsuch of a palace, Sir John. They say that, once it is complete, he will abandon his capital and live only there. He has no happy memories of Paris, sir, which has rebelled so ungratefully and so often against his family. He is, even now, contemplating tearing down the city wall – he says, because France is so safe now that no wall is needed. But I think he wants to be sure that, if the citizens rise again in revolt, they will have no stones to hide behind. So perhaps you should also tour the ramparts before they vanish into legend.'

'I'm sure that is all good advice,' I say. 'We are most grateful to you. Coincidentally, we met somebody quite recently returned from Paris who told us about Versailles and its fountains. Elizabeth Needham. Perhaps you know her?'

Father Christopher opens his mouth, then closes it again. We do not, after all, just want advice on the sights of Paris. That could be awkward.

'We met her at Lord Ashley's house,' I continue blandly, as if the priest's response was an entirely normal one to such a casual question. 'Mistress Needham seems to be a very good friend of his . . . as indeed my wife and I are.'

He takes a very deep breath. 'And what did she say of her time in Paris?'

'She said that her mother, Lady Byron, lived here in the 1650s. Her ladyship returned to England and sadly died there. Elizabeth stayed with the English nuns until she was old enough to make her own way in the world. She led me to believe that you would know that?'

'Yes, of course. I visit the convent often.'

'There is a strange rumour circulating in London,' I say, 'that Mistress Needham is actually the daughter of the King. Is that possible?'

He swallows hard. I hope that he does not collapse before he tells us what he knows. 'I have no idea what they say in London.'

'We saw another friend earlier today. Lord Clarendon. He seemed to confirm it.'

Father Christopher says nothing.

'There is actually a rumour circulating that the King married Lady Byron here in Paris. Can you believe that? I suppose you would know better than anyone, though. You would have been chaplain here in the 1650s?'

'Yes. I was.'

'So perhaps you would have had the honour to officiate? If such a thing happened?'

A lesser clergyman might have blustered and denied any knowledge of a wedding, but this one is tougher than he looks.

'I'm sure that my Lord Clarendon will clarify matters for you, if something he said was unclear. Since you are such a good friend of his and of Lord Ashley's.'

'Clarendon has said you will swear to it if necessary. Is that why he remains in Paris? To make sure that you do?'

'Sir John, I am an old man, and have no further ambitions for this world, other than to be left here in peace. You have visited me under false pretences, which is unkind. I do not know what lies behind these strange questions, but let me assure you that you possess nothing that you can use either to bribe me or to threaten me. If I am asked to give evidence – I mean to a properly constituted court – I shall do so. But it is pointless to ask me further questions that you know I cannot answer.'

'Thank you. We shall of course do as you say.'

'Do as I say?'

'We shall visit the Notre Dame, Father Christopher. That large church just outside the window. I have always wanted to go there.'

Father Christopher smiles. He seems relieved that we would rather be in the cathedral than here with him. But we leave him less happy than we found him.

Chapter Nineteen

In which we continue our interesting discussion concerning the laws of succession

The interior of the Notre Dame is a miracle of stone and light, Gothic arches piled on Gothic arches, all rising in carefully judged stages to the vaulted roof so very high above us. The Parisian sun, filtered by coloured glass, cascades to the glowing floor.

'Father Christopher is a frightened man,' I say. 'Or at least a very cautious one. He could have told us outright that he had conducted no wedding. Why not say so, if it is true? But he chose not to. I suspect that he agreed to swear to what he knew when he thought that the Byron girl was dead – as she is. Then Ashley and Clarendon managed to conjure an Elizabeth Needham out of thin air, much to the consternation of Father Christopher, who probably still has not been let in on the secret that she is Kitty Burgess.'

'To the consternation of a number of people who know

that Elizabeth Needham would be the King's rightful heir, had she lived – including the Duke of York.'

'I'm surprised Pepys didn't let us have an entire fleet to take us across the Channel. Moreover, as we've said, Catherine of Braganza is no longer the King's lawful wife. The treaty with Portugal must be torn up. There is also the small matter of our having to return the wedding gift of the ports of Bombay and Tangier. The appearance of a legitimate Protestant heir sends ripples out across the Mediterranean and the Indian Ocean.'

'Can the King be prosecuted for bigamy?' asks Aminta.

'I have no idea, but he will appear a rogue and, more damaging, a fool. He may be swept from the throne as his father was. Clarendon's revenge would be complete and, incidentally, Arlington's life's work is destroyed. I can see why my Lord thought it worth our while to come to Paris.'

'Arlington trusts you a lot.'

'No, I'm just the best he can afford on his current budget. So, in due course Kitty Burgess becomes Queen of England, Scotland and Ireland. Queen Elizabeth the Second.'

'She was right – her new job is better than acting in one of my plays. It's a big role that Ashley's handed her.'

'But there's still something I don't understand,' I say. 'For Ashley it's straightforward. He gets to control the future Queen of England. After all, he knows she's only Kitty Burgess, a jobbing actress, and he could expose her at any time. And without danger to himself. Even if she was revealed as an imposter, he would simply tell everyone that she took him in with her lies; once he realised she was a fraud and a traitor, he loyally denounced her so that she could suffer the appropriate punishment. He'd be there in the second or third row to watch her execution, but that's as close as he'd get. Ashley has an heir to the throne who, unlike Monmouth, will have to do exactly as he says. But it's very different for Clarendon. Clarendon is potentially removing not only his son-in-law but also his own grandson and granddaughters from the line of succession. It is at the best a pyrrhic victory for him. I doubt that he really wants to be restored to the post of Lord Chancellor. He knows he'll just get his windows broken again by the mob, which hasn't forgiven him. But his hopes of seeing his descendants on the throne will have gone for ever.'

'Perhaps that was never important for him?' says Aminta.

'Perhaps. He always claimed it wasn't. But it's difficult to believe that a man like Clarendon is planning to set aside all worldly ambition. I think we should go to the English convent this afternoon – another address that Arlington had foreseen we might need. As soon as we have eaten, we will try to locate the rue des Fossés-Saint-Victor.'

It is now almost midday and the sun is warm as we leave the cathedral and mingle again with the crowds outside. There we see, once again, our Mister Green. It is strange how often he seems to be in the same part of town that we are ourselves. He is hurrying in the direction of Father Christopher's house. Either he does not see us or he chooses not to greet us. He bangs urgently on the front door and is quickly admitted. He is still unaware he is too late to stop Father Christopher failing to deny that he conducted a wedding service.

'Ashley's agent has correctly divined our next move,' I say, 'but this time we have got there before him, by a good hour and a half. Mister Green will however now realise that we have dangerous knowledge. I think it may be best not to linger here in search of a good Parisian dinner – we'll go in search of some English nuns.'

I give our real names to the nun who opens the wicket gate and we are respectfully shown up to meet the Abbess of the English Augustinian foundation of Our Lady of Sion.

Abbess Mary Tredway does not seem to be somebody to trifle with. For over thirty years she has laboured to establish this convent and to ensure that it is funded adequately. From beneath the black veil and white *serre-tête*, two steely blue eyes meet mine. We both know that her title of abbess outranks my insignificant knighthood by some way. Of course, that doesn't mean we are planning to be entirely truthful with her, any more than we were with Father Christopher.

'Sister Alice said that you were seeking a friend and that you believed I might be able to help you?' She raises an eyebrow. I think she is expecting our visit. Us or somebody very much like us. We may have got to Father Christopher first, but Green got to the Abbess.

'Elizabeth Needham,' says Aminta. 'She is the daughter of Lady Byron, who was an exile here in Paris during Cromwell's usurpation in England. My father and I were forced to flee to Brussels at much the same time. We knew Lady Byron, a fellow royalist, and thought that we might call on her daughter. Is she still with you, my Lady? Or at least living in Paris?'

Aminta smiles sweetly, as if lying to abbesses was second nature.

Mary Tredway smiles back with equal sincerity. 'A charming young woman,' she says. She opens a leatherbound book that just happens to be lying on the table by her capacious black sleeve. 'Yes, you will see here the record of her arrival at our convent in 1653. Her mother was, for various reasons, unable to take care of the child, her husband having died some time before the girl's birth. You will notice that we took her at the request of Father Christopher, the English chaplain. How could we refuse? Father Christopher has been instrumental in securing a number of substantial donations for us, from English families who support our work. We are grateful to him in so many ways. And to the families. And she was such a small child. It was no trouble.'

'And she is still here?' asks Aminta.

'I am afraid not,' says the Abbess. She opens a second book that just happens to be lying next to the first. 'We are careful to record both when we take on a new responsibility and when we relinquish it. You will see here that one Elizabeth Needham departed from this convent two weeks ago.'

'Alone?' asks Aminta.

Though the event is a recent one, the Abbess consults her ledger carefully and very visibly to refresh her memory. She wants us to know she would not wish to misinform us by failing to check her facts. 'Our records show that she was accompanied by one of the servants of Lord Ashley – the Chancellor of the Exchequer of England. I assume that you know him?' She turns the book slightly so that we do not have to read it upside-down. That's kind of her. The name of Lord Ashley is as clear as you could possibly wish for.

'So she is now in England?' says Aminta.

'I could not say. But she is no longer here.'

'And in good health?'

'We would not have allowed her to depart otherwise. One of our duties is, after all, the care of the sick.'

'She has much to thank you for,' says Aminta. 'I mean, for bringing her up and overseeing her education.'

The Abbess smiles but says nothing.

'Elizabeth was a good pupil?' asks Aminta.

'Yes. Most apt at languages and music. Music is important to us here at the convent. As Saint Augustine himself said: *Qui cantat, bis orat.*'

'So he did. I am sorry that we have missed her by so little time, but I am much relieved to find that she is well. It was rumoured some time ago that she had died. We were not sure what to believe.'

The Abbess's face still gives nothing away, but with an almost imperceptible motion of her delicate white hands she invites us to reinspect the brief entry recording Elizabeth Needham's departure. She couldn't have done that if she'd been dead.

'I am pleased to be the bearer of good tidings,' she says. 'Did you also know Lady Byron, Sir John?'

'I never met her,' I say. 'I remained in England throughout the time of the Republic, except for occasional visits overseas at the request of the government.'

'The Republican government?'

'Yes.'

'You were not a royalist, then?'

'No.'

'Nor a Catholic?'

'No.'

'You are a member of the Church of England?'

'To the extent that the law requires me to be.'

'Well, you at least speak plainly.'

'When I am permitted to do so,' I say.

She smiles sympathetically. We are not always free to speak as we wish.

'Thank you, my Lady,' says Aminta. 'We should take up no more of your time. In any case, we were thinking of travelling out to Versailles, weren't we, John? There is so much to see in Paris.'

When the wicket gate has closed behind us, I say to Aminta, 'Do you really think we have time to get to Versailles today?'

'Of course not. But I am fairly sure that she will be reporting back within the hour to Clarendon or Father Christopher or Ashley's agent, and I'd rather they went on a wild goose chase to Versailles than otherwise.'

'She is in their pay?'

'Not in the base and servile way that you were in Lord Arlington's pay. But I think that it is a permanent battle finding the money to pay for an institution such as the one she has founded. She relies on donations from rich English families and I have no doubt that Father Christopher is active in persuading people to release funds. She might feel an obligation to help where she can. I don't think she lied to us even once, but there may be many entries in her records between the arrival of a small girl named Elizabeth and the departure of a grown woman also named Elizabeth. She was careful not to say that the woman who left here was necessarily the same woman who is currently Lord Ashley's guest. She showed no surprise that we were seemingly unaware that a woman calling herself Elizabeth Needham was now in London. I think she has been well briefed.'

'But,' I say, 'if she is knowingly abetting Ashley's schemes then she will be mindful that she is conspiring to keep the

Catholic Duke of York from succeeding King Charles. As an abbess, why should she do that?'

Aminta nods. 'I think Saint Augustine, in addition to claiming that singing was praying twice, also said that everything was ultimately God's will. She may feel that it's down to God rather than to herself to ensure that the Duke succeeds. God has considerably greater resources at his disposal, even without Father Christopher's active support. Or she may just think that the Duke of York will make such an inept king that it is in the interests of the Pope to keep him from succeeding. Of course, it must still weigh on her conscience that she is knowingly putting an imposter on the throne of England.'

'She was helpful anyway and we have discovered a little more about the real Elizabeth Needham. For example that she was a good singer,' I say. 'We shall see in due course if the lady in London is.'

'You're hoping we can stop her by catching her out on some minor detail?'

'Yes,' I say.

'Kitty is an excellent singer,' says Aminta. 'In substituting her for the real but sadly dead heir to the throne, Lord Ashley was nothing if not careful about the minor details. And the big details. Kitty could have been the greatest actress of her age. She's more than capable of carrying this off. Moreover, she has no living family – except my cousin in Hampshire – and has made few if any friends in either of the companies she's worked in. There's little chance of a brother or sister suddenly realising what she's done. Ashley was quite right to look smug. He couldn't have chosen better.'

*

We arrive back at our lodgings in the late afternoon. Hopefully anyone looking for us will still be out at Versailles.

'A man came for you,' says the butcher.

'Did he give his name?' I ask.

'No. He just asked if a Mister and Mistress White were staying here.'

'And you said?'

'I said no. Then he asked if Sir John and Lady Grey had taken a room.'

'Had they?' I ask.

'I said I'd never heard of them. But he said he'd leave the letter anyway, just in case I was lying.' He hands me a folded and sealed sheet of paper. 'If you were hoping nobody knows you are here, maybe it is time for you to return to England.'

I look at the letter. The seal bears a coat of arms carefully applied to the wax. I don't recognise it, other than to note that it is not Lord Ashley's. I break the brittle red circle and unfold the document.

'I should be grateful if you would visit me again before you leave Paris,' I read. 'I have changed my mind. Clarendon.'

'Could it be a trap?' asks Aminta.

'The police often forge such things,' says the butcher, knowledgeably. 'Whether you should be worried depends on whether you think anyone here might have betrayed you to the authorities. There will be coaches leaving tomorrow for Calais and Dieppe. Or you might travel to the port of Caen. They cannot watch all of the roads and won't expect you to go westwards into Normandy when the fastest route is the northern one.'

'I'll visit Clarendon first,' I say. 'I need to know what he's changed his mind on. If I am not back by tomorrow morning, Aminta, leave on one of those coaches. I'd suggest Caen.'

'I'll come with you to Clarendon's lodgings,' she says. 'If you're arrested, as you probably will be, you will need somebody who speaks French much better than you do.'

'I need you safely back here, to tell Lord Arlington that I am a prisoner in Paris.'

'You have greater faith than I do that he would spend money trying to free you.'

'I have faith that you'd find a way to persuade him. With luck, however, I'll be back before dark.'

The long, early evening shadow of the city wall has already placed its cold hand on the rue de Montagne-Sainte-Geneviève. The shops are closing, with a hard clatter of wooden shutters. The streets all around are almost empty. A smell of supper hangs in the air. Again I pause at the corner, though with only myself to speak to I cannot again act out this morning's pantomime. I approach the shop slowly, calculating carefully which way I shall try to escape if I am suddenly attacked from this doorway or that. But I reach my destination without disturbing anyone in any way.

'Lord Clarendon asked to see me again.'

The tailor simply nods in the direction of the stairs. He has been warned that I have business with his lodger.

Clarendon, too, scarcely looks up as I enter his chamber. I am not judged a threat. The air is still hot up here after a long summer day that may have ended in the street but lingers on in attics and garrets. Clarendon has discarded his coat and sits in his long waistcoat and shirtsleeves at his desk.

'So you received my message, Sir John? Very well. This will not take much time. I should like you to carry a letter for me to Lord Ashley. I am placing a great deal of trust in you

– both to deliver it and not to read it en route. Lord Ashley will of course suspect you if the seal is broken. And I do know that Samuel Morland believed that he could open and reseal letters without a trace, but I would still suggest that he does not try it with mine.'

'Of course not,' I say. 'But could you not have entrusted it to Lord Ashley's agent? He has been following us around Paris.'

'Lord Ashley has no agent here,' says Clarendon blandly. 'I wish you a pleasant journey back to London, Sir John. Unless you plan to visit Versailles?'

'No, I did that today. Didn't Ashley's man see me there?'

We look each other in the eye. Neither of us blinks.

'I shall take my leave of you, then, my Lord,' I say.

Well, Arlington should be happy to receive the paper that I now have in my hand. And even if Morland's technique with wax is not perfect, I'd back him to fool Ashley. I pause on the stairs, fold the letter carefully lengthways several times and, being careful not to break the small red seal, I insert it into a slit in the already padded bottom seam of my coat. It sits there comfortably. I descend to the ground floor and step out into the cool evening air with relief. My job is finally done. I have discovered all I can for Arlington. I have got him his letter, and in a couple of days' time I shall be safely back in our house in London, and will be looking forward to returning to Essex.

Then I feel a hand on my shoulder. I turn quickly. A gentleman in a black periwig, wide-brimmed hat and a shabby black velvet suit is smiling at me. Behind him are four armed soldiers in blue and red uniforms. I think they are all probably French.

'*Vos papiers, monsieur?*' he asks politely.

I hand him the passport provided by Williamson. I smile and try not to swallow too hard or do anything else that might suggest I am ill at ease. The gentleman in black takes the document and inspects it very slowly. It seems to amuse him in a way that Williamson may not have intended.

'Mister White? You are English?' he says.

'As you can see.'

'A clerk at the Office of Works?'

'Yes.'

'It is your first time in France?'

'Yes.'

I hope he will now return my passport to me and wish me a good evening, in English or French as he pleases, but he does not.

'I trust you are enjoying your stay in our capital city,' he continues, 'and your visit to this tailor's shop in particular. I have always regarded it as one of the most interesting sights in Paris. So many people foolishly choose to visit the cathedral or Versailles instead. How wise you are to include it in your tour.'

'I needed to order a new coat. French tailoring is so much better than English tailoring.'

'But the tailor works on the ground floor. From the sound of your feet on the stairs, you would seem to have descended from one of the upper storeys. We counted your footsteps most carefully. There were sixty-seven of them. So, Mister White, how was the Count Clarendon? Is he also enjoying his visit to Paris?'

I narrowly avoid saying, 'I don't know what you mean.' It rarely sounds convincing. And it is unlikely that they're not aware Clarendon has been in town for some time and that

White is a false name. Once you know you've been successfully betrayed, it's wise to assume your betrayers have done a better job than you have yourself.

'You'll have to go and ask him,' I say. 'I could offer to wait here while you do.'

'We'll ask him tomorrow,' says the man in black, who seems to trust me even less than Clarendon did. 'In the meantime, you must come with us. As you are almost certainly aware, the English King has asked that anyone attempting to carry messages from the Count Clarendon should be arrested and punished according to our own French law. But be of good cheer, Mister White. If you have no letters about you, you have nothing whatsoever to fear.'

Chapter Twenty

In which, under threat of torture, I discuss Lord Arlington's views on a French alliance

It is dark and my captors have not seen fit to provide me with a candle, even one made of tallow. Occasionally the white walls are lit by the blood-red glow of a torch, flickering briefly through the barred window, as some citizen, free to go wherever he pleases, makes his cautious way along the street outside. The room I am being kept in is small and bare. From what I can hear and smell, my captors are jovial and have had a good supper. They may be about to torture me but do not intend to do so on an empty stomach. My passport has not been returned. My other possessions have all been taken somewhere, including my watch, though they have not yet detected Clarendon's letter in the hem of my coat. Of course, they will. It's only a matter of time, and they have all the time in the world.

I decide I shall not pace up and down like a caged beast. It would be best to reserve my strength for whatever is to come. I am therefore sitting in a corner, on the stone floor, with my back against the wall and with my eyes closed. The evening is passing slowly, but it will get slower. By the day after tomorrow, with luck, Aminta will be in London. In a week or so, Arlington may put in a polite request via the French Ambassador that I should be released and returned to him. The French Ambassador may be prepared to overlook Arlington's recent slights and insults and send a suggestion to Paris that my freedom should be restored. And, God willing, I shall still be alive when somebody finally comes to let me out.

Then something happens. A key turns in the lock and one of the soldiers orders me to stand. It's a while since I've been somebody's prisoner. I'd forgotten how few decisions are left in your own hands.

I rise and allow myself to be led to another small room, this time with a desk and the man in black sitting behind it. There is only one chair and it is not mine.

He rubs his nose thoughtfully and pushes my lying passport across the table.

'You would seem,' he says, 'to be in possession of somebody else's papers. I find I have reason to doubt you are John White. If you consider the matter carefully, you will probably find you have reason to doubt it too. So what is your real name? It will save you a certain amount of unpleasantness if you simply tell us now.'

'Why don't you ask whoever told you I'd be in the rue de Montagne-Sainte-Geneviève?'

'I never entirely trust informers. And the gentleman concerned is elsewhere. If it helps you at all, we think you're John Grey. Is the name familiar to you?'

'It sounds as if your man was worth whatever you paid him,' I say. 'I suppose you wouldn't like to let me know who it was that informed on me? So that I can congratulate him?'

'I am afraid not,' He smiles apologetically. 'So, then, you are Mister John Grey?'

'Sir John Grey,' I say.

'*Sir* John Grey. An English knight. We are honoured. And I have never had the good fortune to question a knight. I assume knights are very brave under torture. I shall have to make a special effort if I can hope to impress you.'

'I wouldn't wish to put you to any trouble. As it happens, I'm quite easily impressed.'

'Nothing is too much trouble for my guests. So, what are you doing in Paris, Sir John Grey? Do you work for the Count Clarendon? You clearly know him.'

'I have been sent here by Lord Arlington. I am surprised your source didn't tell you that.'

'You never quite know what to believe. It is helpful that you are able to confirm things. We do of course enjoy the most cordial relationship with Baron Arlington. But he has not mentioned your visit under either name.'

'An oversight no doubt. He is a busy man, as I'm sure you are. Well, now you know the full facts of the matter, I am anxious not to take up any more of your time. It might be best if I just left you to your work and returned to my lodgings.'

'Why did Baron Arlington send you here?'

'He wished to know the state of Lord Clarendon's health.'

'He could have asked us. *Monsieur* Clarendon's doctor is in our pay. For your information, he is in good health, but suffers a little from gout and a great deal from melancholy. The climate of Montpellier would be much better for him in all respects. We intend to impress that on him when we next speak to him.'

'Thank you. Lord Arlington will be much reassured. The sooner you release me the sooner I shall be able to tell him.'

'Why not question the Count Clarendon under your own name?'

'In England we say "Earl" not "Count".'

'How very interesting. I must remember that. And do you have an equally interesting explanation why you are called "White"? Is that another old English custom?'

'It's one of Arlington's customs, certainly.'

He looks at me over steepled hands. 'Does your master favour a French alliance or a Dutch one?'

'Dutch,' I say. 'But he will do whatever the King wishes.'

'Not what his wife wishes?'

'No. He fears the King slightly more.'

'Is it worth bribing him?'

'He'd like the money but would be too cautious to accept it.'

'And his wife?'

'She is less cautious. Offer her some money by all means. You will need to do so in a way that her husband could deny all knowledge of it. That should not be difficult.'

'You are remarkably free with information about your master.'

'It isn't worth being tortured for facts that you could obtain in ten minutes from any footman at Whitehall Palace.'

'Good. Let me ask you once again: why are you really here? Arlington doesn't care if Earl Clarendon is in good health or dead of the plague. He wouldn't send a knight like you just to find out something that simple.'

'I'm a cheap knight. You'd be surprised how cheap. Arlington also wanted to know why Clarendon is in Paris.'

'And did the Earl tell you?'

'No. I think somebody had warned him I was coming. Possibly the same person who told you where to find me.'

'Did the Earl Clarendon give you any letters to take to England?'

'Did you find any amongst my papers?'

'Not yet. There's no point in searching, when you'll tell us soon anyway. You'll be pleasantly surprised tomorrow just how much you'll tell us. You came here alone?'

'Yes.'

He nods. He doesn't seem to know that Aminta is also in Paris. That at least is in my favour.

'Do you believe in God, Sir John?' he asks.

'Yes,' I say.

'So do I,' he says. 'Against all logic, of course. I look at the world and it is a confused mess – storms destroy crops, houses burn to the ground, soldiers bayonet women and children, men die of disease and hunger in the winter mud. Where, I ask, is God's plan for us all? And yet, when I look at a flower, I see only God's perfection. Without such small instances of God's wisdom, I would find it hard to believe in anything at all. Do you understand me, Sir John?'

'Yes,' I say.

'It is the same with your master, Arlington. When I look at his broader policy I find it almost impossible to fathom his design – sometimes he favours Spain, where he was ambassador for so long, sometimes he favours his wife's homeland, sometimes he favours us, the country of his master's mother. All is flux and confusion. Yet, I would still hope to see perfection in the small things of Arlington – his sending an agent of your rank and undoubted experience to Paris, for example. You are not some soldier of fortune that he has dragged from the gallows and pardoned so he can do his dirty work. I would expect him to send you only if he needed information that he could obtain in no other way. And yet you are here, Sir John, to do what? Nothing, according to you, except talk to a man who is already forgotten in England. And so my faith in Lord Arlington fails. There is a lack of harmony to your story that troubles me.'

I say nothing. He's right, though. I wouldn't believe it myself.

'That is why I really cannot let you go. Tomorrow we shall have you transferred to the Bastille – another of the great sights of Paris, incidentally – where we may question you more privately and with the aid of whatever devices and machinery we have there to help your memory. Perhaps you will then find you have more to tell us. Or perhaps, as a knight, you will be brave. I am curious to find out which.'

'I've told you all I know,' I say. 'But if I am to remain your guest, could I ask that I should be furnished with some sort of supper? And perhaps a glass or two of wine? And my gold watch? If you haven't sold it yet?'

'I shall enquire whether you did in fact have a gold watch when you came here. But, sadly, I think we have no food in the house. Perhaps they will provide you with dinner tomorrow at the Bastille. Or perhaps you will not feel as hungry then as you do now. I shall ask my men to escort you back to your room, Sir John.'

'Would it be too much to ask for a bed? Or at least a mattress?'

'You'll soon get used to sleeping on a bare floor, Sir John. After a few years. Unless you'd prefer to tell us a little more about your visit to Paris, in which case you may not need to. We'll give you the night to think it over, shall we?'

I dream that I am in a cage of Arlington's making, stretched out on a perch made of particularly hard wood. The cage door is open, but, without wings, I cannot fly away. The birds outside skim past the bars in ever-increasing numbers, mocking me. They make so much noise that I wake up.

It is daylight outside and the dawn chorus floats in through my window. My mouth is very dry, but then I recall that this is the least of my problems. One thing at least is clear in my mind. I really do know nothing that is worth dying for. Arlington would probably prefer the matter of the Byron girl to remain secret from the French, but if he wanted his agent to remain silent under torture then he should have sent somebody else. I'll hand over the letter as soon as we're at the Bastille and they can do what they wish with it. Then I'll probably admit Ashley wants to make Elizabeth Needham the King's heir, setting aside the Duke of York. I'd be surprised if the French Ambassador doesn't report the same thing very soon, along with the interesting implications for Tangier and Bombay. Out in the corridor there is the noise of feet and a key turns in the lock. They have come for me sooner than I expected.

Chapter Twenty-one

In which I almost go to Caen

Two soldiers escort me through to the room with a desk. My friend in the shabby black velvet suit smiles at me as I enter. He's up early. And, standing in front of him, is Mister Green. I think they have both been there some time and I don't think Green is a prisoner in any way, in spite of his having visited Clarendon. The last wisp of smoke from a difficult conversation still hangs in the morning air. The gentleman in black seems well pleased with the way things have gone. Green, conversely, appears nervous, on edge; but at least there is no doubt he is friendly with my jailers.

'Well, Mister Green, we meet again,' I say.

Green nods. Whatever has been agreed in the room, he thinks it could all still go wrong for him or me or both. 'I have been speaking to Inspector Leclerc,' he says to me. He is choosing his words carefully. 'There has been a misunderstanding. He was unaware that your visit was known about and approved of at the highest levels.'

'I must have failed to mention that,' I say. 'I apologise pro-fusely. The fault, Inspector, is entirely my own. How fortunate it is that I did not put you to the trouble and expense of inter-rogating me further.'

'Please think nothing of it, Sir John,' says Leclerc. 'These mistakes happen. I was of course sorry that we were unable to provide you with more comfortable accommodation while you were our guest.'

'Am I to understand that I am free to go?'

'Of course,' says Leclerc. 'Until next time. *Au revoir, monsieur.*'

'Thank you. And you are therefore about to return my watch, passport, purse and other possessions?'

'*Mais bien sûr.*'

Leclerc removes some objects from his desk drawer and passes them across the table. It seems I did have a gold watch, after all. I place the papers in my pockets, one by one. I count my money, which is mostly still there. I wind up my watch. I bow to Leclerc. He bows to me. I am not, it would seem, going to visit the Bastille today.

Green and I walk some way along the street before either of us speaks. The first few shops are beginning to open for the day. There is a smell of baking bread.

'I must thank you,' I say, 'for arranging my release – unless you were also responsible for my incarceration.'

'Your arrest was nothing to do with me,' he says. 'Somebody decided to make a little money on the side by informing the authorities of your presence. Fortunately the tailor witnessed your arrest and informed me.'

'So it was not the tailor who told Inspector Leclerc where to go?'

'I couldn't say. It is not uncommon for an informer to work for both sides. It may be that you are right that he betrayed you. But it wasn't on my orders.'

'Then I must thank you for your kindness and your persuasiveness.'

'It was a simple commercial transaction,' says Green. 'The Paris police are ill paid and are as keen as their own informants to supplement their incomes from all available sources.'

'I should naturally be happy to reimburse you,' I say.

'It will not be necessary. A trifle to help a friend. One day I may need you to do the same for me.'

'In that case, I shall simply express my gratitude once again and go on my way. Should we ever meet in London, shall I call you Mister Green or something else?'

'Green is good enough for the moment. Let me give you some advice, Sir John. It is more than possible that they will try to arrest you again if somebody pays them enough. You and your wife must leave Paris today. They will be expecting you to travel via Calais or Dieppe. You should head west to Caen on the Normandy coast. It will take longer – maybe an additional day or two – but they will check many other ports before that one.'

'Somebody else recommended the same route. I'm sure that is good advice.'

'I hope that the police did not retain anything of value?'

'Nothing that I know of. Certainly nothing that should cause Lord Clarendon any loss of sleep. And I was obliged to tell them very little. Only that Lord Arlington's wife probably favours a Dutch alliance and the Queen Mother a French one.'

'Arlington's views may be less important in future than they were in the past,' he says.

*

'I was about to book my seat on the Caen coach,' says Aminta, looking up briefly from her packing.

'Well, you can now book two. If you give the butcher's boy the money, he can do it more discreetly than we can.'

I explain briefly what has detained me.

'Caen it is, then,' says Aminta, shutting the trunk. 'If that's what both your butcher and Ashley's agent advise.'

'You sound doubtful. I don't think it was Green who betrayed me. Or, if he did, then I can't see why he should have arranged for me to be freed so quickly. He thought it might be Clarendon's tailor. But the person I really don't trust is Clarendon. After all, it was his invitation that led to my arrest.'

'Well, it was probably him or somebody else. Sadly we really don't have time for a long discussion. We would seem to have hours at the most before they come to arrest you again. Forget what I said. Caen's probably as good a route as any.'

'No, you're right. We need to check it's not a trap.'

'I may have wondered briefly whether it could be a trap, but I also said that we should leave as soon as we can. Anyway, who could tell you?'

'Clarendon.'

'Returning to the rue de Montagne-Sainte-Geneviève to ask him that question may be even more unwise than returning direct to Calais.'

'It's the last thing they'll expect me to do,' I say.

'Hopefully I can get a refund on your coach ticket when they lock you up a second time,' says Aminta.

For the third time I pause at the corner of the street. There is no sign of the Paris guard. No sign of Monsieur Leclerc. No sign of Mister Green. I enter the shop as if I were a respectable

Parisian customer intent on buying half a dozen shirts or a new pair of breeches, cut in the French fashion.

The tailor looks up from his work. 'Milord Clarendon has left,' he says. 'You can go up to his room if you don't believe me. No charge.'

'And Inspector Leclerc?' I ask. 'Is he here?'

'What about him?'

'Somebody informed him that I was to visit the Earl yesterday evening.'

'Well, I didn't. Nor did the Earl. He wanted you to carry the letter for him. It worried him when I told him you had been arrested.'

'Somebody certainly told the police. If not Lord Clarendon, then who?'

He looks at me for a long time.

'The priest was here,' he says. 'Yesterday afternoon. Milord spoke to him for a long time.'

'Father Christopher?'

'The English priest. I don't know his name. The old one. The worried one. He was here. Then he went away. He wasn't happy. But he never is.'

'He came here a lot?'

'No. He doesn't like danger, that one. But I have seen him climb those stairs more than once.'

Obviously I should have thought of Father Christopher. And I think I can persuade him that it may be safer for him to confess everything to me now than to risk upsetting Lord Arlington. It's probably safer for me too.

'That's helpful to know,' I say. I offer him a silver coin.

He looks as if he is about to refuse it, then he shrugs, silently pockets the money and returns to his sewing.

I am outside the Notre Dame again. I wonder briefly how cross Aminta will be that I have not yet returned. If I am quick, then I may be able to get back to the butcher's shop before she decides to sell my ticket for ready money. I do not need to knock at the front door of Father Christopher's house, however. It is already slightly ajar. That is odd in a crowded city, full of thieves. I proceed carefully up the stairs. I can hear the noise of somebody in his rooms, but I have no way of knowing who it might be. There is the sound of a chest being slammed shut and then heavy footsteps crossing the floor quickly. Just one person, I think, but not Father Christopher. I enter the room as silently as I can. Mister Green is searching through a pile of documents on a desk.

'Good morning,' I say. 'Have you lost something?'

He looks up. His face is red and his periwig is slightly awry but he is not particularly upset to be caught in the middle of whatever he is doing. He thinks he has a right to be there and that I don't. He would rather be left alone.

'I thought you were going to catch the first coach to Normandy?' he says.

'It may have been Father Christopher who betrayed me to the Parisian police. I thought I'd discuss the matter with him.'

'Who says it was?'

'Lord Clarendon's tailor. You might be in a better position to judge than I am, but he seemed to know what he was talking about.'

'He usually does. Well, Father Christopher has gone, as you can see, so you'll need to have that discussion with him some other time. And my advice to you is still to leave for the coast today. I paid Leclerc enough to stay away from you for twenty-four hours at the most. He's got a short memory once his purse is empty.'

'I'm grateful for your advice, Mister Green. In return, can I possibly assist you in finding whatever you're searching for?'

'He's taken it with him,' says Green. 'He must have done. It's not here anyway. But he can't get far. And he won't destroy it. He'll have promised not to, and that's one promise he'll keep.'

'Then I shall be on my way,' I say. 'I hope we shall meet again, Mister Green. Perhaps at Lord Ashley's house?'

He laughs. 'I look forward to it,' he says. 'So long as you get to London alive.'

'You have decided to accompany me after all?' says Aminta. 'I have already sent the boy ahead with our box. Another five minutes and I would have followed him, so as to have enough time to sell your ticket and spare shirts at the inn.'

'It seems likely it was Father Christopher who informed on me,' I say, 'but he has fled – not I think because he imagined I would come looking for him. Bearing in mind what he knows, I think a number of people may want to talk to Father Christopher. Anyway, he's gone and taken some papers with him that Mister Green very much wanted to find – proof of the marriage, I would guess.'

'Tell me in the coach,' says Aminta. 'I think we too need to leave Paris as soon as we can.'

'That's what Green said.'

'He seems a well-informed man. Whoever he really is.'

We have stopped to dine at a place called Mantes – a pretty little town on the green banks of the Seine, specialising, according to one of our fellow passengers, in the manufacture of violins. It is well past noon, but the driver hopes to be in Évreux tonight and Caen by late tomorrow, barring accidents.

'We could have been in Dieppe in time to sail this evening,' says Aminta.

I nod. 'What worries me about our speed of travel is not that we won't be back in England for a couple of days, but that it will be easy to overtake us. Even if they are checking the other routes first, the police will only have to ask a few questions at the inn we left from and they'll have a description of everyone who boarded the Caen coach. And we still have a lot of road to cover before we reach safety. I noticed there's another coach in the yard about to set off for Rouen. If there are seats available, I'll get our luggage transferred to that. Though I hate to waste more time and the better part of the fare we've already paid, it is nevertheless always a good idea to keep your enemies guessing. And I would like to live long enough to meet Mister Green in London and discover his real name, as he has discovered ours.'

We spend the night in Rouen before finding another coach to take us on to Honfleur, a small, out-of-the-way port, where we discover a smack is about to sail to Portsmouth. Nobody there accuses us of being anything other than Mister and Mistress White. Nobody is interested why we should have travelled back by the twisting route we have taken. Nobody tries to stop us buying places on the boat. The weather is again fair and the crossing not unpleasant.

'Well,' I say, as we finally disembark on to English soil, 'we have at least avoided being arrested again but my caution has landed us many miles further from London than we would have been if we'd crossed to Dover.'

'But all is not entirely in vain,' says Aminta. 'We are in Hampshire, are we not? I propose that we pay a long overdue visit to my cousin Reginald. In view of all we have done for Kitty, I think he owes us a little hospitality. His village is only a short distance off the main road. And we still have four or five hours of daylight.'

Chapter Twenty-two

In which I meet a cousin of my wife's

This is the vicarage that Kitty was so eager to leave. In the last slanting sunshine of an August afternoon, it is a neat and symmetrical stone house, set in a small paradise of a garden. Ferny, wooded hills rise above and cradle it tenderly. After our drive along the hot, dusty roads of Normandy, there is a pleasant softness in the very English air this evening.

'I can see why she was so keen to leave,' says Aminta. 'Just think about it. She could have been happy and secure here for ever. Visiting the sick of the parish, with a scented handkerchief pressed firmly to her nose. Reading drafts of my cousin's weekly sermons. Listening to the final version of my cousin's sermons. Working on her latest embroidery while she waited for Reginald's curate or the squire's least-repulsive son to propose to her. Which of course one of them would, in the fullness of time. Then the long succession of constantly shitting babies and bad-tempered servants to be cautiously disciplined and house-trained. That was her future. Who wouldn't risk their life and reputation pretending to be the King's bastard daughter?'

'Pretending to be his legitimate daughter,' I say. 'It's a much bigger prize, but comes with a bigger penalty if she's found out. The question is: will she get away with it?'

'If Ashley's written Kitty a good enough script, and she's bothered to learn it, I think she may succeed. Unless we can find a way to stop her. Who would have thought that the daughter of such a pretty little house could topple the rightful King of England?'

The front door opens and a clergyman appears. He looks at us suspiciously, then he smiles.

'Aminta?' says the Reverend Reginald Norris. 'I'm sorry – I didn't recognise you at first. It must be almost two years since we last saw each other? And you've done your hair differently?'

Aminta looks at me and nods. It's not that difficult to become somebody else. Even she can do it.

'And this is your husband?' Norris adds. 'Sir John, I am delighted finally to meet you. Have you come about Kitty? I hope the silly girl is all right . . .'

Aminta holds up the hand of reassurance. 'As far as we know, my dear cousin,' she says. 'But we were travelling up from Portsmouth and thought we would stop here on our way.'

'Ah,' he says, clearly trying to work out how a modest clerical supper for one will stretch to three. 'Well, that will be very pleasant indeed. A surprise but . . . pleasant. Very pleasant. Come in. Come in. You must tell me about your journey from Portsmouth. We get so few tidings here about anything, that I am eager to devour whatever scraps of news you have picked up on the road.'

*

We tell Aminta's cousin a great deal about Notre Dame, in which he arguably has a professional interest, the enviable number of bridges that Paris possesses, the French King's plans for Versailles and the proposed destruction of the city walls. We tell him about the food and he expresses amazement that the French don't roast and boil everything before slapping it down on the plate as they do in Hampshire.

'Perhaps I should be surprised,' he says, 'that Kitty has chosen to impersonate the King's daughter. But it's no more surprising than that she should choose to act upon the stage, I suppose. And she always did have . . . how can I put this?. . . strange ideas of her own importance. I fear my wife may have encouraged them, in a way that I have not. But surely nobody is going to believe her? I realise that she has Lord Ashley as a patron – no friend of the Church, of course, but a powerful man. Even so, she must realise that somebody will reveal who she really is.'

'What do you know about Kitty's past?' I enquire.

'You may well ask, Sir John!' he says. 'She was my wife's kin, not my own. And then I think not close. I was never sure exactly where the Burgesses fitted into her family tree. It is the greatest of pities that my wife is dead and so cannot help you. Had I known all this would actually matter one day . . . But from the little my wife had told me over the years, I do know that the Burgesses were royalists, who I believe were exiled for a time during Cromwell's rule. They died when Kitty was about six, and there was nobody more closely related who could afford to look after her.'

'Did you ever meet the Burgesses?'

'Meet them? I don't even remember hearing of them until the question arose of looking after Kitty. They appeared out of nowhere, so to speak, already dead. My wife and I had no children. It was not unnatural that we should take her in and bring her up as our own daughter. I saw her as a blessing from God that I should not seek to refuse or question. Later, I felt somewhat differently, but not at the time.'

'But your wife was also happy to take her on?' I ask.

'Indeed. She pressed me to do so. Pressed me strongly. During her life, she looked after Kitty with immense care and concern for her education and her welfare. She taught her some French, for example, though it was little use to her here in Hampshire. She was most opposed to Kitty's desire to take to the stage, on moral grounds I think. I was quite surprised by her vehemence. But there you are. Such were her concerns. After she died, I allowed myself to be persuaded that Kitty should be allowed to go to London to become an actress. And, to be fair, she seems to have achieved some success in that trade. As for our stopping her doing what she is doing now, Kitty always was very determined to get her way, even as a little girl. Supper should be ready in a moment. I have had my cook kill a chicken in your honour – a stringy old bird but at least not stewed to rags as they do in France, eh, Sir John? We'll have something to chew on properly.'

It is late the following day when our coach finally rattles through Southwark and we disembark and take a ferry across the wide, dirty Thames with its brackish water and one solitary bridge, choked with traffic of every possible sort. We hire a man to transport our box in his barrow and walk northwards to our lodgings.

Our maid hands us several letters that have arrived during our absence. One is from Arlington, reminding me to report to him immediately on my return, with any incriminating evidence that Clarendon may have been foolish enough to entrust to me. Another is in a hand that I recognise, even without Sir Samuel Morland's assistance. It is addressed to Aminta and I pass it to her unopened.

'Kitty's writing and Elizabeth Needham's signature,' she says. 'She's been to the theatre, it would seem.'

From my Lady Grey's celebrated comedy, *The Summer Birdcage*

Act 2 Scene 2, The Palace gardens – later that day

Enter Bellair and Snarkly

BELLAIR: They say you are a rich man, Snarkly.

SNARKLY: How so?

BELLAIR: Have you forgotten so soon? Only last night you won a large diamond from my Lady Fortinbras.

SNARKLY: Yes, I won the diamond, but I . . . ah . . . lost it again playing with a group of young sparks later that night. I cannot remember who. It was but a trifle.

BELLAIR: I should not so lightly bear the loss of something that I had dug so deep into my pockets to win. Indeed, I should not.

Enter Emilia, dressed as a man.

EMILIA: *(Aside)* When I was a woman I was brave enough. But now I am a man my legs tremble in my new-cut breeches. How shall I deceive these fellows who know me so well? *(To Bellair and Snarkly)* Good day, sirs. I am recently arrived here from France and was told to introduce myself to Prince Bellair and Mister Snarkly as soon as I reached this court. Do you know where I might find 'em?

SNARKLY: Your arrow has hit the bullseye at your first shot. But who are you, young sir? What is your name?

EMILIA: Ah yes, a very good point ... clearly I do have a name ... I am called ... Bonnedame.

SNARKLY: Bonnedame? I have not met with one of your family before.

EMILIA: It is a very old family. We can trace our ancestry back to Adam and Eve. *(Aside)* Eve especially.

BELLAIR: You are very welcome. Who did you say introduced you to us?

EMILIA: A friend in Paris. *(Aside)* I hope he has one!

BELLAIR: That must be Monsieur de Chantilly?

EMILIA: So it is. The very same. You do not know how pleased I am that you remember him.

BELLAIR: And how did you leave him? Well, I hope?

EMILIA: Well? I should say so! He and I were carousing and wenching until past midnight!

BELLAIR: You amaze me! At his age?

EMILIA: *(Aside)* Too young? Too old? Help me, somebody! *(To Bellair)* He is a remarkable man. For his age.

BELLAIR: Remarkable indeed. When I last heard he was at death's door and had sent for his confessor.

EMILIA: I tell you, good sir, he has a lot more to confess now! I saw to that.

SNARKLY: Well, Bonnedame, you have a very pretty face. I wish I could get my barber to shave my cheek as smoothly as yours shaves you. And you have a fine leg. The young wenches must swoon just to look at you.

EMILIA: *(Aside)* I am like to swoon myself. Whatever next?

BELLAIR: If you can near raise the dead with your carousing, Bonnedame, then we'll follow you ourselves, shall we not, Snarkly?

SNARKLY: It is a while since I did something that really shocked my confessor. And he so enjoys being shocked. But young Mister Bonnedame may wish for quieter entertainment.

BELLAIR: Nonsense. I can see that he is a rake-hell in the making. A roisterer in the egg. Where will you take us, Bonnedame?

EMILIA: Where to take you? That is a better question than you can imagine. I am but newly arrived. To be frank with you, gentlemen, I have never been wenching in this city. *(Aside)* Or any other, on my life! I would ask you gentlemen in Wits' Row where to go, but I am sure none of you could possibly tell me, since you all have a very Presbyterian air about you.

BELLAIR: Well, well. Then we shall take you, shall we not, Snarkly?

SNARKLY: But of course! *(Aside)* I can see how this will unfold. Better I go and watch over Bonnedame than I leave him to the tender mercies of the Prince! He will end up with the pox and an empty purse.

BELLAIR: Meet us here after supper, Bonnedame. You will have an evening such as you have never had before.

EMILIA: That I do not doubt! I mean, I shall be there, my brave sparks! *(Aside)* I beg you all to be there too. I am in sore need of advice. And, for some reason, you seem to know all my thoughts.

Chapter Twenty-three

In which my wife claims I should have been more careful

'To Lady Grey,' the letter reads. 'As you know I much admire your work and was able to pay a further visit to the theatre yesterday, though I fear Lord Ashley did not approve. I thought that *The Summer Birdcage* was a very fine play indeed, and I was particularly taken with the character of Emilia, who gets into so much trouble by assuming a false identity. I was very much reassured by the way you manage to extract her from her predicament, since sometimes people do inadvertently find themselves in such a position and look to their true friends to save them. Lord Ashley tells me that we are to set out for Wimborne St Giles tomorrow morning. I think he may still be, quite rightly, angry that I visited the theatre without his authority. I do so hope to see you on our return. Your true and most humble friend, Elizabeth.'

'I think,' says Aminta, 'that Kitty has finally realised that this is more than a joke on Ashley's part and that there is real danger for her. Even now I suspect she hesitates, wondering if it would not be a glorious thing to be queen. But she is afraid all the same. And rightly.'

'The letter is a very clear message that she is hoping you will step in and save her if everything goes wrong. A little too clear. If Ashley had seen it, I think he would have understood its supposedly hidden meaning as well as you have.'

'It's just another example of Kitty believing she is much cleverer than she is. Oh dear. It is so much easier to save a fictional character than it is to save a real actress hesitating on the edge of high treason,' says Aminta. 'But I think Ashley is getting nervous too. He didn't want her to visit the theatre again, where people would have now noted her presence and there was a completely unnecessary risk of her being recognised by somebody as Kitty. He realises, as she doesn't, that she is still not quite the finished article. But she, as ever, has decided to improvise her part and go anyway. Never a good idea. He has wisely whisked her off to Dorset before she can do any more harm.'

'So, what do we do now? I am, after all, about to tell Arlington and Williamson that the real Elizabeth Needham was almost certainly the true heir to the throne, and to show him Clarendon's letter, which may reveal a great deal more. Depending on what it says, Clarendon's letter could seal Kitty's fate.'

'It would be easier, of course, to judge what was right for Kitty if we had read the letter in question,' says Aminta.

'My thoughts exactly,' I say. 'I'll get a candle and a knife and some sealing wax. It's not only Morland who knows how to open and reseal a letter.'

I heat the knife in the candle flame and run the thin blade carefully under the wax seal, taking great care not to crack it.

The seal obligingly releases its grip on the paper. I open the letter, ready to read Clarendon's treasonable words.

'I have had reports both from your messenger and from Arlington's creature,' it reads. 'I am pleased that Mistress Needham has been restored to her rightful place. The Duke of York is clearly aware of all aspects of the plan, but he is powerless. Clarendon.'

'That is less than nothing,' I say. 'Ashley needs to know none of that. Maybe the real message is hidden?'

I hold the paper up to the light. There are no telltale traces of invisible ink.

'Maybe Morland can make sense of this,' I say. 'But I'd say Clarendon has deliberately given us an almost meaningless text, perhaps as a test of whether I can be trusted to bring it home unopened, perhaps because it amused him to think of Arlington's face when he opened it. I'll take it to Arlington, however, and show him. I'll also tell him what Kitty has told us. She's having doubts and would welcome finding an exit, stage right or stage left. And for her sake we should find one as soon as we can. The stakes have become too high to do otherwise.'

It is already quite dark as I set out. Hopefully Arlington will be home at this hour.

I proceed on foot – it is not far and I shall travel faster and less noticeably, along the many twisting lanes. It is not impossible that I shall be followed and I do not wish to be waylaid as I step from my carriage. I first take the road southwest, through grimy, tumbledown St Giles, then onwards to the more open countryside beyond Westminster. I check behind me often to see whether there is a figure lurking in the shadows. An almost full moon has risen by the time I turn off Piccadilly and enter Upper Saint James's Park. The King has newly laid out the Park with paths, though not with flowers. Rumour has it that the Queen forbade flowers after he picked some there for Nell Gwynne. Or for Frances Stewart. Or for Lady Castlemaine. Or for all of them – it's a big park and there's no point in having only one version of a good story. The gravel paths are raked smooth and shine pale gold in the moonlight, but the bushes and trees that flank them are still unkempt and overgrown. It is a strange world of ghostly yellow light and grey shade. I watch carefully but little stirs except the occasional bird, disturbed in its leafy slumbers. Ahead, I can now see the warm glow from the windows of Arlington's house. That was easier than I expected. I breathe a sigh of relief. Just another few bushes to pass and then ...

I open my eyes. My head is throbbing. I put my hand up to see what can be the matter. My hair feels slimy. I look at my palm and it is bright red.

'I wouldn't touch it if I were you,' says Arlington. 'I've sent for a surgeon, of course. Now we know you're alive.'

'Why?' I say. My voice is very loud. 'How?' I say more quietly.

'You were attacked. They hit you over the back of the head. Somebody must have been waiting for you on the edge of the Park. They knew you would come to the house tonight or some other night. I am not sure what I'm paying you for when you are so careless and unobservant.'

'You're not paying me,' I say. Even now my voice is still much too loud. I'll have to remember to whisper. I try to pull myself up. The room moves around alarmingly, but after a while it doesn't.

Arlington shakes his head. 'You'd be better staying completely still until the surgeon comes.'

I look around carefully. I'm in a bed in a fine oak-panelled
room. I don't recognise it but, since Arlington's also in the
room, it's probably his house. The bed hangings are heavy
Chinese silk – he's made some money somewhere – more
perhaps than Pepys. I pull myself up a little more and rest
against the headboard.

'Could you try not to get blood on that? The pillow is
already ruined.'

They're definitely Arlington's pillows, then.

Somebody carefully pushes something soft behind my
back. That's a bit better. I turn slightly. Williamson nods at me
in a friendly way.

'I suppose you didn't see who it was?' he says.

'No. If I had, I wouldn't have stood there waiting to be hit.'

'That's a pity,' says Arlington.

He doesn't mean that it is a pity for me.

'Did you have any letters from Clarendon with you?' asks
Williamson.

'Yes,' I say. 'One, addressed to Ashley.'

'Well, you don't any more,' says Arlington.

'You searched me?' I say.

'We intended no disrespect. We thought you were dead.
It goes without saying that we were very pleased to discover
you were not, but we did want that letter. You didn't open it
and read it by any chance?'

'Yes. It just said that, on the basis of what his various
informants had told him, Clarendon was happy that Mistress
Needham was now in her rightful place, or something of the
sort. The Duke of York was powerless.'

'So Clarendon actually believes she's what she claims?' says Arlington. 'That seems unlikely.'

'He can't possibly. He, above all, knows exactly who she is. And Ashley would know the position as well as he does. There must have been something else on the sheet of paper.'

'Invisible ink?' asks Williamson. 'Or a message hidden in plain sight in the text? Using alternate letters, say?'

'I was hoping Morland might tell us,' I say.

'I'm sure he could have done if you had not lost it,' says Arlington. 'All you had to do was walk across London with it. A child might have done better.'

'It's not Sir John's fault,' says Williamson.

'I can't see whose fault it is, then.'

'Perhaps we were intended to see the message?' I say. 'If so, Clarendon was laughing at us. He referred to me as your creature. I don't understand what the joke is, but my head hurts so much that nothing seems very funny at the moment.'

Arlington's look tells me I have only myself to blame for that.

'What happened in Paris?' asks Williamson. His voice is somewhat quieter than Arlington's.

'We saw Clarendon,' I say. 'He had, at great risk to himself, travelled there in order to ensure that he fulfilled his part in the plot. We spoke to the English chaplain, Father Christopher. He was quite frightened, I think. Then he vanished and took some document with him. We spoke to Mary Tredway, the Abbess. She told us that Lord Ashley had arranged for Elizabeth Needham to be sent to England. She was not in any fear, but was very cautious. A Mister Green, probably working for Ashley, travelled through Kent with us in the coach, tried to delay us at Dover, visited Clarendon and

Father Christopher in Paris, freed me from the clutches of the Paris police and urged us to travel back via Caen while he wisely took the shorter route via Calais or Dieppe. Oh, and the Duke of York thought it was worth sending Pepys after us to persuade me to pass any letters I was given to the Duke rather than to you.'

'Well, in the end you gave it to nobody,' says Arlington. 'So, what are your conclusions?'

'I think Elizabeth Needham was almost certainly the King's legitimate daughter. At some time in the early 1650s, the King married Lady Byron, a few months before Elizabeth was born. Clarendon disapproved – on pragmatic rather than moral grounds – but all he could do by the time he found out was to try to conceal what had happened. His Majesty was obliged to promise Lady Byron regular and surprisingly generous payments to keep quiet. Elizabeth was brought up in a nunnery in Paris, away from public gaze. We thought Clarendon and Ashley wanted Kitty to impersonate the King's bastard daughter. In fact, they plan that Kitty will be acknowledged as the King's heir and in due course be crowned as queen – a Protestant queen. The Duke of York will effectively be disinherited, as will his children.'

'So if the King was legally married to Lady Byron between late 1652 and early 1664 . . .' says Arlington.

'His marriage to the Queen is invalid,' I say.

Arlington and Williamson look at each other. The consequences of that are not lost on them.

'Will Ashley be able to prove it?' asks Arlington.

I explain briefly why the answer to that question is probably yes.

'Ashley has two problems, however,' I add. 'First, Kitty

is as overconfident as ever of her ability and still inclined to improvise rather than stick to the script. Recently she thought it would be amusing to revisit the theatre to watch my wife's play – a chance literally to look down on her former colleagues. Ashley found out and was not pleased. She has been taken to the country, partly as a punishment, partly for further instruction in languages or court etiquette or politics.'

'How do you know about the theatre visit?'

'A letter was waiting for us when we got back from France – it's probably about four or five days old. It also made it clear Kitty is having doubts that she has acted prudently in taking on the role. That's Ashley's second problem. She is looking for a way out.'

'Acted prudently? Of course she hasn't. Impersonating the heir to the throne is a capital offence.'

Williamson coughs. Perhaps, in his view, it isn't. Time will tell who is right.

'I should add we know a bit more about Kitty,' I say. 'We visited Hampshire on our way back to London. According to Kitty's guardian her real parents were a Colonel and Mistress Burgess, royalists from the west country. She was adopted when her parents died and has since lived in a small Hampshire village, until her arrival in London.'

Arlington pulls a face. 'Interesting, but knowing her ancestry doesn't help us a lot. What I still don't understand is what Clarendon hopes to get out of it. Revenge, certainly. It will greatly embarrass the King and, as you say, it may effectively disinherit the Duke. But, as you also say, it cuts off the Duke's surviving children – young Edgar, Mary and Anne – Clarendon's own grandchildren. Why would he do that? And it generously hands power to Ashley with no clear gain for the Earl. Yet most of the effort and the risk so far seem to be Clarendon's.'

'That was what we failed to understand too,' I say. 'But maybe revenge is enough?'

'Not for Clarendon. It won't be sufficient that the King loses more than he does. He'll want to win. There has to be something more. Another twist in the tale.'

The door of the room opens.

'He has a habit of doing this,' says Aminta to Arlington.

'Not deliberately,' I say.

'I have our carriage outside,' says Aminta. 'The messenger implied you might not live, but he was clearly mistaken. I'll need to cancel that order for a black dress and veil. If you've stopped bleeding, John, I'm taking you home. Oh, and the Duchess of Cleveland presents her compliments and asks that you should attend upon her at your earliest convenience.'

'She would scarcely expect him to go tonight,' says Williamson.

'I assume she is in London,' I say. 'Not at her palace.'

'She finds her Nonsuch increasingly inconvenient,' says Williamson. 'She's back in Westminster – in her old rooms in the Palace of Whitehall, much to the King's annoyance.'

'Wherever the Duchess is tonight,' says Aminta, 'John is going no further than our lodgings. And he is going now.'

'I have summoned a surgeon,' says Arlington. 'Perhaps Sir John should remain here for a little longer.'

'While you continue to interrogate him?' says Aminta. 'I think not, my Lord. Do send the surgeon on to us if he'll come. But, lawks-a-mercy! You'd have thought somebody had been slaughtering cattle in this bed of yours, Lord Arlington. My dear husband has certainly made a shambles of your pillow.

I'll have to get our maid to look out some old ones when we get back to our lodgings, if John is not to sleep standing up. Who would have thought the old man to have had so much blood in him? As a certain Scottish lady once said.'

Chapter Twenty-four

In which Lord Ashley does not appear

It is in fact two days later when I am finally allowed to stop bleeding on the bedlinen and venture out with a bandage round my head. The treatment of my wound has necessitated the removal of my hair – at first, some of it, and then, after a judicious appraisal of my appearance, the rest of it. My scars shine red through the black stubble. Perhaps I shall finally need to purchase a periwig. But first I must call on the Duchess of Cleveland.

She too looks at me as a possible source of unwanted bloodstains. Her dress is, after all, cream watered silk. It will not wash. She pulls in her ample skirts, just in case. She doesn't ask why my head is bandaged. Either she's heard already or she doesn't think it's important. I probably won't bother to tell her how much my head still hurts. She has more important concerns.

'So, is Elizabeth Needham really Kitty Burgess?' she demands.

'Yes,' I say. 'There is not the slightest doubt.'

'Good,' she says. 'The King has become far too attached to the so-called Mistress Needham. He is cross that Ashley has taken her off to the country. I shall await with interest how you intend to expose her to the ridicule and scorn of the town.'

'It may not be that easy to prove she is not who she claims to be,' I say.

'Of course it is. A babe in arms could do it.'

'She has been well coached in her new role. Her past life has been utterly wiped clean. The Abbess of the English convent in Paris will swear that she has been with her since she was a small child. Lord Clarendon is about to swear she is the King's legitimate daughter.'

'The King married Lady Byron?'

'Yes.'

'Is there a marriage certificate?'

'We believe there is and that it's with the English chaplain – we just don't know where he is.'

'So the girl is about to claim to be the King's lawful heir?'

'Yes,' I say. 'With Ashley's full backing.'

'They're still saying I murdered Kitty Burgess. Did you know that?'

'But you didn't. Just ignore them. She's clearly alive.'

'No. Legally she's still dead. I want that Burgess woman exposed as a living fraud. Exposed and utterly humiliated. Made to crawl back to Hampshire, or wherever she came from, on her hands and knees. You have to act, John. My reputation depends on it.'

'Possibly, but I am more concerned about the attempt to impose a false heir to the throne on the country.'

'I care about my reputation. I don't particularly care who rules the country after the King dies in the arms of his latest tart. Do you know, he actually told me to go away and take whatever lovers I liked, so long as I did it quietly?'

'Do you not do that anyway?'

'Quietly? *Quietly?*'

'I see your point,' I say.

'I'll not sneak around Whitehall, conducting my business in dark corners, like some silly little maid of honour. Is that how the King behaves?'

'Not usually,' I say.

'I'm a duchess.'

'Undeniably.'

'With my own palace.'

'A large and imposing one. A masterpiece. Unlike any other before or since. Built by one of the King's illustrious forebears and hence much cherished by him.'

'Do you know the price of second-hand bricks by any chance?'

'No, but if it's only a penny a dozen, you're sitting on thousands of pounds. Not to mention the stucco, tiles and timber.'

'Exactly,' she says. 'Tens of thousands. That's what I thought too.'

'A friend of mine at court,' says Aminta, 'tells me that there are already rumours there that Elizabeth Needham is the legitimate daughter of the King. I did no more than express surprise. But word spreads quickly.'

'It depends who spreads it.'

'The Duchess of Cleveland, to name but one.'

'Perhaps I shouldn't have told her,' I say.

'Ashley will have spread plenty of rumours himself,' says

Aminta. 'The Duchess is useful in that respect but not essential. And obviously the King will have worked it all out, though he may choose to keep it quiet.'

'Where is Ashley now?' I ask.

'He's still in Dorset,' says Aminta.

'I wonder what he's planning?'

'I am pleased you are so much recovered,' says Arlington. 'And so very quickly.'

His tone implies that I bled so much the other night just to vex him. I might have done, if I knew how. I doubt, however, that his visit today is just to enquire about the state of my head.

I smile. 'The pain is almost gone. But my wife says that where there's no sense, there's no feeling.'

Arlington nods. He thinks so too. 'That periwig suits you, by the way. You should have got one before.'

'My periwig maker says that it will sit better on my head once I am able to remove the last of the bandages.'

'I imagine so. You have no better recollection now who might have attacked you?'

'None. I assume your agents have discovered nothing?'

'Nothing at all. And I've asked everywhere. I've threatened. I've promised. Mainly the latter, of course – most of my budget for the year is already spent. It must have been Ashley's men, though.'

'Why?' I say.

'Because it must.'

'But why steal a letter that he would have known was intended for him anyway?'

'To stop me reading it.'

'But Clarendon probably wanted us to read it.'

'I'd have liked to have shown it to Morland anyway. He might have got something out of it.'

'Maybe Morland already has it.'

'What do you mean?'

'I've been thinking who really betrayed me to the police in France. The tailor told me it was Father Christopher, and Green thought that was likely, and that's what I believed too, especially when he fled. But Morland also knew I was going there. He could have been behind both my betrayal to the police and, when that didn't work, the attack on me in the Park.'

'You think he's in the pay of who . . . Ashley?'

'Ashley or somebody else. Morland told me that, newly married as he is, he needs all the money he can lay his hands on. He won't get it from you.'

'Where is Ashley now? Do you know?'

'I understand he's still at Wimborne St Giles.'

'I wonder what he's planning?' says Arlington.

'There's a letter for us,' says Aminta. 'From Lord Ashley. He is inviting us to dinner next Monday.'

'In Dorset? That would be a long way to go.'

'No, at his London residence. He's clearly back.'

'With Kitty?'

'I must assume so. He seems determined to keep her on a short rein. I can't see that he'd risk leaving her behind.'

'And who is invited to dinner? Just us?'

'He doesn't say. But I imagine not. Ashley likes to make an impression. He'd need more than you at the dinner, with the greatest respect, John.'

'I am surprised he is holding another entertainment so soon after the ball.'

'So am I. He's not a dancing man.'

'No,' I say. 'Far from it.'

'He's Chancellor of the Exchequer, for God's sake. He wouldn't spend money without a very good reason.'

'I wonder what he's planning?'

Chapter Twenty-five

In which the Chancellor of the Exchequer spends some money

Once more the candles burn bright at Exeter House. You can almost count the cost of them, inch by waxy inch. A confusion of gilded carriages, arms bravely painted on the doors, unload their owners at the entrance. Our rather plain coach and four joins the long queue and at length we too descend, with the ostentatious assistance of our postillion, who rarely gets to display his scarlet livery under such gratifyingly public circumstances.

'It will be a large dinner,' says Aminta. 'And everyone is here. Or, at least, I saw Arlington's coach departing empty as ours arrived. And the Duchess of Cleveland's coach is somewhere behind us, still full of a duchess and whoever she has chosen to appear with tonight.'

'That's Prince Rupert four or five places ahead of us now. I thought he was half dead of the pox.'

'I hope not. He has my very good friend, Peg Hughes, with him. Like Kitty, she seems to have abandoned the stage for something more profitable.'

'He won't marry her.'

'Of course he won't. She's merely an actress, after all. Her status is scarcely above that of a writer. But he is rumoured to be not ungenerous and relatively faithful. And Peg is thought to have held out some time for the best possible terms.'

'Lord Ashley is greeting them both now. It won't be long until we reach the end of this line. Perhaps he will then tell us why we've all been invited.'

'I doubt he'll say anything until he wishes to. I do wonder what he's planning, though.'

We have eaten well at his lordship's expense. I am seated next to Williamson's wife at the more obscure end of the table. Again, I think Williamson is less at ease at these events than he might be and is slightly resentful that Arlington, as Secretary of State, has his place at the top table. Our position does not trouble me, when so many dukes and earls are present, though not, I notice, the King or the Duke of York. Ashley wishes to shine brightly tonight, in the shadow of nobody.

Aminta, on the other side of me, nudges my arm. 'Do you see who is three places down from Ashley?' she says.

'Kitty,' I say. 'At least she is still safe. And very nicely turned out. Only the Duchess of Cleveland will owe her dressmaker more.'

'And, more interestingly, four places to the other side?'

'Well, well,' I say. 'Mister Green has managed to evade Leclerc's police and reach England safely.'

'Others, more observant than you, are already pointing him out to each other. To sit there he should be a viscount at the very least. And they are looking at Kitty. Ashley hasn't dressed her up like that out of charity.'

'Green has spent some money at his tailor's too,' I say. 'Most of the men will be trying to calculate what he paid for that lace cravat.'

The room is in fact abuzz. Now that eating seems to be at an end, the conversation has turned to discussing the other guests and one in particular. After all, she is strongly rumoured at court to be our next ruler. Ashley rises to his feet and has to tap his wine glass with a knife several times before the room is quiet. But then the silence is profound. We all want to know why we're here.

'My lords, ladies and gentlemen,' he begins. He surveys us all and smiles crookedly, though perhaps no more crookedly than usual. 'I believe that there has been some speculation in town as to why I have invited you all here. Well, for the pleasure of your company and nothing else. I am an old man and not in the best of health. It is rare for me to have the joy of seeing so many of my friends together. Some of you, I know, do not think well of me. My views are not your views. I am not French enough. Not Italian enough. Not pliant enough. Too Polish, some say. Too Dutch. Too Protestant, if such a thing were possible. But are we not all patriots? Are we not, deep down, all of the same religion? Do we not wish this country and its monarch well? I, for one, must profess my complete loyalty to our gracious monarch and the house of Stuart. I therefore give you a toast. To His Majesty, the King!'

We all stand and drink, then look at each other. Is that it? Or is there more to come?

'You will all be wondering,' says Ashley, 'is there more to come? Does this old, dried-up Chancellor have anything to say that is not about taxation or foreign treaties? Do softer feelings ever stir in him? Well, my good friends, since you are already gathered here, out of love for me and nothing else, I should like to share with you some very good news. You might have heard it sooner or later but, you being all so dear to me, I wish to share it with you now. You will know that my kinswoman, Mistress Elizabeth Needham, has been on a visit to England from her home in Paris, where she has dwelt continuously since her birth and whither I had expected her to return in due course. But, to my great joy, she will not. It is my pleasure and privilege to tell you that she is about to marry into one of the most distinguished and illustrious families in the country. And the gentleman concerned is present in the room.' Ashley turns to request that the gentleman concerned should also rise. Four places to his right, Mister Green stands, resplendent in his silver coat and breeches, yards of lace at his neck, an embroidered silk sword belt across his front. 'The marriage will take place very shortly – within the next few days. I am delighted to tell you that Mistress Needham has, with my consent, accepted the proposal of Lord Cornbury.'

'Cornbury?' I say. 'That is *Lord Cornbury?*'

'So,' says Aminta. 'Finally we know what Lord Ashley's plan is. We finally know what Clarendon's plan is. That explains everything.'

But Arlington has already pushed aside his chair and joined us. Over my shoulder, he exclaims, loud enough for everyone to hear, if anyone was still listening to anyone else: 'He's marrying the Byron girl to Lord Cornbury? He's marrying her to *Clarendon's eldest son?* He's going to make Clarendon's son, what? King? Clarendon's son will be my master, your master and master of everyone in the room? Clarendon will not be merely the father-in-law of the next king – he is actually founding his own dynasty. The House of Clarendon will succeed the House of Stuart. Well, that was worth the risk of a visit to Paris. God damn him to everlasting hell.'

'Clarendon ensured that King Charles was restored to the throne,' says Aminta. 'Now he's made the king who will succeed him. He hasn't lost his touch, has he?'

'Nor has Ashley,' I say.

We look at Ashley, his face wreathed in smiles. He doesn't think he's lost his touch either.

Chapter Twenty-six

In which we discuss Maud the Empress and other notable precedents

We do not notice Pepys in the throng, until he accosts us as we are about to get into our carriage.

'Ashley intends to depose my master, the Duke of York,' he says.

'You must have suspected that for some time – hence your ride to Dover and offer of a frigate?'

'Possibly. There were things I was not at liberty to tell you.'

'Well, King Charles happily still lives and will live for many years yet,' I say. 'Nobody has actually been deposed.'

'But the intention is clear. Ashley will force the King to repudiate his marriage to the Queen, which he has long wished for anyway, and to acknowledge Mistress Needham as his heir.'

'That certainly appears to be the plan,' I say.

'With Ashley as the chief minister?'

'Who else? If he lives that long.'

'What does Arlington say about Cornbury's future position?' Pepys asks. 'I mean, if Mistress Needham is recognised as heir presumptive?'

'She still has some way to go to achieve such recognition,' I say. 'Her status as legitimate heir seems to be an open secret, but it is not yet formally recognised by His Majesty. Arlington's view is, however, that, subject to the necessary formalities, Cornbury would in due course become our king.'

'I'm sure that's what Cornbury hopes,' says Pepys. 'But it is far from certain, Sir John. It is true that Philip of Spain was King of England for the duration of the reign of his wife, Queen Mary. But he was already King of Naples in his own right. And Guildford Dudley did not live long enough to claim a royal title in respect of his wife, Lady Jane Grey. Moreover, while Maud the Empress, in the brief time she ruled the country, described herself as *domina Anglorum*, her husband Geoffrey was not called *dominus Anglorum*. Still less was he was he *rex Anglorum*. He retained the title of count, which he had inherited from his father.'

'I fear,' I say, 'that most of the country will not care greatly what title Geoffrey of Anjou held. Parliament, as we know, can make and break kings. It requires only a bare majority of the members of both houses to make a man the anointed of God.'

'The King is determined his brother will succeed him. He will dismiss Parliament and not call another for the rest of his reign if he has to.'

'His father tried that,' I say.

'His father lacked the subtlety and cunning of our present king. Nevertheless I must go and warn the Duke of this development. Ashley can and must be stopped. At any cost. Good evening to you, Sir John. Good evening, Lady Grey.'

As Pepys leaves, another familiar face presents itself.

'A masterstroke by Ashley,' says Williamson.

'At least we now know what the plot is,' I say.

'Do we? I think there may be a twist or two in the tale yet to come. In the meantime, if I were Kitty Burgess, I should be very worried that it could all unravel very quickly. Ashley has made it difficult for us to prove who Kitty really is, with Neville's death. But it is far from impossible. He must know that sooner or later we will be able to provide proof she is an imposter. And yet he is very, very confident. Far more confident than he should be. What have we missed, Sir John? What is the obvious thing that we haven't yet seen? Why does he think he is so secure when he isn't?'

'Mister Morland conversely looks very unhappy,' says Aminta.

We turn and see Sir Samuel and his wife departing on foot. He cannot afford a carriage of his own and will have to try to find a coach plying for hire in the surrounding streets.

'He has backed the wrong horse again,' says Williamson. 'As I told you, it looks as if he has established contacts with the Duke of Monmouth. Morland was hoping to rise with Monmouth when Ashley made him king. But it is now clear that will not happen. Morland is out in the cold again.'

'I can see that the Duke of Monmouth has lost more than anyone,' I say. 'If the King proves to have a legitimate Protestant daughter, nobody will look to Monmouth to save the country from the papists.'

'Which means that Monmouth has more cause than anyone to stop Elizabeth Needham in her tracks. And indeed to stop you. I think that you were right about Paris – Morland, working for Monmouth, must have betrayed you. You were lucky Cornbury was able to intervene and offer Leclerc more than Morland was able to. And you are probably right that it was also Morland who had you attacked in the Park outside my Lord's house – on Monmouth's behalf, not Ashley's. They doubtless thought you were carrying proof that Elizabeth Needham was the King's legitimate heir. They will have been very sorry to discover they have a bland couple of lines from Clarendon.'

'I doubt Morland attacked me in person,' I say. 'And Monmouth wouldn't have got his hands dirty.'

'Morland has also been seen with Philip Herbert. Think about it: Monmouth, Morland and Herbert could be a dangerous combination, when you look at their various talents – bravery, cunning and an utter contempt for the rule of law. They'll look to act quickly now – before the King formally recognises a new heir to the throne. Yes, if I were Kitty Burgess, I think I would be quite worried. It is not only the authorities that she has to fear. Well, good night to you, Sir John. Good night, Lady Grey. I hope you both have a safe journey home.'

From my Lady Grey's comedy,
The Summer Birdcage

Act 2 Scene 4, The Palace

Enter the Queen and Snarkly

SNARKLY: Take this, Your Majesty, and guard it well.

QUEEN: You have recovered my diamond for me! I am eternally grateful to you, dear Mister Snarkly. I bless the skilful hand that won this jewel back from that evil woman. *(Takes his hand and kisses it.)*

SNARKLY: *(Withdrawing his hand quickly)* That must be a private matter between us, and one that is concluded with the thanks you have just given me. For your sake and mine, the King must not learn what I have done. I pray you speak no more of it.

QUEEN: Nevertheless, I am for ever in your debt. If I can ever perform a like service for you, then I shall.

SNARKLY: I hope never to need it. But you must excuse me

now, Your Majesty. I have an engagement this evening and must go and dress.

Exit Snarkly L, Enter Livia R.

LIVIA: *(Curtseys)* Your Majesty! I am sorry to have disturbed you. I did not know you were here. I was looking for my friend Emilia.

QUEEN: I have not seen her. Is it some urgent matter?

LIVIA: Yes . . . no . . . yes. I needed her advice. On a difficult subject.

QUEEN: Can I assist you?

LIVIA: No . . . yes . . . no. Perhaps I should mention it to you least of all. It concerns your stepson Prince Bellair. And I do not wish to shock you.

QUEEN: Nothing about Bellair surprises me. Speak to me as one friend to another.

LIVIA: Very well. As one friend to another. I have just heard, from another friend, who heard it from the Prince himself, that Bellair intends to take some innocent young man – Bonnedame, newly arrived from Paris – on one of his debauches this evening. Bonnedame will end up being robbed or worse. Bellair should be stopped and the young man rescued.

QUEEN: Are you certain the young man wishes to be rescued? Whatever the young man stands to lose, he may not wish to keep it.

LIVIA: When he is old enough to grow a beard, he will thank me.

QUEEN: Can you not speak to Bellair yourself?

LIVIA: Oh, he will just tell me that it is none of my business or he will promise to take the young man to listen to some uplifting sermons, and then do just whatever he likes.

QUEEN: Then we must find a way to teach my stepson a lesson. He'll go to the Park, I have no doubt, and not to pick flowers. We'll follow him and keep him on the straight and narrow paths.

LIVIA: But he will quickly recognise us and find a way to escape our attentions.

QUEEN: Therefore let's don some hoods and vizards so we cannot be recognised. We'll meet him and his new friend there. He'll think we're ladies of the night. We can lead them a merry dance. Find your disguise and meet me here again in an hour.

LIVIA: I'll do it. *(Aside)* If Emilia saw me in the Park, it would greatly surprise her. Indeed, I am rather sorry that will not happen.

Chapter Twenty-seven

In which I am given a small job to do

Another day has dawned and those, like our maid, who have a need to be up and about early, have already heard of Lord Cornbury's engagement to the lovely Elizabeth Needham, reputed though not yet acknowledged child of His Majesty the King. Her fellow servants are whispering that Mistress Needham may actually be the King's heir presumptive, even if many are not sure what an heir presumptive is.

It is mid-morning before Arlington arrives in his coach with three demi-lions on the door.

'Mister Williamson and I have devised a plan,' he says.

'I am pleased to hear it, my Lord,' I say.

'It seems to us that it will be Father Christopher's evidence that will be critical in proving that Mistress Needham is legitimate.'

'I imagine so. If he has the wedding certificate.'

'He therefore needs to be stopped.'

'I think he is in hiding. Probably in Paris.'

'We need to persuade him to travel to England.'

'How?'

'You will write to him and assure him that it will be safe to come here. You will say that you will conduct him to Lord Ashley, who will reward him for his efforts.'

'I said he had vanished from his house. Unless you have an address for him, I shall be wasting my time writing.'

'We believe he has taken refuge at the convent. If not, the Abbess will certainly know where to find him if we write to him there.'

'I doubt that I have sufficient eloquence to tempt him to cross the Channel.'

'That's why we have drafted this letter on your behalf.'

I read it. It is short and to the point. I am pleased to find that I am plausible and trustworthy.

'I agree that it is persuasive enough,' I say, 'but Father Christopher has merely been obliged to do various things by the powerful men around him. I would be reluctant to sign something that may lead him to his death. I assume that's what you're planning to do to him?'

'We have not yet decided.'

'I think not, then.'

'You are becoming very nice about killing the King's enemies. How many men have you dispatched on the King's behalf?'

'I have only ever done so in self-defence – to protect myself or one of your other agents. I've never been party to killing a priest. I'm safe enough without killing Father Christopher.'

'But Kitty Burgess is not safe. The longer this farce is allowed to run, the more danger she is in. I can tell you, in the most absolute confidence, that the King is enchanted by her. He is seriously considering announcing that she is his heir, even though he knows that invalidates his marriage to the Queen. I leave you to imagine what he will feel if he does all that and finds he has been duped by an actress. His rage will know no bounds. Every day, Ashley drags Kitty another couple of inches closer to the block.'

'And what happens to Kitty if we manage to extract her from Ashley's grasp? Does she just return to her life as an actress? Or do you have other plans? I won't help you destroy her any more than I'll help you destroy the priest.'

Arlington decides not to lecture me on my loyalties. He knows how little time we all have. 'Look – all we need is that she doesn't allow herself to be declared the King's heir. Let her be a royal bastard if she wishes. Let her marry Cornbury if he wants her. None of that makes any difference. But she can't be queen. She has to understand that. And the priest has to understand it too.'

I nod. 'I'll find a pen and sign the letter for you,' I say.

'There is no need. That is merely a draft.'

'And the original?'

'We signed it on your behalf earlier this morning. It is already on its way to Paris.'

'That is very thoughtful of you,' I say.

'Think nothing of it,' he says. 'All you need to do now is to wait for him to come to you, and tell us you have him. We can deal with things after that. In a kindly and understanding manner, of course.'

'I agree,' says Aminta, 'that we have to try to save Kitty from the dangers that threaten to overwhelm her. She's not in control of her destiny any more than Father Christopher is in control of his. Arlington is right that it is a declaration that Kitty is the King's legitimate heir that could kill her. At that point, both the Duke of York and the Duke of Monmouth will feel that she must be removed by any means available. But why does Arlington imagine that the priest will be taken in by his letter? Father Christopher has survived more than twenty years of plotting and counter-plotting in Paris. He may appear to be a frail old man, but he's as skilled a survivor as Morland. You saw him in Paris. He was frightened and very careful what he told us, but he never lost his nerve.'

'We'll have to wait and see what happens,' I say.

'Perhaps, but in the meantime I would propose another visit to Mistress Elizabeth Needham,' says Aminta, 'now she is back in London. I think she may be a little more cooperative than she was before.'

'It is very kind of you to call,' says Mistress Needham.

'We merely wished to congratulate you on your forthcoming marriage,' says Aminta. 'A very advantageous match.'

'I have Lord Ashley to thank for that,' says Mistress Needham. 'He helped in all sorts of ways. He has provided a dowry, for example.'

'That is very generous of him, then. When will the wedding take place?'

'Quite soon, I believe. I cannot stress too strongly that I am very much in Lord Ashley's hands. Totally in his hands. I have to make very few decisions for myself. Is your play enjoying a successful run, Lady Grey?'

'It is indeed. Thank you for your letter about it. Betterton thinks it may continue to the end of the year – along with other plays, of course.'

'I wish I could come and see it again, but Lord Ashley considers the theatre an unsuitable place for me to be. I have to be careful where I am seen now that . . . now that certain rumours are circulating about me. And about my future prospects. Would you be so good as to have a copy of the script of your play sent to me so that I may at least read it?'

'But of course,' says Aminta. 'I shall have it sent.'

'Increasingly I empathise with Emilia's predicament,' says Mistress Needham. 'Assuming a false identity and then finding that she is no longer in control of events around her.'

'In a sense she has nobody but herself to blame,' says Aminta.

'Yes, I do realise that, as I didn't before. And I am sure that she therefore feels very foolish as well as frightened. Snarkly, however, was a true friend, was he not – assisting her, even though she had perhaps not treated him as well as she should in the past?'

'You feel there are lessons to be learned for us all there?'

'Oh, I hope so. Drama sometimes has so much to teach us.'

From my Lady Grey's celebrated comedy, *The Summer Birdcage*

Act 3 Scene 2, The Park

Enter the Queen and Livia, both in disguise

LIVIA: I have never visited the Park so late. Everything is very strange. I am in fear for our lives and reputations alike. There is no sign of Bellair or the young French gentleman. Let us go back to the Palace, Your Majesty. I shall find another way of rescuing Bonnedame.

QUEEN: Not so fast, Mistress Livia. If Bonnedame is worth saving, let us not give up before we have gone a dozen steps into the Park.

LIVIA: But he is not here to be saved.

QUEEN: On the contrary, madam, I think I spy Bellair now and a young gentleman with him. We shall do a good deed and make Bellair suffer at the same time.

LIVIA: But there is a third – and I think it is Mister Snarkly! What now? I am sure he will recognise me!

QUEEN: Mister Snarkly! I would have expected this of Bellair, but not Snarkly. *(Aside)* Disaster! I could have chastened Bellair to my heart's content, but I owe Mister Snarkly too much. What do I do?

LIVIA: Indeed, madam. I am shocked at Snarkly's being a party to this. *(Aside)* And how I despise him for't! To think I was almost considering falling in love with him!

QUEEN: Let us step back into the shadows, lest they see us too soon. I would hear what they say to each other. We must consider before we act. Perhaps, after all, we should retire to the Palace and think again.

Enter Bellair, Snarkly and Emilia, disguised as before.

SNARKLY: The Park is almost empty tonight, Bellair. Let us go back to my lodgings. I have some bottles of rare Canary there, a pack of cards and a purse full of gold, ready to be lost to a more skilful player. *(Aside)* I'll get the Prince drunk while we play, and then I'll let the young boy slip away.

BELLAIR: Wait a while, Mister Snarkly! There are always some ladies who come here at this hour. *(Sees the Queen and Livia)* And what do I espy there under the trees? A promising pair of wantons in their vizards! Good evening to you, ladies!

QUEEN: *(To Livia)* You answer him! He will know my voice.

LIVIA: *(To the Queen)* You answer, madam! Mister Snarkly most certainly knows mine.

QUEEN: *(To Livia)* Oh, very well. *(To Bellair)* My name, sir, is Mistress Jones and this is my good friend, Mistress Davis. We were taking a walk in the Park. Nothing more.

BELLAIR: Then we'll take a turn with you. And perhaps you'll join us for some wine? My name is ... er ... Cromwell. This is Mister Fairfax and that is our good friend Mister Richelieu from France.

EMILIA: *(Aside)* So, I'm Richelieu now? Another name to remember! I pray you, if I forget myself, remind me who I am!

QUEEN: The path, sir, is uneven. Perhaps, after all, we shall go home.

BELLAIR: Then hold on tightly to us, ladies, and you shall not fall. Or if you do, we shall provide you with something soft to fall upon, eh? I doubt it will be the first time you've taken a tumble in the Park.

SNARKLY: Let them go, Mister Cromwell. They do not wish to join us.

BELLAIR: Of course they do, Mister Fairfax. Why else are they here? *(To Snarkly)* They merely seek to drive up their price with a show of reluctance. *(To Queen and Livia)* Come ladies. Let's away! There are places in the Park where the blushing moon scarcely dares to show its face! Let me guide you there. Or do you know the way already? I fancy that you may!

LIVIA: *(Aside)* Horrors! Suddenly I love moonlight above all else! And I do not love Mister Snarkly at all.

EMILIA: *(Aside)* Horrors! My worst fears are confirmed! I shall never marry Bellair now! But how do I make my exit from this comedy?

SNARKLY: *(Aside)* Horrors! It is easier to win a diamond at cards than preserve a young man's virtue! At least Emilia will learn nothing of this!

BELLAIR: Why do you all stand there? Our young friend wishes to have fun, don't you, Richelieu? Richelieu?

EMILIA: Oh, sorry, yes, of course, you spoke my name. *(Aside)* Or one of 'em. Further and further into danger. If only I could admit to being Emilia again, I'd never try to be anyone else!

All exit.

Chapter Twenty-eight

In which I have a visitor

'And because Kitty Burgess mentioned Emilia it means she now wishes to escape?' Arlington looks doubtful.

'In my wife's play, Emilia entraps herself by pretending to be somebody else. Kitty doubtless thought we might be overheard.'

Arlington frowns and taps the feathery end of his pen against his lips. 'Why can't she just walk out of Exeter House?'

'Ashley has turned her into a powerful weapon. Like a retreating general who spikes his guns or a captain who scuttles his ship to avoid its capture, he won't risk her falling into the hands of a rival if he's forced to abandon his plan. Not now he's all but established that she is the rightful heir to the throne. He'd kill her before he allowed her to go over to Buckingham or to you, and she knows it. I think that it was only when she was in Dorset that Ashley explained the full plan to her – that she is to be made queen. Kitty sees this as one risk too many but she will be aware by now just how ruthless Ashley can be. She certainly knows what happened to Neville. We'll have to find a way of extracting her, by force or guile, and sending her somewhere safe.'

Arlington considers this for a long time. Could he use Elizabeth Needham if he could get her? Use her more skilfully than his rival would? Probably. But would she cooperate with him any more than she would with Ashley? Eventually he says: 'I should tell you that I have just come from the King. He is more than ever convinced that the lady really is his daughter – his legitimate daughter.'

'He said so in so many words?'

'The King, as you know, rarely says anything in so many words. He likes the safety of ambiguity. But his meaning was clear to me. There were rumours as you know that he married Monmouth's mother. He has always denied that, even at the expense of losing the legitimate son he has always craved. He'd do things differently now, of course, but he can't go back on what he has so often claimed was a lie. It's too late. And the evidence has in any case been destroyed. He regrets missing his chance of a proper heir – a child of his own to succeed him. That is why he is willing to accept what now seems inevitable. He is thinking of declaring Elizabeth Needham, as he believes her to be, his daughter, born in lawful wedlock. And he wishes this to be done openly and handsomely – not as a result of a nasty campaign of whispering and rumouring by Ashley. The stumbling block, of course, is the Queen, who will clearly no longer be Queen because His Majesty was not free to marry her.'

'And the King will need to surrender Tangier and Bombay back to the King of Portugal.'

'Perhaps. Both ports are well fortified and held by English troops. We might let him have Tangier without a fight, but

Bombay is another matter. That, however, is not the problem. The King feels guilty about the Queen. He has humiliated her with one mistress after another, but repudiating the marriage will be an insult too far. However much he has betrayed her with other women, however much he may have slighted her, he has always loved her. She has always remained Queen. She has retained the right to wear a crown – to walk with him arm in arm. Now she will not even have that.'

'Could he not just remarry her? After all, Lady Byron is now dead. This time it would be valid.'

'But would she agree to it? Or will she insist on the validity of her original marriage or nothing? Will she appeal to the Pope to intervene on her behalf? Or to the King of Portugal? Or to the King of France? We could find ourselves with enemies all over Europe and our friends laughing at us behind our backs. That is even less desirable than losing Bombay. So nothing can happen until the King has decided how and what to tell his wife. But very soon, however much he wants to delay, his hand will be forced. Clarendon will swear Elizabeth Needham is the genuine article and most people will think Clarendon ought to know. So will Father Christopher. Then we shall have very few choices in front of us.'

'In that case the King simply has to be told that Elizabeth Needham is an imposter,' I say. 'That will clarify things for him. And save the Queen from humiliation that she has done nothing to deserve.'

'Yes, of course. The problem is that the King is prepared to believe certain things but not others. He had long resigned himself to having no heir of his body. Now, suddenly, he wants more than anything to believe he has a legitimate daughter. Simply telling him won't do the job, I'm afraid. What he believes will all be a lie, of course, and at some point, after a great deal of damage has been done, to the King and to the country, the lie will be exposed and Kitty Burgess will lose her head for falsely claiming to be the heir to the throne.'

'She has made no claims of any sort yet,' I say. 'And she would like to find a way out before anyone makes one on her behalf. I think she too is worried that she will end up with her head on the block, like Lady Jane Grey.'

'True,' says Arlington. 'Well, whatever the King wants, my duty is very clear. We simply can't let Ashley put an imposter on the throne of England. If Mistress Burgess wishes to escape his clutches, then I would give her every possible assistance – make every possible concession to ensure that we can detach her from Ashley. Tell her that if she cooperates with us – if she makes a claim to be nothing more than His Majesty's illegitimate daughter – then no harm will come to her. She'd be a fool to refuse such an offer. She still has the marriage to Cornbury, who can hardly back out of something announced so publicly and who will in the fullness of time become the next Earl of Clarendon. I mean, she's not actually the King's daughter. She's a nobody from some village in Hampshire. An actress! To marry an earl – or at least the heir to an earldom – must exceed her wildest dreams. All she has to do is marry Cornbury and then refuse to go through with the rest of the plan.'

'That may not work,' I say. 'She tells us Ashley rules her while she is with him. And then, once married to Cornbury, she will belong even more completely to her husband. That's the law. He can lock her up and beat her or starve her into submission. And I have no doubt Cornbury wants to be king. Like Lady Jane Grey, she is already part of something that she cannot control herself.'

Arlington is silent for almost a full minute. 'Then I can see a compromise won't work either. We'll find a way of kidnapping her back. Then Elizabeth Needham must disappear every bit as thoroughly as Mistress Burgess did before her. Without trace. Without any hope of a further resurrection. It won't be easy to hide her. No one wants to be cut off from their old life completely – their friends, their parents, their brothers and sisters. That's how we have caught renegade republicans hiding out in the Netherlands. A loving wife pays a visit and the trap snaps closed. The next thing you know, we've got our man dangling from the end of a rope.'

'I agree. That's why only you could do it, my Lord.'

'True, Sir John. Very true. Let me give it some thought. Then you must convey the plan to her and make sure she sees sense.'

'And Father Christopher?' I ask.

'There is no sign of him in Paris. Perhaps Ashley has already had him killed because he refused to testify, perhaps Monmouth has killed him because he agreed to testify. I think you wasted your time writing that letter to him. It's a dangerous game we all play, Sir John, and the priest has lost the final hand. Still, there we are. His death means that I have one less problem. We must be grateful for small mercies.'

The weather has changed. A late summer rain lashes against the windows. I am safe and dry but I fear for Aminta on her visit to a cousin on the other side of town, even though she has taken our carriage. She still has to get from the coach to the front door and lutestring dresses do not like being rained on, even a little.

I am not expecting visitors on such an afternoon, but our maid surprises me by ushering into our sitting room a very wet and dishevelled clergyman.

'Father Christopher!' I exclaim. 'But you can't have got the letter already?'

'What letter?'

'If you didn't receive it, what are you doing in England?'

'Things got a little difficult for me in Paris.'

'As they did for me. You must tell me about it, but first you must change into some dry clothes. I'll also ask our maid to make you some tea or coffee as you prefer.'

'And some food. Anything, Sir John. I haven't eaten since Dover. I have money, but I couldn't be sure where Arlington's spies were. Or Ashley's. Or Monmouth's. It seemed safer to keep moving. I've scarcely stood still or slept since I left Paris.'

Father Christopher is now dressed in one of my older suits of clothes – an unclerical burgundy red – and is sipping some very hot coffee. An empty plate, once more than adequately covered in ham, is on the table in front of him.

'The problem,' he says, 'is that I promised too many people too many things. That's always a mistake in my experience. Lord Clarendon got me to say I'd work for him and Ashley – I didn't want to, for obvious reasons, but it seemed easier to say yes. And Sir Samuel Morland had contacted me to point out that it would be to my advantage to throw in my lot with the Duke of Monmouth, who is, he says, certain to be the next king. He hinted that I might be made a bishop. I mean, I have no worldly ambitions, but it would still be nice to be a bishop and have my own cathedral somewhere. Of course, he may have been lying. He seemed like the sort of person who would. Then, at the same time, I was getting letters from the Duke of York reminding me of my loyalty to the present king, and to himself as the future monarch, and to the Church. Well, I could hardly deny that I didn't have loyalties to the Church. Last, and most of all, there are my loyalties to Mistress Needham. I promised Lady Byron, you see. I said that no harm would come to her. That's why I need your help. I have to speak to Lord Ashley and beg him not to do what he is planning to do. Only he can release her. When you came to me in Paris, I thought you seemed the sort of person I could rely on if I needed help.'

'You overestimate my ability to help you,' I say. 'But what I really don't understand is why should you care what happens to Mistress Needham? Or how a promise to Lady Byron years ago affects anything? If you are in the confidence of Lord Clarendon, you will know exactly who the lady calling herself Mistress Needham really is. She's Kitty Burgess. And you owe that lady nothing at all, whatever you may have promised Elizabeth Needham's mother.'

He blinks at me a couple of times. 'I'm sorry – you think that the lady at Lord Ashley's house is Kitty Burgess?'

'I know she's Kitty Burgess,' I say. 'She's Kitty Burgess impersonating Elizabeth Needham.'

'No, she's Elizabeth Needham impersonating Kitty Burgess,' he says. 'I thought you understood that?'

'No,' I say.

'Ah, well, she is,' he says.

'You'd better tell me the whole story,' I say. 'Then I'll decide what, if anything, I can do for you.'

'I am not sure, even now, I should tell you everything. There were, as I say, many promises that I made.'

'Then you can change back into your wet clothes and go out into the rain to see if there's somebody you trust better.'

He looks at me. He doesn't trust me, but he doesn't want to give up a dry coat. Not now he's got one.

'It all begins with Lady Byron,' he says. 'You know that much at least? I thought so. Well, in the early 1650s she and her husband, Lord Byron, arrived in Paris, having fled from Cromwell's rule in England. Lord Byron died in August 1652, but fortunately the King was there to comfort Lady Byron in her grief. The result was a baby girl – towards the end of the year, actually, suggesting that the King had been comforting Lady Byron even while her husband was still alive, which showed great prescience on his part.'

'So Elizabeth was definitely his child?'

'*Is* his child. And, yes, I'm sure.'

'And did the King marry her mother?'

'I thought you knew that too. You told me you did. Yes, as soon as the husband was decently buried, there was a wedding. That would have been in September, I think. I conducted the service, just as you said.'

'Who else was there?'

'The witnesses, you mean?' He frowns, as if trying to recall the event twenty years ago. 'Daniel O'Neill was one.'

'The spy? The man who tried to kidnap the young Duke of Monmouth?'

'I suppose he was a spy then. But he became Postmaster General after the restoration.'

'The two posts were never incompatible,' I say.

I did, of course, know O'Neill. Though it was Clarendon who threatened to have me shot in Brussels, O'Neill would probably have been given the job of shooting me.

'Anyone else?' I ask.

'Yes, what was his name? Allen Brodrick, that's it.'

I nod. I know him too. Brodrick would probably have been responsible for tying me to the post and checking the knots were tight enough. The witnesses were two of the King's most loyal servants and agents of the highest skill and deviousness. One is now dead and the other certainly won't talk. But that won't help me.

'What about Clarendon?' I ask. 'I assume he was there?'

'Certainly not. He could not possibly have approved. He knew that the King needed allies and that the best way of getting allies would be for him to marry into one of the other royal families. The King couldn't do that if he was already legally bound to an amiable but impoverished female member of the English gentry. No, Clarendon was not pleased. Heated words were exchanged. The King was lectured on his duty to the country. In the end, it was agreed that the baby should be sent to a convent, as soon as it could be done, that the fact of the marriage should be hidden away for ever and that Lady Byron should be bought off as cheaply as might be. I think she proved quite expensive in the end, but she did know an awful lot that wasn't to the King's credit. Yes, she was in a position to demand a great deal of money from him.'

'So Elizabeth Needham was entrusted to the nuns? With your help?'

'Indeed. I was delighted to be of service to His Majesty in any way I could. I had, after all, with the very best of intentions, created the problem in the first place.'

'But surely Elizabeth Needham – the real Elizabeth Needham – died there? That's what the convent records apparently said.'

'Died? No, not a bit of it. She was just moved elsewhere. The King had got nervous. He wasn't sure that little Elizabeth would remain quietly with the nuns for ever, helpful though that would be. He began to wonder if Lady Byron would not use her, once the child was old enough to cooperate, as a bargaining counter. Just as he tried to have Monmouth kidnapped in 1658, so he tried to have Elizabeth kidnapped at about the same time. The nuns were more than capable of seeing off the King's agents, but it did worry Lady Byron. She had the child sent to England, while the nuns were to say, if anyone asked, that she was dead. I found an old royalist couple to take her there – a Colonel and Mistress Burgess, who had been in exile in Paris but were returning to England having made their peace with Cromwell, as so many royalists were forced to. Elizabeth travelled as their daughter. But they knew they would not live long enough to bring her up and guard her until she reached adulthood. They therefore in turn passed Elizabeth to a distant relative of theirs – the wife of a clergyman in Hampshire. Whether anyone told Elizabeth who she really was I couldn't say. Maybe they did. Maybe they didn't. I don't think that Reginald Norris's wife ever trusted him with the information, so he wouldn't have been able to tell her anything. Or to tell anyone else. I suppose you don't have any more of that excellent ham? Travelling from Paris has given me quite an appetite.'

Chapter Twenty-nine

In which we see the truth

'Well, that explains a great deal,' says Aminta.
'Yes,' I say. 'It does.'

Aminta has returned from her visit and I have summarised my conversation with Father Christopher.

'And where is Father Christopher now?'

'Upstairs,' I say. 'Asleep in the small chamber. I doubt we'll see him until it is time to eat again.'

Aminta nods. 'So what happened to Kitty's supposed parents, the Burgesses? Are they in fact still alive?'

'They seem to just vanish from the picture at the time the child was handed over to Mistress Norris. The Burgesses had fully discharged their duty by passing her and her secret on to another, younger protector. Your cousin's wife was to tell nobody who Kitty really was – not even, it would seem, her husband or the child herself. But Mistress Norris knew she was bringing up a future queen and some of that rubbed off on Kitty. It's not surprising the young girl came to the conclusion that she was somebody rather special. Mistress Norris was also determined that no hint of scandal should attach itself to her charge. The young men of the district might admire her from afar, but it could go no further than that. And, of course, she could not possibly become an actress – a profession that was actually illegal until a few years ago. Sadly Mistress Norris died, taking her secrets with her and leaving Kitty in the sole charge of your cousin, who could see no objection to her going to London to seek a new career.'

'I'd thought all of the subterfuge was needed because Ashley had discovered the real Elizabeth was dead and needed an actress to play that role.'

'But in fact,' I say, 'Clarendon had somehow discovered, from his sources in Paris, that she was alive, had been taken to England and had then become an actress. That last piece of news presented problems. Actresses can become the mistresses of noblemen, but they don't become nobility themselves. Still less do they become queens. He had to cover up the fact that she'd ever been near a theatre. So, he and Ashley arranged a neat little death for Kitty Burgess, so that she could be reborn as herself. So we know why Clarendon not only had to take the risk of visiting Paris, but had to risk staying there. It needed somebody of his weight to persuade the Abbess to cooperate – to get her to retract her former lie and not waver. It needed somebody who could ensure Father Christopher remembered the right promises rather than the wrong ones. It needed a master of detail, which is one thing we know Clarendon most certainly is, to oversee all of the comings and goings – including our own – until it was clear things were well in London. And it also explains why Clarendon and Cornbury wanted me to get safely back to England, with the evidence we had found for Elizabeth Needham's legitimacy. In a sense, we became witnesses too. The brief letter he sent with me, knowing I'd show it to Arlington, must have amused him a great deal. He more or less told us Elizabeth was the genuine article, knowing we wouldn't believe it.'

Aminta nods. 'And I now understand Ashley's inexplicable confidence. He knew Arlington couldn't prove Kitty wasn't Elizabeth, because she actually is. I did well to have her cast as the Queen in my play, when you think about it.'

'And we know exactly what was in it for Clarendon, subject of course to various constitutional precedents, dating from the twelfth to the sixteenth centuries, that Mister Pepys will doubtless be prepared to summarise if you wish. His son marries not an imposter to the throne but the real heir.'

'All went well until Kitty started to have reservations,' says Aminta.

'Yes. I don't know what Ashley told Kitty to begin with – he may well have said that he wanted her to impersonate somebody for a while. But it would have become clear, bit by bit, how much of her early life had been kept from her. As I say, she'd grown up, quite rightly, with a conviction that she was a very special person. She just never quite knew why. I think Ashley revealed the plot in its entirety at about the time we left for France – hence the letter waiting for us when we returned. Of course, she still thought she could play around with the script. She decided she'd go off to the theatre as an act of bravado, and was very quickly reined in. Ashley didn't like her improvising any more than Betterton had done. I can see how, some days, becoming queen might have seemed quite attractive to Kitty – or perhaps we should start calling her Elizabeth again since that's her real name – but how, other days, it might fill her with dread. She'd face years of being told, by one man or another, exactly what she could and couldn't do. She'd be constantly worrying about assassination, wondering which plate of food the poison was in. Then when the King dies, who knows who Parliament and the people will actually decide to back as his successor? There are plenty of people who still hate Clarendon enough not to want his son as King at any price. If they declare for the Duke of York after all, he's unlikely to be in a forgiving mood. Dying a traitor's death is an easy mistake to make, as a lot of my mother's ancestors discovered.'

'What next?'

'I've told Father Christopher that I'll consult Lord Arlington on how we can extract Kitty from the mess she has got herself into, now we know what the mess actually is. She may not exactly deserve our help, but it's the right thing for everyone.'

'Will Arlington agree to be helpful,' asks Aminta, 'when he knows exactly what Ashley has?'

'He said that he would, when he thought the lady was an imposter. We'll just have to see what he says when he knows she's the real heir. As for Father Christopher, I can't see why he shouldn't simply be returned to France, once he has done what he needs to do here.'

'Excellent,' says Arlington. 'Now we can crush that traitor priest.'

'I told you that he is under my protection. And as I have just explained, he has provided us with some very useful information.'

'That Ashley has the genuine Byron girl? I'd wondered about that for some time.'

'Had you?'

'Of course. Why would Ashley select some lowly actress for his scheme? No reason at all, unless he had no alternative to choosing her. Because she really was Elizabeth Needham. And what about that letter you brought back from France in which Clarendon appears to think that Elizabeth Needham was the real heir? You mocked it. Well, I trust you can see what the joke was now. Yes, it was obvious all along, when you think about it. To me anyway. We can't let Ashley get his hands on the priest as well as the girl. Not now the stakes have been raised. I hope you will concede that, very sadly, he has to die. Is Father Christopher obviously a papist? I could find an informer or two to discredit him. Plant a letter on him urging the gentry of England to rise up against the Protestant king. It won't be difficult to get him hanged.'

'I think it would be better to try working with him. As we said, we can try to get Elizabeth Needham away from Ashley by force, but it won't be easy. Perhaps Father Christopher can simply appeal to Ashley's better nature, if he has one. Or maybe he knows some reason why the service he conducted was invalid. With such a clandestine affair, there must have been some technical irregularity he could find. Perhaps in calling the bans? If we can, we must persuade Ashley to abandon the scheme, drop his claim and give the girl up. If not, then we have to revert to ensuring that Kitty can escape to somewhere beyond his clutches. But there will be danger for everyone in doing it.'

Arlington nods. 'It would need to be further away than Amsterdam or Geneva,' he says. 'Virginia or Maryland, I think. Both perfectly comfortable. Not the place we've just taken from the Dutch, of course – too rough and uncivilised for a member of the King's family.'

'I agree that it would be cruel to send an actress somewhere like New York. With the lady's consent, however, one of the older colonies should be acceptable. But we'll try to persuade Ashley to drop his scheme first. I'll take Father Christopher to Exeter House tomorrow around noon. Hopefully it is not being watched by the Duke of Monmouth or the Duke of York or any of the many people in London who would prefer it if Elizabeth Needham vanished even more comprehensively than we are proposing.'

'I'll send two of my men over there, at noon, just in case. You've already been ambushed once.'

'Twice. I was also incautious enough to be captured in Paris. I told you that you should send somebody else. I'm getting too old for this work.'

Chapter Thirty

In which Lord Arlington is proved right

'There is still much damage from the Fire,' says Father Christopher as we cross the city. 'Truly I had not realised that dear old London had suffered so much. We heard reports of it in Paris, of course, but so many fine, ancient churches have gone . . . And all these new buildings in place of what was there before. I do not recognise where we are at all. This modern London is a strange place.'

'I suppose you're right,' I say. 'I am so used to it now that I scarcely notice how it has changed since the Great Fire. The streets are all much where they were, but the houses and shops are now clean red brick rather than plaster and timber, and there is still a great deal of rebuilding to be done – the new churches, for example, are scarcely started. Wren has only recently completed his designs for Saint Paul's. The building work may take thirty years.'

'Then I shall not live to see it,' says Father Christopher.

'Perhaps I shall not either. But, for the moment, we should concentrate on still being alive this afternoon.'

'You think we are in danger, even now, on a mission to resolve matters peacefully?'

'It depends on whether there is anyone lying in wait for us and whether Lord Arlington sends his men as promised.'

'Nevertheless, I have to do this,' says Father Christopher. 'I should never have married them, you see. I knew that was wrong. And the King knew it was wrong or he would have ensured that Clarendon was there. Then I should never have allowed the nuns to admit that Elizabeth was alive and well. Her ability to grow up into a healthy adult depended on her having died as a child. I have, through my own weakness, put her into such danger. I have sinned, Sir John, against God and against so many people and so many things. That's why we must do what we can, you and I, even if we die in the attempt.'

'I've no plans to die,' I say. 'And if Lord Arlington's men are there at noon, then hopefully we shall not.' I check the gold watch that I so narrowly avoided losing in Paris. It is, here in London, exactly a quarter before midday. But hopefully our friends will be in place early. If we keep walking, we shall be at Exeter House in five minutes and standing around here in the open is more dangerous than pressing on, though we are now beyond the last of the ruins and into the streets that were untouched by the Fire four years ago.

'You know,' says Father Christopher. 'That thing you asked me before we set out. I said that I couldn't see any objection to the marriage I performed – I mean, something that would make it invalid. But I have just thought of something – just this moment. It's funny it hadn't struck me before, but it would make a great difference to things. You see, it's like this . . .'

'Tell me later,' I say. 'I think there is trouble ahead.'

Just short of our destination, I have spotted three men, who had been inoffensively lounging in a doorway but who have now, in a very leisurely manner, started to walk towards us. They are not ruffians, but well dressed in velvet coats and periwigs and with feathers in their broad-brimmed hats. For a moment, I hope that they are friends, but when they reach us they stop and the tallest of the three says: 'We'll take the traitor priest from here, if it's all the same to you, Sir John. We have business with him.'

'And who might you be?' I ask.

He's young and his face is smooth. His false locks flow over his shoulders in a mass of glorious curls. He smiles that I do not recognise him. He thinks most people would.

'Don't worry. We're old friends of his,' he says.

I look at Father Christopher. He shakes his head. His friends don't usually refer to him as 'the traitor priest'. Though he has expressed a general willingness to die, I think he feels that I have let him down with regard to the specific timing. I hope Arlington's agents are not too far off. Still, I may be able to keep these gentlemen talking for five minutes.

'I realise the streets can be dangerous,' I say, 'but I think we'll be safe without your help, if you'll excuse us. And we have urgent business of our own to attend to.'

'You'd be best advised to give him up, Sir John, much though I like you.'

I turn to the man who has just spoken. Ah, yes. I know him all right. I've just never seen him sober before. It's my drinking companion, Philip Herbert. Arlington's probably right that he could out-fence me any day of the week, even without the help of his two friends. And he probably won't mind killing me. After all, I turned down his offer of a cheap whore. But who is the tall man who spoke to me first? He has an aristocratic confidence and a self-assurance that even Herbert lacks. And I suspect he may be able to handle a sword as well. A church clock, very slowly, starts to strike midday. I hope that it, rather than my watch, is giving the correct time.

'Well, I'm delighted to meet you again, Mister Herbert,' I say. 'But I would not wish to delay you gentlemen and keep you from your dinner.'

'We keep London hours, Sir John,' says Herbert. 'We'll not dine before two o'clock. Plenty of time to deal with your priest, clean our swords on his backside and find a suitable tavern. Ha! We have no argument with you, Sir John. You can go on your way, sir, in your fine new periwig. It's the scurvy little cleric we have business with.'

I've occasionally wondered how I shall die. Usually I've concluded that the most likely place would be a dark alleyway or the back room of some low inn, while engaged in some largely pointless, unpaid mission for Lord Arlington. It had never occurred to me that it would be in the Strand at midday, at the hands of a madman, while trying to protect the English chaplain in Paris. How was I supposed to guess that? I draw my sword, more for something to do than in the hope of frightening anyone off. With luck I may damage one or two of them before they run me through. And that may give Father Christopher time to get away, taking with him whatever objection to the King's marriage he has just thought of. The problem is, I suspect he does not run as fast as he will need to. I scan the street for anyone who may have been sent to help us, but there is nobody – just a few onlookers, who are keeping their distance. The three men blocking our route don't seem too worried about killing us in front of witnesses anyway. They think they'll get away with it when they show the judge their family trees. Herbert draws his own sword. It sits very comfortably in his hand. Nicely balanced, I'd say. And probably very sharp. He's going to enjoy this.

His first lunge at me is perfunctory, at chest height, and I am able to parry it with ease. But we both know he wasn't trying. He's giving me a chance to run if I want to. Not an honourable chance, but a chance for all that. The second stroke is more considered and I have to step back and defend against a thrust to the gut. I try to keep myself between Herbert and the priest, but a sudden sweep of his sword, aimed at my head, makes me stumble backwards on the cobbles. There is a silver arc through the air, and the next thing I know, Father Christopher is clutching at his chest, or perhaps at what can still be seen of the blade of Herbert's sword, and a lot of blood is flowing between his fingers. He falls to his knees, much of the blade still in place inside him, his hands clasped before him, as if in prayer. Herbert gives me an amused smile, twists the weapon in a very practised manner and carefully pulls it out. He wipes the shining steel on Father Christopher's right sleeve to remove some of the blood.

The third man, who has not yet spoken, is on to the priest straight away, his fingers in Father Christopher's right-hand pocket.

'Try inside the coat,' says the tall man. 'It will be there.'

But behind us, I hear the sound of running feet. Arlington's men have apparently finally arrived and in force.

Herbert looks at them, then at me, then plunges his sword again into Father Christopher's ribs. It is a piece of pure spite, which almost severs the hand of his companion, who is still trying to search the inside pockets.

'Sorry about your priest, Sir John,' says Herbert. 'But no hard feelings, eh? We'll share a bottle of Canary when you are next in town, by way of apology.'

'Have you got the papers?' asks the tall man.

'They're not here,' says the man on the ground. 'Not in either of his outer pockets or inside the coat.' He is watching Herbert cautiously before he risks trying anywhere else.

'Let's go then,' says the tall man. 'We've done all we can.'

I look round. I was sure that there had been some onlookers when this began, but they all seem to have vanished.

Arlington's men wisely decide not to pursue Herbert and his two friends. There are, after all, other things that need doing. They assist me in carrying Father Christopher to a nearby tavern, from where we send for a surgeon. I kneel beside the low, beer-covered table on which he has been laid. I try to reassure him that help is coming, but the chaplain shakes his head.

'Important,' he says. 'The papers they wanted – the marriage certificate . . .'

'Yes?' I say.

'Never had it. Too dangerous. My rooms in Paris. Too easy to break into.'

'Who has it?'

'Reginald Norris,' he says. 'Hopefully. The Burgesses said they gave it to his wife anyway . . .'

'But there is an objection to its validity,' I say.

'Yes,' he says. 'So it doesn't matter after all. I hadn't thought of that. That's very reassuring. We don't need to worry.'

He smiles and closes his eyes.

'So what is the objection?' I ask. 'For Kitty's sake . . . for Elizabeth's sake . . . for everyone's sake . . . I need to know.

Father Christopher? Can you tell me? Why wasn't the marriage valid?'

But Father Christopher, for so many years the English chaplain in Paris, has spoken his last words on this earth.

I stand very slowly. For a few minutes there I had the solution to my problems, but now I don't. 'At least I know who killed him,' I say. 'Philip Herbert. We may still be able to get him convicted for this.'

'You won't. Not unless you can also convict his master.'

'Yes, who was the tall man?'

'I'd have thought you'd have recognised him, sir. That was the Duke of Monmouth – the King's eldest bastard, sir. He's a very popular man in London, is my Lord Monmouth. Quite an honour to have met him. You're lucky it was only Herbert who drew his sword on you, though. He wasn't really trying, was he? I think he likes you for some reason. But Monmouth would have killed you in an instant, begging your pardon, sir. And you'd have hardly seen him do it. He's a pretty man, with that smooth face and those curls, but he's the very devil of a swordsman.'

'So, they've attacked you in the Park when you weren't paying attention. Now they've hoodwinked you and killed the priest, who knew why the marriage was invalid – but you couldn't even be bothered to ask him about it before he died.' Arlington shakes his head sorrowfully. 'At least they don't have the papers they were after.' He's less annoyed than I expected; but he was, after all, always in favour of having Father Christopher neatly disposed of. And, if Herbert is unfortunate enough to hang for it, that is a bonus of sorts. His lordship certainly seems willing to overlook my carelessness on this occasion.

'They clearly thought Father Christopher had proof of the marriage about him,' I say, 'just as they had previously thought that I had brought the same thing from Paris.'

'They were probably quite disappointed, having gone to the trouble of stabbing Father Christopher, to discover his pockets were empty – especially when they had already hit you over the head, only to find it was merely a letter from Clarendon that you were carrying. Proof of the marriage of Monmouth's own mother, if it ever existed, has long since been destroyed. But he's still hoping the King will acknowledge him as his heir one day. He wouldn't have wanted anyone else to have, for their own claim, the very evidence that he lacks for his. The production of a marriage certificate now for Lady Byron would have been very inconvenient.'

'If it exists, it would seem to be in Hampshire,' I say. 'I could try to retrieve it and bring it to you. Perhaps if we had it, we could find out why Father Christopher doubted its validity.'

'If that's where it is, I would prefer you destroyed it there. I don't want you bringing it to London and dropping it in the street for anyone to find.'

'Of course,' I say.

'You'll have made an enemy of Monmouth. But hopefully he'll never be crowned. You may not suffer for it. You'll also have made an enemy of Herbert.'

'Oh, I don't think so,' I say. 'He gave me quite a friendly wave as he left.'

'Reginald said nothing about any papers,' says Aminta.

'He may not know he has them. I remember when Pepys's wife died he said that he couldn't bear to throw away many of her possessions – the tapestry wool that she had just purchased, for example. It may be that Reginald has yet to go through all of his wife's papers and throw out the ones that aren't needed. It's easy to put these things off.'

'Perhaps we should travel down to Hampshire – before anyone else does?'

'No, I think that particular secret is safe for the moment. But we do need to speak to Elizabeth Needham and somehow tell her what's happened. I think we're back to having to extract her by force, and I need her to be prepared for it. I'll go tomorrow morning. I can take that script she asked for. Ashley can hardly object to my doing that.'

'I'll come with you.'

'It may be dangerous.'

'That's why you'll need me to look after you. You've been ambushed three times now, remember?'

'Thank you for the script, Lady Grey,' says Ashley. 'I shall make sure she gets it. But Mistress Needham cannot see you and your husband. Unfortunately, yesterday, she witnessed the stabbing of a priest, almost outside the house. She saw it very clearly from her window. It has unsettled her a great deal. She feels London is unsafe at present. Even before yesterday, she wished, very vehemently, to change some plans we had made together – plans to attend the court and speak to the King. I reminded her that I did not like indecision and eventually suggested to her that a stay in the country might be appropriate. For a few weeks. Perhaps longer. Until she had calmed her nerves a little. She hesitated but the death of the priest has finally made up her mind. She is even now packing to go to Dorset. I will not interrupt her – nor can I permit you to do so – but I shall of course pass this document on to her.

Do not worry for her safety, Lady Grey. On her journey she will be accompanied by two of my men. My coachman and my postillion. Both good strong fellows. And very, very loyal to me.'

'Will she be gone long?' I ask.

'Who can say?' says Ashley. 'Who can possibly say?'

'If Kitty did see the attack on Father Christopher,' says Aminta, 'it will most certainly have heightened her fears for her own life. As Arlington said to you, the stakes are being raised all the time. Kitty will have seen you couldn't protect the priest and will have concluded you and Arlington won't be able to protect her either. If she recognised Monmouth, she will have realised how many people are determined to prevent her becoming queen. I can see why she wants to leave quickly.'

'It's a long way to Dorset and a lot can happen on the road. Let's hope that Ashley hasn't already decided that she is no further use to him.'

Three days later a letter arrives.

'It's from the coroner in Salisbury,' I say. 'They've found a body. They think it's Elizabeth Needham. We're both needed to identify her.'

Chapter Thirty-one

In which I talk to another coroner

'She was found dead beside the road, just outside the city,' says the coroner.

'Why do you think it is Mistress Needham?'

'It's a strange story,' says the coroner. 'She was travelling down to Dorset in a coach belonging to Lord Ashley. They were passing through a wooded area and Mistress Needham banged on the roof to ask the driver to stop. He did so and went to the right-hand door to see what was the matter. The postillion also descended and went to the same door. When they opened it, the coach was empty. This perplexed them very much, then they noticed that the far door was not latched properly. They went round to check and thought that they saw a lady in a red dress vanishing into the wood. The coachman gave chase while the postillion looked after the horses, but in vain. She had gone. They both reported this strange incident at the next town, mentioning that the lady had recently witnessed a brutal murder and was perhaps not in her right mind. Night was already falling and it was too late to begin a search for her. The following day the constable and some townsmen were dispatched in the direction of the woods and a body was quite easily found. The coachman thought the victim had been overtaken and murdered by footpads. But we cannot rule out other perpetrators, including the coachman and postillion themselves.'

'Why did you send for us?'

'The coachman suggested it. He said you knew her well. Were you aware of any threats to the lady's life?'

'If it proves to be Elizabeth Needham? More than enough. Shall we look at the body?'

'I am not sure that viewing it will help one way or the other. She had been beaten about the face so much that identification will be very difficult indeed. If you insist on trying to do so, perhaps it would be better, sir, if you did so on your own. It is not a sight for a lady.'

'My husband is not good at identifying bodies,' says Aminta. 'He has made embarrassing mistakes in the past. You'd better show us both.'

'At least, this time, we weren't asked to pay for a coffin,' says Aminta.

We have retired to the nearest inn, where we shall spend the night before we return to London.

'No,' I say. 'But, unlike Kitty, Elizabeth Needham was not supposed to be kin of any sort.'

'You are right,' says Aminta. 'It's easy to lose track of these things and who is supposed to have been killed where. The coachman and postillion were clearly acting under Ashley's orders. In a way, I feel sorry for them, having to recite that ridiculous story. Running through the woods in petticoats, doubtless with brambles on every side, would not have been easy. They should have realised that.'

'The coroner was correct, however, in saying that, in the absence of witnesses, there was no evidence that they were the killers.'

'I doubt that he wanted to implicate Lord Ashley in the killing.'

'And I don't blame him. Coroners are hard-working public servants and nothing like well paid enough to take on the Chancellor of the Exchequer.'

'As an author, I still feel Ashley might have come up with a more plausible story.'

'But in all other respects, he could not have arranged it better,' I say. 'Under the circumstances, I mean. Once he realised he had no possible further use for Elizabeth Needham, she had to die.'

'I suppose I can't blame him for the parody of Kitty's death,' says Aminta. 'From a literary point of view, that bit at least is well structured. He's laughing at us, obviously. But she is gone, for all that.'

'For once, he and Arlington would have been in agreement that it was the best thing all round. Should we travel back via Hampshire and see if we can retrieve the wedding certificate from your cousin, if he still has it?'

'I don't really see the point now, do you?'

'No,' I say. 'It's not much use to anyone, now Elizabeth Needham is finally and indisputably laid to rest.'

'According to this letter, Lord Cornbury is to marry Mistress Flower Backhouse,' says Aminta.

'Really?' I say. 'When?'

'Next month. October. She's a widow twice over. A rich one. She owns nine shares in the New River Company, apparently.'

'He has got over his grief for Elizabeth Needham quite quickly, then.'

'Money is a great healer.'

'Who is the letter from?'

'The Duchess of Cleveland. In London. She thought, here in Essex, we wouldn't have heard.'

'We hadn't.'

'She also says that Lord Ashley is suddenly very friendly with the Duke of Monmouth again.'

'Perhaps having seen off the threat of a potential rival, Monmouth will decide to accept Ashley's offer to establish him as the Protestant heir. Morland should be capable of forging the necessary proof of legitimacy. Does your friend Barbara have anything else to say?'

'She asks if we need stucco panels. Do we?'

'I don't think so.'

'I'll let her know.'

Chapter Thirty-two

In which we visit a theatre

Autumn has given way to winter and winter to spring. The roads are passable again and our coach has trundled southwards to London. *The Summer Birdcage* is still being performed by the Duke's Company and Aminta wishes to discuss with Betterton why she's not being paid more than she is.

It is pleasant to enter the theatre from the cold air outside. Unseasonal snow fell last night, surrounding the yellow daffodils with a powdering of white – a white that is slowly turning grey with London soot.

Betterton greets us enthusiastically. Aminta has made him more money in seven months than he usually makes in a year and a half.

'Welcome back, my Lady!' he says. 'I am sorry we don't have warmer weather for you. Thank you for your suggestions for amendments to the script. As you will see tomorrow night, I hope, we have incorporated them all and brought the play thoroughly up to date. Unfortunately the actress who played Emilia has just defected to the King's Company, but we should have rectified matters by then.'

Aminta enquires after his family and after the members of the cast who have not defected. She would have gone on to make certain financial demands, but we feel a draught on our necks as a door opens and closes behind us. We turn to see who the newcomer is – a lady in a black cloak. She throws back her hood, revealing her face and a lining of red silk. For a moment nobody says anything.

'Kitty?' says Aminta.

Yes, of course. I almost didn't recognise her, but that's who it is. She wears her hair in the simple English fashion, and she has gained a little weight since I last saw her as Elizabeth Needham. Her hair is blonde again. When she speaks there is no trace of any accent except – or am I imagining this? – a slight west country one.

'Good morning, my Lady,' she says. 'I did not know you were in London, but I returned only yesterday evening. I hope you got my letter, Mister Betterton?'

'Letter?' says Betterton.

'The one I wrote last August – apologising that I had needed to leave London so urgently. A niece of mine was very ill – I was called by the family to go and nurse her. They sent a coach to take me and, to my dismay, told me that I had to come at once, so badly was I needed. I didn't even have a chance to come back into the theatre and find you and say goodbye.'

Betterton frowns, trying to reconcile this with any part of his own recollection of Kitty's departure. Didn't she say she had an offer from an important gentleman? Or was that just what Meg thought she'd said?

'And you haven't been to London since then?' he says.

'Not once. I have been in Somerset the whole time.'

'And how is your niece?'

'Little Elizabeth? I am sorry to tell you that she is dead. She was a delightful child. I very much enjoyed her company and will always think of her with such fondness. Happy days, Mister Betterton, but gone for ever, I fear. Elizabeth is now safe with God and his angels. And I am back in London.'

'So what can I do for you?' asks Betterton cautiously.

'I wondered if you had any work for me? I had heard that you needed somebody to play Emilia in my Lady's most excellent comedy.'

'You can't just walk in and demand any part you fancy.'

'I should not dream of doing so, Mister Betterton. I should be happy to audition for it. As it happens, I took a copy of the script with me and have had a chance to study the part. If you permit, I shall refresh my memory and come back tomorrow morning at the same time. You may judge then if I am in any way suitable.'

'Since Mister Betterton seems lost for words,' says Aminta, 'I'll just say that that sounds fine. I'll be there too and if you get a single word wrong, we'll give the part to the first person who walks in off the street – man or woman or child.'

'Thank you, my Lady,' says Kitty, dropping a very respectful curtsey. 'I won't let you down. Not after all you've done for me.'

'And for little Elizabeth,' says Aminta. 'Just so that we understand each other fully. We helped tidy up a few loose ends for her too. When we were in Salisbury.'

'Of course, my Lady,' says Kitty. 'I learned a lot from my time with little Elizabeth. Such a great deal. Sometimes you don't realise how fortunate you are. Then something happens, and you do. You'll see. Once I'm on stage . . . you'll hardly recognise me.'

Postscript

Spring 1671

From his box, high up in the theatre, Samuel Pepys had a fine view of the stage and the audience, both lit by the flickering light of he knew not how many dozen good wax candles. Outside, it was still daylight, and on his desk at the Navy Office there was much work for him to do, but the King could scarcely begrudge him a few hours' peace and innocent recreation here.

The stage was empty, though a painted canvas indicated that the first scene would take place in a garden – as Pepys knew well, having seen the play three times before. *The Summer Birdcage* had enjoyed a good run, though Betterton had obviously interspersed other plays from the company repertoire in between performances. Music was playing, but the voices of hundreds of theatregoers below made it difficult for Pepys to tell what the music was – a country dance, he thought. Most of the unwanted noise was coming from the pit – to be precise, from Wits' Row, where Sackville and Herbert had planted themselves. They looked ready for trouble. Pepys reflected that he'd been wise to pay the extra money to sit where he was.

In a box opposite him sat Lord Ashley and the Duke of Monmouth. They seemed to be close friends these days. In the next one along was the Duchess of Cleveland, whom he had long idolised as the beautiful Lady Castlemaine. She had a new young man with her – he was called John Churchill, apparently. Pepys needed to speak to her. She'd written to him recently offering him a load of high-quality building materials, if the Navy Office needed any. It didn't, but it might still be possible to use Navy Office funds to buy them and then re-sell at a profit to another government office that did. That needed careful consideration. Only one box was empty and that was reserved for the King. He would be here shortly to watch Kitty Burgess in her role as Emilia. Rumours that he planned to make Kitty his mistress had proved false, but he still took what seemed to be a fatherly interest in her. The strange story that Kitty's body had been found at Bishop's Stortford last summer – a stupid mistake by the coroner – had almost been forgotten in the rising tide of praise for her acting, from both the public and her fellow players. There was no doubt – she owned the stage every minute she was on it. She would, Pepys thought, have made a most charming queen in real life. It was a pity that a mere accident of birth prevented any such thing from happening.

But the music had now stopped. The actors were entering from the wings. The play had begun.

Lady Grey had, Pepys noted, added some new material since the play first opened. But the plot remained the same. And, he was pleased to note, Emilia still appeared in breeches, showing two very fine legs. The scene in the Park was as he remembered it, as was the lovers' subsequent falling out and Bellair's noble gesture in eventually admitting to everyone that he, not Snarkly, had tried to lead Bonnedame astray. That was followed by the reconciliation of Livia and Snarkly and by Emilia's acceptance that perhaps Bellair was the sort of man she might possibly marry – a series of touching scenes that caused the King to be wholly reconciled with the Queen, though Lady Fortinbras being exiled, weeping and cursing, to a crumbling palace in the country seemed to be a new development that Lady Grey had added. For the most part, however, the characters had emerged better people. That, after all, was the point of the story.

It was Livia who had caught Pepys's attention this afternoon, however. He'd see if he could speak to her after the performance and perhaps invite her out for supper somewhere. Yes, she was a pretty little thing, with a roguish glint in her eye. He ought to talk business with the Duchess of Cleveland, of course; but on reflection the demolition of that crumbling pile of quite valuable stone and timber, Nonsuch Palace, could wait a day or two.

Notes and Acknowledgements

Nonsuch was not in fact demolished for another ten years, leaving behind the park that is there today. The palace was really like nothing else – or nothing that has survived from the period in this country – a sort of English Chambord. A whole village had been flattened to make way for it and no expense had been spared in its construction. Only a handful of drawings remains to show how splendid it was, along with a few artefacts such as some wood panelling that was rescued and installed in Loseley Hall. Had Nonsuch survived, it would have been at least as well known and visited as Hampton Court. Its loss to later generations, architecturally speaking, was a tragedy. Contrary to what the Duchess of Cleveland confidently states in my book, however, Henry VIII doesn't seem to have liked it very much at all. He didn't even finish the building work, and his daughter Mary sold the partly completed house to Lord Arundel. Queen Elizabeth, who did visit it often, reacquired it in the 1590s, but it passed back to various non-royal owners until Charles II found himself presented with it on his restoration. Its position was always inconvenient for anything except hunting – unlike most of the royal palaces it was not on the Thames. A survey of Nonsuch in 1650 had noted that the estate was already in need of repair and by 1670, when it passed out of royal hands for the last time, it must have become quite a liability to anyone who owned it. The only surprise is that it took the Duchess of Cleveland so long to decide that it was better to knock it down and sell off the assorted building materials to pay her gambling debts.

It is not clear whether the King's intention was to exile the Duchess to her palace, but her relations with Charles II were by then more or less at an end, and he did indeed tell her (as she indignantly reports to John Grey) that he didn't care what she did as long as she did it quietly. Even then she managed to hang on around court as a lady-in-waiting to the Queen until 1673. The King took other mistresses and she took many other lovers of her own, including John Churchill, the future Duke of Marlborough, of whom we catch a brief glimpse at the end of the book.

Her earlier escort 'George' (if that is indeed his name) is pure invention, but many of the other minor characters are real, including Philip Herbert, later seventh Earl of Pembroke, who was notoriously violent and was eventually charged with the murder of Nathaniel Cony, whom he kicked to death in a tavern for no reason he could ever explain. He was found guilty of manslaughter but was able to plead 'privilege of peerage', since he was a peer and it was his first offence. Or, to put it another way, at that time a nobleman was permitted to kill one commoner during his lifetime without any penalty. Herbert was duly set free but warned that 'his lordship would do well to take notice that no man could have the benefit of that statute but once'. Earlier the same year he had been committed to the Tower by the King 'for uttering such horrid and blasphemous words, and other actions proved upon oath, as are not fit to be repeated in any Christian assembly'. And Charles II was a difficult man to shock. A couple of years later Herbert killed William Smeeth, an officer of the watch, and this time, having already used his 'Get Out of Jail Free' card, was obliged to flee the country, though he was later pardoned and allowed to return. You would be right to conclude that in the seventeenth century, if you were of sufficiently noble birth and avoided outright treason, you could get away with almost anything.

It was not only the King who was relatively unshockable. Restoration theatre audiences enjoyed plays that later generations banned from the stage and were not performable again until the twentieth century. Aminta's play, quoted in the book, reflects the audiences' love of both *double entendre* and world-weary cynicism. Readers may like to compare it (for example) with Wycherley's *The Country Wife*, and the famous 'china' scene in particular. Wits' Row was a genuine phenomenon, and those who considered themselves wits had a great deal of licence to comment on the play and the actors during the performance. The audiences put up with it, doubtless seeing it as part of the entertainment, rather like hecklers today on the comedy circuit. Actually being in the pit with the Wits, however, was probably not a pleasant experience.

One problem with quoting from a fictional play, with your characters telling each other what a wonderful play it is, is that the reader may imagine that you, the author, truly believe that the fictional extracts you are offering them are something very special indeed. Let me hasten to reassure you that I believe no such thing. As with the scenery of a play, I aimed to make them just good enough to stand inspection from a distance. You, the audience in this piece, must imagine the genuinely witty dialogue that was in the scenes that I do not quote. Still, I had fun writing the other stuff.

The King had many illegitimate children, plus the Duke of Monmouth whose mother he may or may not have married. That he should have had a daughter by Lady Byron (another real person whom I have included in the book) is not impossible. She certainly managed to extract a lot of money from the King for no very clear reason, enraging Pepys (who occupied no moral high ground of any sort) in the process. The King must have paid her so much for some reason and, if not that, then what? Had there been a real Elizabeth Needham in the 1670s, then I do not doubt that Lord Ashley would have taken an interest in her, just as he did in real life support the Duke of Monmouth. And he would have found any connection between Elizabeth/Kitty and the theatre somewhat awkward. Actresses did not enjoy a high reputation morally and many became the mistresses of the aristocratic patrons of the theatre. The country would not have been happy to see one marry into the royal family. There are possibly some today who still think it would be a mistake. The King himself seems to have distinguished carefully between his mistresses from good families (who often ended up with titles themselves) and actresses like Nell Gwynne and Moll Davis, who didn't. Their children were another matter – they were half royal, after all. The Dukes of St Albans are descended from the orange seller Nell Gwynne (though half the British aristocracy can probably trace their ancestry back to the many children of the Duchess of Cleveland, by one father or another). I don't know of an instance of the King's friends ever attempting to kidnap a mistress for him, but that too would not be impossible. Pepys reports in his diary that a committee had been set up at court 'for the getting of Mrs. Stewart for the King; but that she proves a cunning slut . . . and so all the plot is spoiled and the whole committee broke'. It is not clear, by the way, what Frances Stewart had done to Pepys that he felt she deserved to be called a slut. Though noted for her beauty rather than her intelligence, she successfully resisted the King's advances for some years before eventually marrying the Duke of Richmond. But, as you will gather from the book, Pepys's judgements could be somewhat harsh.

One of the problems with including real people in a work of fiction is that they are rarely where you need them to be to accommodate your plot. John Churchill, for example, was supposed to have a much bigger role but I discovered, from one source or another, that he was inconveniently serving in the Mediterranean, as my narrator says, during the summer of 1670. Would it really have mattered if I had placed him in London? Probably not – it's only fiction, after all – but having dug up that particular fact, I felt I couldn't ignore it. Sometimes it's better not to know. Lord Cornbury was more obliging. He was temporarily single, and therefore could have married Elizabeth Needham that summer. His first wife had died in 1661 and he didn't marry Flower Backhouse (another real person, with very valuable New River Company shares) until October 1670. Had he married her a few months earlier, it would have shot a massive hole in the plot. It was good of both of them to delay.

*

In the process of writing this book I have consulted many sources, including the following, just in case you want to read further on any of the above topics. On the licentious activities of the court, I would strongly recommend Linda Porter's excellent *Mistresses, Sex and Scandal at the Court of Charles II*. R. E. Pritchard's *Scandalous Liaisons, Charles II and His Court* is also good, including some material on aristocratic misbehaviour. On plotting and espionage during the period, Alan Marshall's scholarly *Intelligence and Espionage in the Reign of Charles II* is probably still the definitive work. Julian Whitehead's *Rebellion in the Reign of Charles II* is more recent (and easier to find). On theatrical matters I consulted *The Cambridge Companion to the Restoration Theatre* and *The Restoration Theatre* by Montague Summers. Ships feature only briefly in this book, but I can't resist also mentioning J. D. Davies's sumptuous *Pepys's Navy*. Turning to individuals mentioned in the book, I would recommend Elizabeth Hamilton's *The Illustrious Lady*, on the subject of the Duchess of Cleveland, though at least one other biography of her is being written at the moment. For a long time, Violet Barbour's *Henry Bennet, Earl of Arlington, Secretary of State to Charles II* was the standard text on Lord Arlington. There is now also *Henry Bennet, Earl of Arlington, and His World: Restoration Court, Politics and Diplomacy* by Robin Eagles and Coleman A. Dennehy, which (during the pandemic) I was regrettably unable to get to the British Library and read. I must add it is rather expensive as a casual purchase. Alan Marshall's lecture entitled 'Sir Samuel Morland and Stuart Espionage' can be found online, and is the best account I know of for that slippery character. Though John Churchill in the end appears only briefly, for the reasons stated, Winston Churchill's *Marlborough, His Life and Times* is also worth reading, both for its insights into the workings of the Stuart court and as literature. More general texts on the period include Alexander Larman's *Restoration*, Ian Mortimer's *The Time Traveller's Guide to Restoration Britain* and (as ever) Liza Picard's detailed and very readable *Restoration London*. Pepys's diaries (and the biographies of Pepys by Claire Tomalin, Stephen Coote and Arthur Bryant) are also invaluable in understanding the Restoration period, its politics and its morality. If only one out of Nonsuch Palace and Pepys's diaries could have survived (not a likely choice to have to make in real life, I admit), I'd have to vote to save the diaries every time.

Many people have helped in the production of this book. I should like to express my gratitude, as ever, to my agent David Headley and the team at DHH; to Krystyna Green, Amanda Keats and Howard Watson at Constable; and of course to my wife Ann, who was as usual the first to read the manuscript. My deepest thanks to all of you – I most certainly could not have done it without your advice and support.

The acknowledgements for previous books in the series have frequently included the much-loved Thalia Proctor, who died, far too young, as this one was being edited. She was helpful, efficient, warm and funny. She will be missed enormously by her many friends, including everyone who is published by Little, Brown.